A Rumor of REAL IRISH TEA

Other Works by Kate Stradling

The *Annals of Altair* Series
A Boy Called Hawk
Oliver Invictus

The *Ruses* Series
Kingdom of Ruses
Tournament of Ruses

Goldmayne: A Fairy Tale

The Legendary Inge

Namesake

Brine and Bone

Soot and Slipper

A Rumor of REAL IRISH TEA

ANNALS OF ALTAIR, BOOK 2

KATE STRADLING

Eulalia Skye Press
MESA, ARIZONA

A Rumor of Real Irish Tea

Copyright © 2019 by Kate Stradling
katestradling.com

All rights reserved. No part of this book may be reproduced or transmitted in any form or by any means, electronic or mechanical, including photocopying, recording, or by any information storage and retrieval system, without written consent of the author.

This is a work of fiction. Names, characters, places, organizations, and events are either the product of the author's imagination or are used in a fictitious manner.

Published by
Eulalia Skye Press
P.O. Box 2203, Mesa, AZ 85214
eulaliaskye.com

ISBN: 978-1-947495-07-4

**to the Olivers and Emilys
of the world,
May you find what you seek**

Contents

I: Tail between the Legs. 1
II: Prom-F Again 10
III: The New Routine. 24
IV: A Little Monkey Business 35
V: The Man in the Gray Suit. 44
VI: Forewarned Is Forearmed 55
VII: An Afternoon at the Movies .61
VIII: Spaghetti and Stars. 68
IX: The Shadow Campus 79
X: Of Ducks and Geese. 87
XI: A Meeting of Minds 98
XII: Real Irish Tea. 113
XIII: On the Road Again. 123
XIV: Insufferable Know-It-All. 133

Contents

XV: Misguided Projection 146

XVI: Real Irish Tea (Reprise) 164

XVII: An Unanticipated Snag 180

XVIII: Ten Minutes Too Late 187

XIX: The Ever-Tightening Noose 198

XX: Reversal of Fortunes 205

XXI: Rude Awakening 213

XXII: The Morning After 221

XXIII: Altair is Here 233

XXIV: The Big Break 252

XXV: Turnabout Is Fair Play 265

XXVI: The Long Ride Home, Part 1 276

XXVII: The Long Ride Home, Part 2 281

ed # I
Tail between the Legs

MONDAY, JULY 28, 2053, 5:24AM MDT, IN TRANSIT

THE LOW, CONSTANT thrum of an airplane engine droned in Emily Brent's ears. She half-heartedly tried to ignore it, but after three weeks in confinement, she was actually grateful for such white noise. It meant that she was moving forward, finally cleared of wrongdoing and going home. After three weeks, she could hardly believe it.

Her gaze strayed across the aisle to a reclined chair and the sleeping ten-year-old who occupied it. Oliver hadn't fared much better than her. He had been in the room next to hers, a silent creature left to self-study and retrospection. They hadn't seen much of one another, and she was surprised by how much relief she felt every time she caught a glimpse of him.

Oliver had gotten tangled in this mess because of her. There was nothing she could ever do to make it up to him.

But then, it wasn't *entirely* her fault.

It was hard not to be bitter about the circumstances that had spoiled her first month as an intern with the Prometheus Institute. It wasn't her fault that she had been assigned to work with Oliver, or that he had been summoned to help with a "problem"

A Rumor of Real Irish Tea

at Prom-F the same morning that she got on the train to meet him. It wasn't her fault that she had been sent across the country without so much as a toothbrush. She may have sought out this job, but all the promotional literature indicated that her assignment would be in one location. How could she be expected to traipse around from place to place without any advance notice?

It wasn't her fault.

If she were to blame anyone, it would be the Wests. Right now those four children were the bane of Emily's existence. If not for the Wests, she and Oliver would be tucked snugly in their beds at Prometheus-A in New York, never the wiser that the Government-Civilian Alliance had holding cells in each regional office. Emily could have gone a lifetime without discovering that detail.

After three weeks the Wests were still at large, too. Her only contact with the outside world during her confinement had come in the form of a television attuned to the National Public News Network. The disappearance of Maddie and Alex North—Honey and Happy West, really, and Emily would be glad if she never saw their devilishly angelic faces again—was reported multiple times throughout the day. No mention was ever made of the two older boys, but if Honey and Happy were still out there, Hawk and Hummer were with them.

It didn't matter, Emily told herself for the thousandth time in the last three weeks. It didn't matter what the Wests did. They were gone, and the GCA would continue to chase them until they caught up with them, but Emily and Oliver were done. They had both been disgraced—Emily more so than Oliver—and now, exonerated at long last, they were going home.

At least, that's what they had been told. Nervously her gaze flitted to the front of the cabin where a black-suited agent sat on guard, and then to the back, where another wiled away his time

I

reading a magazine. She and Oliver had both been roused in the middle of the night—just after two, the clock on the wall told her—and informed that they had finally been cleared to go home.

In the scant time they were given to get ready, the agents returned their belongings to them. Emily received with mixed feelings the tailored pants and white shirt she had worn for the first week of her travels. In confinement she had been given a set of GCA coveralls to wear, and it was difficult not to resent being treated like a prisoner. At the same time, though, her clothes had gotten her into this mess: it was while in search of a new set that she'd fallen into the nefarious clutches of Honey West. That encounter had landed her trussed in duct tape and under suspicion for conspiracy to aid fugitive minors. Her returned clothes were clean now, but she wanted nothing more than to dump them into an incinerator.

She was wearing them for the moment, though. It wouldn't do to show up back at Prometheus in a prison-style jumpsuit.

Once dressed, she had shuffled into a waiting car alongside Oliver. He kept a sullen silence throughout the ride to the airport. Emily didn't begrudge him it. He had every excuse to hate her and no reason whatsoever to engage their driver or escorts in chatty conversation.

His taciturn demeanor also stemmed from a second source: he was conditioned to a strict routine that did not include middle-of-the-night awakenings, a fact made readily apparent by his drooping eyelids. He fell back asleep right after takeoff, unconcerned with what was happening around him.

Emily envied him for that. The last month had been like something out of a nightmare, and she couldn't quell that inner suspicion that it wasn't over yet. It shouldn't have taken so long to arrange a flight back to New York. She thought about all the little conspiracy theories she'd encountered over her lifetime, especially the ones about secret government internment camps and people disappearing in the middle of the night, never to be heard from again. She had never been one to entertain such paranoia.

But then, she had never known the GCA could hold citizens in confinement for weeks on end, either.

"Paranoid," she muttered, as though to quell her twisted inner monologue. The guard at the front of the cabin looked up. *Coincidence*, Emily thought as she averted her eyes. There was no way he could have heard her over the thrum of the engines. She needed to stop being so anxious. The guard wasn't watching her every move, and the GCA wasn't squirreling her and Oliver away to some unknown pit for the rest of their lives.

A mere twenty minutes later, though, the intercom chimed and the captain's voice announced their impending descent. Emily's heart dropped into her stomach. A flight to New York would have taken longer than two hours. If this was their final destination, she and Oliver weren't going back to Prom-A.

Her fists clenched against the armrests as the plane landed. All of the windows were covered and she hadn't dared to flip any of their shades up, but a thread of pale light shone at the bottom of them. It was close to dawn.

Her anxiety grew as the plane taxied and came to a full stop. When the seatbelt icon finally switched off, the two GCA escorts proceeded to the front of the cabin to open the door. Emily gingerly arose and shook the still-sleeping Oliver by his shoulder. He didn't respond.

"Oliver," she whispered.

Briefly he stirred, but nothing more.

"Oliver, we're here. It's time to get up."

1

He batted away the hand on his shoulder.

"Oliver Henry Dunn, if you don't wake up right now I'm telling everyone that Hummer West is a thousand times smarter than you are."

His dark eyes shot open and his lips parted to protest a hot denial.

"There you are," Emily said before he could utter a word. "We're here. It's time to get off the plane."

There was this one moment in the day, right when Oliver was waking up, that he acted human. Emily watched it pass with some meager satisfaction before his sullen façade slipped into place. He recoiled from her in seeming disgust, flung away the blanket, and said a very disgruntled, "About time," as though he had been waiting eons for the plane to land.

Emily didn't have the heart to tell him that they weren't in New York and that she had no idea where they were. He would figure it out soon enough. Anemic light spilled from the open door ahead as Oliver snatched up his bag and trundled forward between the empty rows. Emily followed behind, watching, waiting for the truth to dawn on him.

He stopped just short of the door. A breath of silence passed, and then, "What is this?" He whirled on her, glaring as though she had been the one to orchestrate all of their travels. "What are we doing back here?"

Back here. The words echoed in Emily's mind as she edged forward. "I don't know," she said sedately. Through the open doorway she caught glimpse of a gray pre-dawn sky and the restricted government terminal of the airport in Great Falls, Montana. "I don't know," she said again, more bewildered this time.

The two agents by the door exchanged a telling glance. "Your ride is waiting," one of them said in a callous voice.

A Rumor of Real Irish Tea

Oliver was furious. "You said you were sending us home! What's the meaning of this? What are we doing here?"

"Oliver, just go," Emily said quietly. She couldn't stop the slight tremor in her voice, but she knew well enough not to protest to their apathetic escorts. It was a waste of breath to say anything to them. Surely Oliver would understand that much.

To her utmost relief, he did. The outrage on his face contorted into contempt. He favored them all—and Emily most particularly—with a malevolent sneer, but then he wordlessly stomped out the doorway and down the stairs to the black tarmac below. Emily didn't bother a glance toward either agent as she followed. They didn't care how she felt. No one cared. She was a puny underling who would do as she was told or be abandoned and replaced.

As she stepped carefully down the last stair, her eyes traveled to the waiting car and the familiar figure beside it. Maggie Lloyd had met them here on their first trip to Prometheus-F, too. Round-faced and dumpy as ever, she raised one hand in a lackluster greeting. Emily feebly returned the wave.

This had to be some sort of hiccup. Oliver was a fixture at Prom-A, had lived there practically his whole life. Perhaps some news of the Wests had been received and caused the flight this morning to be rerouted. It wasn't as though anyone would tell Emily or Oliver such a detail.

Oliver had already crossed the tarmac to the car, anger in his every step. Maggie popped the trunk in time for him to fling his bag inside. Emily watched his retreat into the back seat, apprehensive of the two-plus-hours' car ride that lay ahead.

"Good morning," said Maggie as Emily drew near. "Toss your things in the trunk and we'll be on our way."

Emily wanted to ask what was going on, why they had been brought again to Prom-F. Instead she quietly followed orders

I

and climbed into the back seat next to Oliver. Maggie closed the trunk and crossed around to the driver's seat.

"All buckled in, hmm?" she asked as she adjusted the rearview mirror to peer into the back seat. She had waxed the unsightly hairs from her upper lip. It must be a special day indeed, Emily thought snidely.

Oliver started complaining before the car was even in gear. "They said this morning that we were going home. What are we doing here? I thought I'd been taken off the West case."

Maggie's brows arched. "Well, I'm sure it's only temporary," she said in a diplomatic voice. "You were loaned to Prom-F until the Wests were retrieved, so the system still has you under our custody. You know how this government red tape is."

If he didn't before this ordeal, he surely had to know by now. Emily shifted her gaze out the window to keep from rolling her eyes outright. Three weeks in confinement had been an enlightening experience. According to the GCA agents that had watched over them, most of that time had been spent waiting for someone to approve their transfer notice back to Prometheus. If the transfer from Prom-F back to Prom-A took anywhere near as long, Oliver would probably burst a vein.

"Have you been keeping up with your homework, Oliver?" Maggie asked in that fake-friendly voice that grown-ups often used with children. "I know they sent your assignments along, but I heard you weren't allowed any electronic devices."

Oliver made an irritated noise. "They gave me a notebook and pencil. It's all done and ready to be graded."

"Is that what they had you doing?" Emily asked. She was jealous—all she'd had was NPNN and her own thoughts to distract her from her surroundings. She'd nearly died of boredom several times over.

A Rumor of Real Irish Tea

A crusty glare was the only answer she received, and she recalled that Oliver despised her with enough energy to keep the western coast lit up for a decade. She snapped her mouth shut and turned her attention back out the window.

"Good, good," Maggie continued, seemingly oblivious that Emily was even in the car, let alone that she had spoken. "We'll give it to your teachers to check when we arrive. I have an envelope here with your class schedule—"

"Class schedule?" said Oliver, sitting up straight. "I thought you said this was temporary."

They were stopped at a red light. She leaned over to rifle through some papers in the front seat. Her voice floated back. "Of course. Temporary. You didn't have to go to classes the last time because we had suspended them following the incident. They're back in session now, so naturally you'll have to attend while things get sorted out."

"I never had to attend classes when I helped with incidents before," he argued.

Maggie's response was methodical, as though she was the very essence of logic itself. "We've never had any incidents like this before. Ah, here we are." She straightened in her seat and extended a white envelope to him.

"Kill me now," Oliver said to Emily. Then he realized who he was talking to, because his face contorted. "Never mind. You'd just botch things up. That's pretty much all you're good for."

Emily nodded sadly. "You can say that again." She deserved every censure his barbed little tongue chose to fling at her.

Oliver had expected more of a fight, if the stunned expression that flashed across his face was any indication.

"Whatever," he muttered, and he snatched the envelope from Maggie's waiting hand. The car started forward again.

1

Emily tried to ignore him as he pulled out the schedule and perused its contents, but he made that difficult.

"What is this? You have me signed up for all the same classes I was taking at Prom-A!"

Maggie's eyes glanced up to the rearview mirror, but she said nothing.

Oliver continued his tirade. "Do you honestly think that Prom-F's classes are anywhere near the caliber of Prom-A's? I'm probably three grades ahead of these yahoos, and you expect me to sit in the same classes? It's an absolute insult! I'd be better off doing independent study, like I have been for the last three weeks!"

"I'm sure you can ask Principal Gates about that when you get the chance," said Maggie placidly.

"You bet I will." Oliver slumped back into his seat with an ill-concealed glower.

Emily somehow doubted that Principal Gates would care to hear the preferences of a ten-year-old, genius null-projector or otherwise. But then, that was a lesson that Oliver would have to learn for himself, sooner or later.

II
Prom-F Again

JULY 28, 8:42AM MDT, PROMETHEUS-F CAMPUS

THE DRIVE FROM the airport to the most isolated of the Prometheus campuses passed in excruciating silence. Emily knew perfectly well that her very presence was a nuisance to Oliver, so she remained as inconspicuous as possible. Maggie, once her errand of delivering the class schedule was complete, focused her attention exclusively on the road. Oliver simply brooded.

A box of shrink-wrapped pastries and lukewarm juice boxes was provided for breakfast. Emily was so sick of pre-packaged food that she barely ate hers. Oliver turned up his nose at the selection, while Maggie contentedly munched away, pastry in one hand and the other on the wheel. The scenery crawled by at a snail's pace, so that it seemed like they would never arrive. When the broad wrought-iron gates of the Prometheus-F campus finally came into sight, Emily was more relieved than she had expected.

"They're working this time," Maggie announced. The gates had had to be opened manually on their first visit here, courtesy of Hawk and Hummer West's exploits with an electro-magnetic pulse generator.

II

"So they've fixed everything?" Emily asked as the gates slid along their tracks. The question was more out of politeness than any desire to carry on a conversation.

"Oh, our maintenance crew still comes across some lingering damage every couple days." Maggie maneuvered the car forward, across the wide driveway to park at the stairs of the main building. As she turned off the ignition, she raised her eyes to the rearview mirror. "We'd probably better hurry. Oliver's first class starts in twenty minutes. I'll show you both where your rooms are so you can put away your things, but we should be quick about it. Principal Gates has very strict rules about tardiness, and they're even more heavily enforced since the incident."

Maggie kept referring to the trouble with the Wests as "the incident," almost as though it was a minor misfortune that had been properly swept under the rug. It was starting to get on Emily's nerves.

"Do I have to go to class with Oliver?" she asked. She didn't have much of a day ahead if the answer was yes.

Next to her, Oliver snorted derisively and shoved his door open. Maggie appeared not to have heard the question, her own door ajar as she gathered up her things from the front passenger seat.

"Is that a no?" Emily asked, more irritated by the second.

"Quickly now," said Maggie. "If Oliver's late to class, he'll have to serve a detention after school."

That was enough to get Emily moving, determined as she was not to cause Oliver any more trouble than she already had. She scrambled out of the car and around to the back to collect her messenger bag. Oliver had already retrieved his things and was stomping away toward the dormitory. Maggie seemed impatient to follow.

A Rumor of Real Irish Tea

"So we're staying in the dorms again?" Emily asked as they hurried after the ten-year-old. "Same rooms as last time?"

"No. You have proper rooms this time, a dedicated place for you and your things. It's best to have your own space."

Emily didn't like the sound of that at all. It seemed more permanent than she or Oliver wanted. "And do I have to attend class with Oliver during the day?" she asked again, intent upon getting a definitive answer on that point at least.

Maggie stopped and stared blankly at her. "You were serious? I thought that was a joke. Oh, you're *new*!" she suddenly cried. Emily wanted to slug her. "I forgot. It's just that . . . new handlers go through this whole orientation, and it really was out of the ordinary that you were sent before you'd done that. But, of course, there were extenuating circumstances—"

"Do I have to go to class with him?" Emily interrupted in a tight voice. All she wanted was one answer to one stupid question, not an exposition on the process of training new handlers about the ins and outs of their babysitting job.

"Not *with* him. You sit in the observation room with the other handlers. Most people use that time to keep up on their reports."

"Reports?" she echoed faintly. Maybe she did need the exposition on how to do her job after all.

"No time to explain now. Here we are, up the stairs and to the left. Come along, Oliver. We'll take your handler by her room and then drop your things off and rush you off to class in a jiffy. Here we are, handler's quarters." She twisted the knob of a sterile white door and motioned Emily inside. "Have a look around, make sure everything's there, and then come back so we can get Oliver to his room."

Emily didn't know what she meant by "make sure everything's there," but she pushed the door open nonetheless. Panic welled in her throat at the sight that met her eyes: stacks of cardboard boxes stood next to a naked bed and empty bookshelf. "What is all of this?" she asked, but her eyes fixed on a familiar chair in the corner. Its presence gave her an answer before Maggie could: it was from her apartment in New York.

Maggie wore a vacant smile. "Your things arrived yesterday. There's a manifest of boxes there if you want to make sure everything's here, but bring it along."

Emily's breath quickened. "I thought this was only temporary," she said, trying to remain calm. Shipping all of her things from the East Coast hardly seemed temporary.

"It's only a two-year internship," said Maggie with a shrug. "That's temporary."

Nausea churned in Emily's stomach. So she was stuck in Montana for the next two years? But she deserved no better. Handlers were shunted around from child to child every two months, so she could just as easily serve out her internship here as at Prom-A. She forced a smile as she resolutely closed the door.

"You don't want to check the manifest?" Maggie asked.

"No point. I didn't do the packing, so I'll have to inventory tonight instead. I don't want Oliver to be late to his class."

She stole a glance in his direction and thought she saw a look of pity on his face. He was going back to Prom-A, but she wasn't. The pity was short-lived, though, replaced with contempt. She could practically read his thoughts: Oliver despised Prom-F, and he despised Emily, so the two would go well together.

His room was the next hall over, in the students' section. Maggie led him straight to the fifth door down, where she twisted the knob and tipped her head inward. "Drop your bag in there, quick, quick. They should have all your new supplies waiting at your first class."

A Rumor of Real Irish Tea

He took two steps into the room and stopped short. "Why are there two beds in here?"

"You have a roommate. His name is Tyler. He's probably finishing his breakfast, so you'll have to meet him later."

Oliver turned wide, outraged eyes upon her. "This doesn't look any more temporary than *her* room did," he cried, and he leveled an accusing finger toward Emily to emphasize his point.

"You're on our roster, so we have to treat you like a regular student," said Maggie with diplomatic calm. "I'm sure you can talk to Principal Gates about it if you get the chance."

"I had my own room last time!"

"That was then. Come on, now."

The message was unspoken but clear: Oliver would be here for some duration, and they had no intention of making special provisions for him during that time. Emily only hoped that it was more government red tape that was gumming up the transfer process, and not that Oliver's residence would be as permanent as hers.

She was free in two years' time. He was at least seven years shy of graduation.

Oliver's thoughts seemed to run along the same lines, for a deep frown worked itself onto his face. Sullenly he dropped his bag next to one bed and returned to the hallway. "Get on with it," he grumbled. "I don't want detention."

The trio trekked back down the stairs and across the lawn to the main building. "First class should be English literature," Maggie said as she held the door for them. "That's third floor, room 315. Did you bring your homework, Oliver?"

His eyes bulged. "You just told me to leave all my stuff in my room! You said they'd have everything I'd need!"

"I can get it," Emily offered.

II

"No, no. Handlers aren't supposed to be more than twenty yards away from their charges during the daytime hours. He'll have to turn it in tomorrow—it shouldn't affect his grade too much."

"*What?*" cried Oliver.

"It shouldn't affect his grades at all," said Emily hotly. "It's not his fault that he got dragged out of bed in the dead of night to travel six hours to a new school. Can't they cut him some slack on his first day?"

Maggie was unfazed by their combined outrage. "Making exceptions creates weakness, Principal Gates always says. There's the first bell—you have two minutes to get up the stairs and in your seat." Then, she motioned to the nearby stairwell. It was blatantly obvious that she wasn't coming with them.

"I think I hate this school," Emily muttered when they circled around the second landing where Maggie could not overhear. Oliver made no response, but just continued to climb as quickly as his short legs would carry him. They were both breathing heavily as they came to the third floor, but he paused to straighten his shirt and futilely brush at the wrinkles in his pants. He seemed determined to enter his classroom with dignity.

"Your hair's falling out of its band," he told Emily, and she suddenly realized that he expected her to enter with dignity as well.

"Thanks," she said, and she quickly pulled out the rubber band and smoothed the offending tresses back into a ponytail. "Is that better?"

Oliver spared her a cursory glance. "Try not to embarrass yourself too much."

They had come up a stairwell at the end of a corridor. Rows of classrooms lay before them, doors open, with children and handlers hurrying to their proper places. Everyone had come from the main stairs or the bay of elevators in the central part of the building, with nary a glance toward the pair of newcomers. Oliver took a deep breath, steeled his nerves, and stepped forward toward the throng.

"Room 315," Emily murmured under her breath. "Here we are. Ooh, hang on! Your shirt's untucked in the back!"

Oliver mechanically fixed the sloppy shirt. "You go into 315-O with the other handlers. That's O for Observation," he said with a sarcastic sneer.

"Thanks," said Emily. "I'd have wondered about that for hours if you hadn't told me."

A breath of silence passed between them. Fear chased across his face in that momentary hesitation.

"Have a good class, Oliver," she said impulsively. "Show all those Prom-F yahoos what a Prom-A genius is capable of."

He snorted, false bravado back in full force. A couple students glanced curiously toward him as they hurried into the room. Oliver followed them at a more dignified pace.

"He'll be fine," said Emily, to no one in particular. Much as she hoped that was true, her anxiety yet fluttered on his behalf. Was this what a mother felt like when she sent her child off to school for the first time?

But she wasn't his mother, and the Prometheus Institute wasn't a typical school. They wouldn't have the discipline problems of the public schools here, or the elitist bullying of the private ones. She had no cause to worry.

The second bell rang as Emily crossed the threshold into 315-O. Within, seated at a long table and on a couple of industrial-style couches, the other handlers had already assembled. Two were typing away on computers in the corner, and three more were reading either books or files. The other three had their attention fixed upon a television screen mounted next to the door.

II

It was broadcasting NPNN. Emily grimaced.

A large picture window allowed perfect view of the classroom beyond. Nine students sat with their backs to the observation room as their teacher took attendance. Emily felt conspicuous standing in the doorway, but her eyes instinctively sought out Oliver. He was seated directly in the middle, surrounded by Prom-F students and the subject of many covert glances.

"Hey, new girl!" a voice hissed.

Emily started. A familiar face stared back at her from the nearest couch. "Oh!" It took her a moment to match the face to a name. "Crystal!" They had interacted only briefly on Emily's first visit to Prom-F, when Oliver had been briefed about "the incident." Crystal had been Honey West's handler at Prom-B. If she was still here, that meant that she'd been transferred to this campus too.

"Come inside and shut the door," Crystal said, motioning her inward. "Those salivating morons will throw a fit if you interrupt their hourly Veronica fix."

Even as Emily obeyed the instructions, her confused attention shifted from Crystal to the "salivating morons," as it were—three handlers, all men, who sat watching the TV. One of them turned and bared his teeth at the insult, but the other two didn't even acknowledge that they had heard it.

The "Veronica fix" referred to Veronica Porcher, a popular NPNN anchor who read the hourly updates throughout the day.

"They just watch NPNN all day?" Emily asked as she took the available seat next to Crystal. "By choice?"

"They're addicts. Not really surprising—Veronica's got her charms, after all."

The beautiful reporter's face flashed on screen and her melodic voice read the latest news. "I used to really like her,"

A Rumor of Real Irish Tea

said Emily with growing distaste. "I guess after a few weeks of nothing but NPNN, I've gotten sick of her."

Crystal quietly laughed. "I used to really like her, too. Then I got assigned to be Honey's handler."

Emily's head twisted sharply. "What's Honey West got to do with it?"

A faint, knowing smile played around Crystal's mouth. "When you encounter a high-grade projector like Honey, I think it must dull your senses to these lower-grade charlatans. At least, that's what it did to me."

"You mean *Veronica*—?"

"Prom-C, class of '44."

Emily shifted her attention back to the broadcast. "That's . . . You've got to be *kidding* me. How many of those monsters are roaming around?"

Two of the entranced males turned and angrily shushed her.

Crystal chuckled again, but when she spoke, she lowered her voice to a whisper. "Think we should tell them they won't be getting their fix during this class?"

"What do you—" Emily started, but her eyes traveled to the picture window and the little boy seated in the center of the classroom beyond. "Oliver," she said with dawning comprehension.

"High-grade null-projector," said Crystal with a nod. "I don't think it's general knowledge that he's been transferred here, and those three idiots certainly wouldn't put two and two together. They probably don't even know that Veronica's a projector, though. It's not like that detail's ever been broadcasted."

So how had Crystal discovered it? "Maybe it's not her news reports they're interested in," Emily said. Even without the ability to project, Veronica Porcher was still an attractive woman.

"Well, they are men," said Crystal with a shrug. "So tell me, is it true that you met my errant little Honey?"

Emily recoiled, wide-eyed. "What have you heard?"

"A lot of things, and most of them are probably false. But it's pretty telling that you and Oliver are here and Honey and the others are still unaccounted for. So what happened?"

It had been a humiliating incident, and what little time had passed had not diminished that humiliation in the least. Emily opened her mouth to deflect the blunt question, but the television on the wall caught her attention. Like a specter that appeared when its name was spoken, the picture of Honey West flashed on screen, alongside one of her little brother Happy. Veronica's news report registered in Emily's ears.

"Authorities are still looking for Maddie and Alex North, who were taken from their home in the early hours of July 1. Their whereabouts are still unknown, but the family announced yesterday that they have increased the reward to fifty thousand ameros for any information that leads to the return of these two children. The case has baffled authorities from the very beginning, but the federal agents in charge of the investigation continue to express confidence that Maddie and Alex are still alive. Anyone with information about this crime or its victims is encouraged to call the National Hotline at—"

"You'd think by now they'd realized that reporting on this story is a waste of time," said Crystal with a frown.

"It's the only way they can track those kids, though," Emily said. "No one who encounters them is going to get anywhere near them, thanks to Honey."

"Thanks to Happy, more like. Honey actually has to talk to you to affect you. Happy can keep people away with a simple glare."

"And Hawk can rain a flock of angry birds down on your head to peck your eyes out while he runs away," said Emily.

Crystal perked up. "Now *that* I hadn't heard. Did he really?"

"In Vegas. I've had nightmares about bird attacks ever since. It was like nothing I'd ever seen."

"Wow," said Crystal, impressed. "Sounds like you guys had a rough month."

Emily couldn't stop the cynical laugh that bubbled up in her throat. "The first week was rough. We've been in confinement for the last three. Thanks to Honey," she added with a pointed glance.

"She must've gotten you good."

"She left me duct-taped in an abandoned office suite, *after* she picked my pockets for any money and my brain for everything I knew about Oliver, Altair, and the GCA's pursuit of her and her brothers. Luckily I didn't know much about any of them."

"Being the new girl paid off, then," said Crystal with an appreciative nod. Her expression shifted into something much more guarded, and she leaned close. "They really asked you about Altair?" she whispered, her voice so low that Emily barely caught the words.

"Yes! What exactly is it?"

Crystal shook her head, her attention flitting toward a security camera in the corner of the room. "Don't talk about it here. Ever. Don't mention the name. Don't ask any questions. Ignorance is your best defense."

"But—" Emily started.

"What little I've heard is enough of a warning," Crystal said with another nervous glance around the room. "If the GCA suspects you're affiliated, or that you know anything about it, you're gone. No questions asked."

II

Her anxiety was contagious. Emily's own gaze shifted from the television-gawking trio to the other four handlers, each seemingly engrossed in his or her work. Any one of them could be a snitch, but even more likely was the chance of a hidden microphone with the surveillance camera that recorded their conversation.

And, of course, each one of them carried a government-issued cell phone that was rigged to perpetually record and transmit sound to a remote database.

"Well, I don't know anything," she said, more because she wanted that on record than because she needed to convince Crystal. "They already confirmed that I don't know anything. Your little monster nearly cost me my job."

That minor shift in topic alleviated the oppressive atmosphere. Crystal sat up with an open smile. "She nearly cost me mine, too. Or did you think I requested to be transferred here? It's not a big deal, though." She fluttered her hand in a careless wave. "My internship is up in less than six months, and there's no chance whatsoever that they'll pair me with another projector between now and then. I'll be fine. I'm assigned to a real gem right now. That's her in the front row, left side: precious little Lucy. She's a piece of work but couldn't hold a candle to Honey's brand of monster."

"You know," said Emily, "the way you talk, I can't figure out whether you love or despise Honey."

One corner of Crystal's mouth lifted in a bitter smile. "Neither can I. She messes with your brain, like a drug. But then, if she had you tied up in duct tape, you already knew that."

Emily sat back on the couch and looked down at her hands. It really had been like a drug, that whole surreal experience where she had allowed a nine-year-old to lead her around and dictate everything she needed to do. She was lucky that the powers-that-be within Prometheus hadn't placed her with a full-blown projector as her first assignment. She hoped they would never place her with one at all.

"I'm worried about Oliver," she said abruptly. "I'm worried that he's going to get stuck here like me, because of me."

Crystal observed her for a full five seconds before she answered. "You can't get attached to these kids. You just can't. Put a wall up around your emotions and let the administrators do whatever they're going to do. You and I have absolutely no say in what happens."

"But it wasn't his fault—"

"Absolutely *no say*," Crystal repeated, her voice firm. "I'll warn you right now, if Oliver's been transferred here, he's probably here for good. Prom-F is the black hole of the campuses: once you're in, you never get out. But *you* aren't going to be his handler forever. Your next rotation will be in another grade level, on a different schedule. You'll barely even see him, so there's no point in worrying about him."

A heavy sigh left Emily's lungs and melancholy settled on her shoulders. Crystal was right. She shouldn't get attached, because she really was powerless. Oliver didn't need her worrying about him. Oliver didn't need anything from her at all.

She looked up to the picture window, to his proud, straight back as he listened attentively to the lecture in front of him. He was an absolute pill sometimes, and the sourest kid she'd ever come across, she told herself. He was a monster, an arrogant, selfish monster.

It made perfect sense to her brain. Deep down in her heart was another story. Oliver was a complex creature, and pinning him down with a label didn't sit right with Emily, no matter how she tried to justify it.

II

Her face must have mirrored her emotions, because Crystal suddenly shook her head. "You're hopeless," she said.

"I suppose I am," Emily murmured, too quietly for anyone but herself to hear.

III
The New Routine

As it turned out, Oliver and Lucy shared the same morning classes. Emily arrived at the second observation room to find Crystal already comfortable on the couch. It was a blessing. Crystal was a new arrival at Prom-F herself, and she was jaded enough not to care that the other handlers seemed intent upon ignoring Emily's very existence. She gladly enlightened her on a number of topics—most of which were pure gossip—and did so with a dry wit that Emily found refreshing.

While Oliver studied post-modern history, Emily learned that she and Crystal weren't the only two handlers to transfer to Prom-F. Todd, formerly the handler of Happy West at Prom-B, had been sentenced as well.

"He's still as bitter and disagreeable as ever," Crystal said in in a hushed voice. "He drew the short straw and had to pull desk work while I got in on the last rotation of transfers two weeks ago. He's up for this rotation, though. They've paired him with a fifteen-year-old named Cody, effective in two days."

"Do handler transfers always happen on Wednesdays?" Emily asked.

III

"Like clockwork."

"How far beforehand do they tell you where to go?" Given the utter lack of notice she and Oliver had received this morning, she worried that that sudden upheaval might be a trend.

"The Friday before," said Crystal. "They put an envelope in your mail slot."

"I have a mail slot?"

This elicited a good-natured laugh. "They really didn't tell you anything, did they? The mail slots are in a room right next to the cafeteria, so that we can check at mealtime without abandoning our charges. The kids are divided into four different groups for transfers, so there's a limited pool of candidates. Every two weeks, one of the groups gets its handlers shuffled around. Over the course of the two years, you won't even shadow half the kids in your group, though. It's all very systematic, and once a handler's assigned to a student, they're assigned until the next rotation—that is, unless something drastic happens, like the student up and disappears."

That explained why Emily was still assigned to Oliver, at least. With everything that had happened already, she had wondered why the higher-ups hadn't separated the two of them.

Still, "It seems like it's too rigid of a system," she said. "What if the handler and the student really don't get along?"

"Tough cookies. There aren't usually any extra handlers floating around, so there'd be no one to transfer a student to without displacing another student. I've never heard of a mid-cycle transfer before—even with Todd and me. I joke that he drew the short straw, but Honey and Happy were in separate groups, and Todd and I ended up transferring at the exact same time as we would have back at Prom-B."

She went on to talk about their required weekly reports

("Useless busywork," she said) and a handful of feuds between administrators and staff.

"Don't get on Maggie Lloyd's bad side. She's just dumb enough to be vindictive. They say the only reason she has this job is because Principal Gates is married to her sister."

"What exactly is her job?" Emily asked. So far she had only seen Maggie act as a chauffeur and what seemed to be a random errand-runner.

"Administrative assistant—every Prometheus principal has one, but they usually have some impressive qualifications for the job. Principal Lee's assistant Michelle has a PhD in organizational behavior. I heard that he's grooming her to take over his position at Prom-B when he retires. No chance of Maggie rising to those heights."

Emily had a hard time viewing the pudding-headed Maggie as much of a threat. "She seems pretty harmless."

"Because she doesn't have any reason to hate you," Crystal said. "She's harmless toward me, too, but there are a couple of handlers whose lives she's made completely miserable. She's in a position to do it. The admin-assistant has access to every file in the Prometheus database, including transfers, room assignments, and weekly reports. And you can't file a complaint against her because every correspondence to the principal has to go through her to get to him. Not that he'd do anything about it anyway. It's crazy that we still have such ridiculous nepotism in this day and age."

"I'm starting to think I should've applied to the children's hospitals again for my internship," said Emily dully.

Crystal slapped her on the back with a grin. "That's the spirit!"

Low morale was contagious among the Prom-F handlers. The few that even acknowledged Emily's existence did so in such a

III

lifeless manner that she had no inclination to speak further with them. Crystal's liveliness, in contrast, seemed fueled by her utter cynicism toward the job. All of the literature about working as a "child-life counselor" for the Prometheus Institute had spoken of exciting opportunities and the invigorating academic atmosphere.

Someone somewhere had done a very creative job of lying.

By the time lunch finally rolled around, Emily was half-starved and more than depressed. The reluctant bites of packaged pastry and boxed juice had long since worn off. She looked forward to sinking her teeth into something warm, even though it was going to be cafeteria food. She was sure that Oliver, who had skipped breakfast entirely, would be absolutely famished.

"We have to go back to the dorms to get my homework," he announced as she joined him after third period, though. "After writing the whole lot of it long-hand in an eight-by-ten cell, there's no way I'm getting marked down for turning it in late."

Emily wanted to protest—and her stomach even more so—but she thought better of it. Lunch was an hour long. They had plenty of time to fetch his homework, deliver it to the interested parties, and get to the cafeteria in time to eat.

"Lead the way," she said grimly.

Her permission wasn't required. Oliver headed off toward the dormitory without any acknowledgement that she had spoken, and with the sure confidence that she would follow.

The dorms were fairly popular during lunch, from the looks of it. Students entered and exited, their handlers trailing sullenly behind them. Emily and Oliver received several curious stares, but no one attempted to speak to them. They climbed the stairs to Oliver's floor, but when they rounded the corner to the correct hall, Oliver stopped short.

"What's wrong?" Emily asked.

"There're three handlers standing outside my dorm room," he said. Her gaze followed his. Sure enough, two men and a woman leaned against the wall, all of them fiddling with their cell phones. They looked like an overgrown group of delinquents loitering around with nothing better to do.

"So tell them to leave," she said logically.

Oliver favored her with a withering glare. "First of all, I'm not allowed to talk to them. Second, if they're out here that means there must be students inside. So why are three Prom-F students congregating in my dorm room?"

"Maybe your roommate's having a party," said Emily with a shrug. Or maybe some malicious-minded students were playing pranks on the new kid, but she knew well enough not to say this out loud. "There's only one way to find out."

A growl rumbled in Oliver's chest. He started forward, brows furrowed. The three handlers paid him no heed as he passed them to open the door. Emily decided that it was best that she wait outside for him.

"Hey!" cried an unknown voice from within the room, a boy. "This is a closed meeting! You can't just barge in here!"

"Can it, Arthur," said another. "I told you guys I had a new roommate. Don't you recognize Prom-A's famous Oliver Dunn?"

"I'm just here to grab my notebook," said Oliver, and from the long-suffering in his voice Emily could tell in an instant that he thought his audience was comprised of morons. "I'll only be here a minute."

"Good," a third voice chimed in. "We don't need a null-projecting Prom-A lapdog in here gumming up our plans."

"What's going on in there?" Emily asked the three handlers.

The two men continued to fiddle with their phones. The woman had the decency to look up. "Our boys are plotting their escape route," she said, tipping her head toward the open door. "They do it every lunch period."

Emily bristled. "And you let them?"

"A month ago they were spending their lunches plotting how to blow up the plumbing system in the handlers' wing of the dorms," said one of the men, his attention still fixed on the little backlit screen in front of him. "I'd say this is by far preferable."

"It's not like they'll succeed," said the other, just as absorbed in whatever he was looking at. "Security here is tight as a drum since the West brothers broke out."

"If it keeps the boys busy, I have no complaints," said the woman, and she returned to the task of thumbing a message on her cell.

"Aren't those phones supposed to be used for official business only?" Emily asked.

"It's not like anyone keeps track of what we do," said the first man.

She experienced some satisfaction in breaking his delusion. "Actually, they do. The microphone is wired for continuous transmission."

The three handlers looked up, startled. They exchanged a nervous glance. "Where'd you hear that?" asked the woman with a faint attempt at skepticism.

"Hummer West. Oh, Oliver. Got your homework?"

Oliver favored her with a sour glare as he shut the door firmly behind him. "Would I have come back without it?" he asked sarcastically.

"Good point," said Emily. She tipped her head to the three stricken handlers. "Have a good afternoon." Then, she followed Oliver down the hallway. "So, what was your roommate like?" she asked him conversationally.

"Would you cut that out?" he said.

"Cut what out?"

"Quit acting like everything is fine. We're at *Prom-F*, for Pete's sake."

She thought about this as they exited the dorms. "I guess I could mope around and glower at anyone who comes near me," she said at last.

"Ha ha."

"I understand why you're upset. It's my fault we're here, so you have every reason to hate my guts, and no one's going to begrudge you that, because you're ten. I'm an adult, and I have absolutely no control over this situation—as Crystal so aptly told me this morning—so I have to make the best of it. I'm sorry. For everything, really."

Oliver stared at her in horror, as though an alien head had sprouted from her neck.

"What?" she asked defensively.

"You're an *adult*. Why are you apologizing to a ten-year-old? You sure the Wests didn't kick you in the head before they abandoned you in that office?" He flung himself away, up the path toward the main building.

Emily belatedly realized that she had embarrassed him. "What a strange kid," she murmured, and she hurried to close the gap between them. Oliver didn't seem to know what to do with a genuine apology, other than to rail at it and insult the speaker. Maybe that meant he didn't hate her entirely.

He paused outside his first-hour teacher's office to tear some pages from the lined notebook. "Hold this," he commanded as he flipped through to find another assignment.

Emily obediently took the pages, and her eyes nearly fell out of her head. "This is your handwriting? It's barely legible!" Most

III

of the letters were malformed, in varying sizes and shapes as though he were a five-year-old with limited motor control.

Oliver flashed a smirk at her. "They start teaching us to type in the first grade," he said as he tore another assignment from the book.

"So this is the best you can write?"

"This is how I write when I don't care about writing nicely. Don't look at me like that. They can't dock points for penmanship—it might hurt my precious self-esteem." He contrived a sad face, but she could tell that he was pleased with himself.

"Passive-aggressive much?" she asked.

Oliver ignored the question. Instead, he snatched the papers from her hands, knocked peremptorily on the door, and opened it inward. "Here's my homework for the last three weeks, Mr. Simpson," he said with a fake smile. "I hope I did everything I was supposed to. I did my very best."

His teacher, Mr. Simpson, was in the process of biting into a large sandwich and could only nod, stunned as he was by the sudden interruption. Oliver dropped the assignments on his desk and shut the door again.

"Two more to go," he said. "Come on, before I starve to death."

"Thank you!" cried Emily. "I thought I was the only one who was dying here!"

By the time they reached the cafeteria, the line for food had cleared out. The room itself was only half-full, which made Emily wonder if there were other children off plotting their escapes in secrecy, or if the lunch periods were staggered. Several of the children present whispered and pointed at Oliver as he passed, but he ignored them like the Prom-A snob he was.

Emily watched with eager anticipation as the lunch lady poured her a bowl of watery soup and slapped a thick sandwich

A Rumor of Real Irish Tea

onto her tray. "Look," she said gleefully to Oliver. "It didn't come out of a vending machine."

"Don't talk to me when we're in here," he replied without glancing at her. "People might see."

That shut her up. She might have been hurt by his blunt tone, but the smell of food disabled any instinct but hunger. So, instead of sulking, she picked up her tray and followed him to an empty corner.

They weren't sitting alone for long. No sooner had Emily taken her first bite than a pair of hands slammed down on the table and a domineering voice said, "Okay, spill it, Oliver."

Emily looked up at the girl who had intruded upon their meal. Black hair framed a familiar, fiercely scowling face. Emily instantly recognized the null-projector and former Prom-A student. "Quincy!" she cried, but since her mouth was full of sandwich, it sounded more like, "Kwnfhee!"

Quincy briefly glanced her direction, incredulous that anyone could be so uncouth. Then she returned her gaze to the ten-year-old in front of her. Oliver peacefully sipped his soup.

"Spill what?" he asked when he was good and ready.

"Is it true that Hawk and Hummer firebombed a GCA office and escaped across the border into Mexico?" Quincy asked.

Emily nearly choked. Oliver remained perfectly calm.

"Not that I know of," he said. "It is true that their little sister charmed an idiot handler and they left her duct-taped in an abandoned office building, though."

"I'll never live that one down," Emily said to no one in particular.

"Duct tape," mused Quincy. "I'll have to try that some time. So you didn't catch them, and now you're stuck here a year ahead of schedule."

III

"What?" Oliver said sharply.

Quincy waved a dismissive hand. "Oh, nothing. Don't mind me. I just wanted to confirm that you failed. I mean, the last time I saw you, you were all ready for the chase and certain you'd have them back within the week."

Oliver scowled, his shoulders stiff. "I didn't fail. The GCA is populated with cretins. We'd have caught them in Vegas if they had only listened to me and held back."

"So what got you shipped back here?" asked Quincy.

Oliver thrust one thumb toward Emily. "I already told you, my idiot handler."

"It's true," said Emily. "It's all my fault."

"You're not supposed to talk to her, idiot."

"Then where's her handler so I have someone I can talk to?" Emily argued.

Quincy tipped her head toward the other side of the room. "Dominic gets transferred in two days," she said to Oliver, though she was obviously answering Emily's question. "He's not being so vigilant anymore, seems to think I can't cause him any real trouble at this point. I was thinking a little surprise was in order, sort of like a send-off present. She gonna tattle on me?" She slid a meaningful glance in Emily's direction.

"Doubtful," said Oliver.

"As long as it doesn't involve backing up the plumbing in the handlers' dorms, I don't really care," said Emily to the ceiling. She probably should have shown some loyalty to her fellow handler, but Dominic had been a sour-faced pill on their one and only meeting.

"I'll have to try that some time, too," Quincy said thoughtfully, much to Emily's dismay.

"Is everyone here a complete delinquent?" Oliver asked. "I

just caught my roommate and his cronies plotting their escape, and here you are planning to ambush your handler. What gives?"

Quincy's eyes lit up with sheer delight. "Hawk and Hummer escaped, that's what gives. They proved it could be done—not just escape from Prom-F, but from the GCA itself. No one thought they'd last this long. And while the admins are running around clamping down on our activities, we're free to dream about the possibilities. The very fact that you're sitting here in total failure of your mission is the beacon of hope that everyone has been looking for."

"So glad to oblige," said Oliver, deadpan.

"The GCA's still looking for them," Emily said to the table, pretending like she was only speaking her thoughts aloud rather than joining the conversation.

"They'll be found and punished, Quincy," Oliver said. "Don't you think that's too much of a risk to take?"

She stepped back and scrutinized him, an odd disinterest in her eyes. "Do you know what happens to the kids that graduate from Prom-F?"

He scowled. "No."

"Yeah, neither does anybody else." She thumped one hand against the table for emphasis and walked away.

"What's that supposed to mean?" Emily asked, bewildered.

Oliver, though, mutely shook his head. His eyes remained fixed on Quincy's retreating form, even after she had rejoined her handler.

IV
A Little Monkey Business

JULY 28, 12:54PM MST, PHOENIX, AZ

"Couldn't we have picked a cooler day to come to the zoo?" Hawk West shifted his eyes from the flamingo enclosure in front of him to his younger brother beside him.

Hummer continued his complaint. "It's, what, five hundred degrees out today? The railings are hot enough to burn you, the sun is beating down, and we're all sweating buckets. Why today, of all days?"

"There's a chance of thunderstorms this afternoon," Hawk said with a half-hearted shrug.

"Not a cloud in the sky," Hummer retorted.

"Blame Happy, then. He's the one who wanted to come so badly."

Hummer made a disgruntled noise and nervously shuffled his feet. A couple yards down the line, their little brother broke his mesmerized gaze away from the flock of pink birds to look apologetically at the pair. A row of tourists behind him did the same.

"Aw . . . it's . . . not so bad," said Hummer under that collective remorseful gaze.

"What's not?" Honey West poked her nose between the pair.

She pinned a suspicious stare on Hummer. "Were you picking on Happy again?"

"No!" he cried.

"He was complaining about the heat," said Hawk. "What's up, Honey?"

"Our group's headed toward the monkey village. Happy, you want to see the monkeys?"

The six-year-old's face lit up. He jogged forward eagerly, followed by the row of tourists behind him.

"Oh, yeah," said Hummer to the sky. "We're not conspicuous at all here."

"The rest of you should go see the giraffes," Honey told the tourists bluntly. They all paused in confusion, unwittingly conflicted by the words of one human-projector and the emotions of another. "Go on," she said. "Happy, tell them how great the giraffes are."

He beamed, and that mute response was enough for the cluster of tagalongs to resolve their indecision. Even as they changed their direction, though, Honey cried a sudden, "Wait!"

The tourists halted. Hawk, Hummer, and Happy all turned quizzical eyes upon her, but she ignored them.

"How many of you work for the GCA?" she asked the tourists. "Raise your hands."

Two men's hands shot into the air. They looked at one another in alarm before retracting their arms again guiltily. Hawk hissed and Hummer groaned.

"You two need to go feed the lions," Honey said, addressing the pair of agents. "Buy a turkey sandwich at the snack shop first and put the meat in your pockets, then climb over the railings into the pen—"

"Honey!" cried Hawk.

IV

"What?" she said in a low voice. "They'll come to their senses before they get near any lions. Probably."

"We don't command people to their doom in this family," he said.

"*Fine.*" She heaved a sigh of long-suffering. "You guys go see the giraffes too. Count the number of spots on the whole herd, and forget that you saw us here. Happy, you want them to go see the giraffes, don't you?"

Happy nodded. "They're really neat!" he said.

The sound of his voice sealed the deal. Everyone within hearing range suddenly swiveled in the direction of the giraffe enclosure, including Hawk and Hummer. Honey snagged their elbows. "Monkeys," she said.

"Why doesn't he affect you like he affects us?" Hummer asked as they turned the opposite direction.

"He does," said Honey. "I'm just more used to fighting it."

"Sorry," said Happy remorsefully.

Honey, though, put an arm around his shoulders. "I'm not. I'm glad you're my little brother. Now let's go see some monkeys, okay? Hawk, Hummer, don't get too far separated from the group, or you'll attract attention," she said over her shoulder as she urged Happy forward.

"Bit late for that," Hummer muttered, but he picked up his pace all the same.

"The group," as Honey called it, was a collection of children from a local public elementary school. Thanks to her wiles, the four Wests had crashed their field trip. The teachers and guides had turned a blind eye on their extra "students," and the crowd of children had provided a decent cover for the four truants. An average visitor to the zoo was far more inclined to stare at the animals than to study a herd of kids.

A Rumor of Real Irish Tea

It wasn't the average visitors they had to worry about, though. Hawk scanned the trees for Revere. Ordinarily he could sense his presence with ease, but the zoo provided a safe haven not only for the exotic birds on display, but also for flocks of native species. Finding one raven in the chatter that buzzed in Hawk's mind was much like trying to find a friend in a crowd solely by the sound of his voice. Revere was on lookout with several of his fellow ravens, and the faithful bird would raise a commotion if he saw anything suspicious. Extensive as this network of surveillance was, though, it couldn't stop undercover GCA agents from milling with the rest of the zoo visitors.

"You going in to see the monkeys?" Hummer's abrupt question drew Hawk back from his search. They had arrived at the monkey village, where the grade-schoolers filed in with great anticipation. Happy was in their midst, his eager eyes the biggest of them all.

"I dunno. I guess I should make sure Happy doesn't start some sort of joyous stampede or something."

"Happy's the only one who can stop himself," Hummer said logically. "If something like that really did happen, you'd just end up getting caught up in the fervor with everyone else. He's really excited about these monkeys."

"Just like he was really excited about the lions, and the tigers, and the rhino, and the giraffes—"

"Yeah, yeah" said Hummer. "You can't blame him. It's not like he ever saw any of that at Prom-B."

Hawk shoved his hands into his pockets with a bitter frown. "No. They just promised to let him go and then reneged."

Honey had disclosed that detail almost a week after their arrival in Phoenix. Happy's grade and the two years above had won a school-wide loyalty contest back in May. The prize had

IV

been a very rare and coveted field trip to the Seattle zoo. Under normal circumstances, the younger grades were not allowed to go on field trips, so this was an even bigger honor for them. When the time came for the children to board the bus, though, Happy was not with them. He had conveniently slept through that morning's wake-up call and was left behind.

"His handler drugged his dinner the night before, under Principal Lee's orders," Honey said in complete disgust. "They couldn't let a little projector out among the public, could they? He didn't wake up until after the buses had left, and he spent the whole day heartbroken. *Everyone* spent the whole day heartbroken. It was the worst day ever."

Once Happy realized that his newfound freedom with his brothers and sister could include a trip to the zoo, the idea had stuck in his head—and an idea stuck in Happy's head was an idea stuck in everyone's head. After three successive nights dreaming of hippos and elephant enclosures, Hawk had finally declared that they were going to the zoo once and for all.

And here they were.

"You go on," he told Hummer. "Make sure Honey and Happy don't wander off or draw too much attention to themselves. I'll catch up in a minute."

Hummer hesitated but then shrugged off his misgivings. He trotted into the monkey village, certain that his older brother would follow soon enough.

Hawk finally spotted Revere perched in a palo verde among a cluster of ravens. The brief contact of their minds made the great black bird turn one beady eye toward his young master, as if to ask, "Did you need me?"

"Keep an eye out," Hawk said. "Honey just sent a couple bad guys to the giraffes. Watch out for anything else suspicious."

A Rumor of Real Irish Tea

Revere didn't need the reminder. He had become their lookout wherever they went, even when socializing with his own kind. His very presence helped to ease some of the paranoia that was second nature to Hawk.

It had been a rough few weeks. After their run-in with Oliver's handler in Flagstaff, the Wests had escaped to Phoenix and, rather than move on, they had worked on blending into the general population. Because they had no set destination to get to, this city was as good a place to hunker down as any. In addition to being a widely sprawled metropolis, the greater Phoenix area was adjacent to several Indian reservations, thus offering the children some options for egress if their situation became too dire.

Upon arrival they assigned each other certain responsibilities: Hawk was in charge of surveillance, Hummer was in charge of research, Honey was in charge of finances, and Happy was in charge of crowd control. In that first week, after some efforts in convincing Hummer and Honey to work together, they rented a series of houses, apartments, offices, and hotel rooms across the city. The amount of money they had spent so far was astronomical, but Honey could collect it back in a matter of hours on a crowded street.

Any qualms about begging—especially Hummer's—had gone by the wayside. Like Las Vegas, Phoenix had a federally mandated curfew of ten o'clock, and the kids had to be off the streets or risk capture by local law enforcement or GCA agents on the prowl. Establishing the network of safe locations seemed to be the logical solution.

They moved from one place to the next as they saw fit. Some were furnished, and others were empty. They didn't remain in one neighborhood for more than a night or two, and they made

IV

concerted efforts not to draw attention from the locals. This was an age of distrust, though, where neighbors tended to mind their own business in hopes that others would do the same. Once the sun set, it was easy to wander into the new location without anyone noticing their arrival.

Daytime presented its own set of problems. Sometimes they stayed indoors, but there wasn't much to do in an unfurnished apartment or an abandoned warehouse. When they did venture out, they had to stay among crowds—the GCA apparently had reservations about tranquilizing small children in front of a large audience—but there were only a limited number of places they could go. Because the schools ran year-round, four children could not simply wander the streets at will. They ended up loitering in public libraries or tagging along after field trip groups, like today. In the afternoons or evenings, they often found a public pool, where a few extra kids raised no eyebrows for the families there.

The whole process had become exhausting, though. The fake kidnapping reports on NPNN had become more frequent, and the reward had been upped a couple of times, which increased the chance that Honey and Happy would be recognized as Maddie and Alex North. So far no well-meaning strangers had approached them, but someone had called in a report of their location. As best as Hawk could figure, it had taken the GCA a week, more or less, to home in on them in Phoenix.

They made no overt attempts to recover the kids, however. Instead, a few low-level agents would begin to shadow them sometime during the day. Honey invariably discovered them and more often than not left them trussed up somewhere—usually with Hummer's ever-present duct tape—after she picked their brains on everything they had been instructed. The agents never knew much, though. The GCA was merely using them as surveillance in much the same way that Hawk used the birds around him.

It made him nervous. They were hanging back, watching and waiting until the right moment to strike.

It was much like a game of chess. Their end goal was obvious, but they needed to get all their pieces in the right places before they went in for the kill, so to speak. So far, the only pieces Hawk and his siblings had discovered were pawns.

Who were the stronger players, then? Presumably Oliver had been neutralized as a threat to the truants. They had done everything they could to cast his loyalties into question, and the government was notoriously untrusting. There were at least two other null-projectors the GCA could call upon for help from among the Prometheus students. There were probably a few more who had graduated from the Institute already, too. If that was the case, those would pose even more of a threat, because the Wests knew nothing about who they were or where they would come from.

The GCA would have to rely on null-projection at some point, though. Tranquilizer darts might take Honey and Happy out of service for a few hours, but when they woke up, they would project their captors into a world of regret. With Oliver out of the picture, the only other null-projector Hawk could identify on sight was Quincy.

She had never talked about her ability except to say that it was localized to herself and those around her, a radius of five to seven feet at most. The subject angered her for some reason that she had never disclosed. Hawk suspected that it had contributed to her transfer to Prom-F, but she never talked about that either. Quincy had been more like a caged bird than any other kid he knew.

IV

He felt guilty every time he thought about her and everyone else left behind. There was no way they could all escape together, but he and Hummer deliberately created a whole mess of chaos when they left. The students at Prom-F would be suffering for it as a result now, through increased restrictions and higher surveillance.

If the escape had only concerned Hawk and Hummer, they might have tried to get a few others out with them. The whole plan had been concocted for Honey and Happy, though. Bringing along anyone else—especially a null-projector like Quincy—would have undermined their purpose.

Still, he was pretty sure she would slug him if they ever met again. Which they wouldn't, he reminded himself as he joined his younger siblings. Not if he had any say in the matter, at least. He hoped, for his sake as well as hers, that the GCA left Quincy out of their plans entirely.

V
The Man in the Gray Suit

JULY 30, 10:32AM MDT, PROM-F

EMILY LIKED THE observation room for Oliver's second period. Even though it had the same taupe walls and industrial-grade furniture as all the other observations rooms, it had an added amenity: a window to the outside world. All the classrooms had windows to let in natural light, but the attached observation rooms usually only had the one large pane of glass that allowed handlers to watch their students. Children assigned to desks did not provide a lot of entertainment.

She was supposed to use her time in the observation room for work-related activities, but there was only so much she could do. She had already watched the orientation videos—a bunch of lies and propaganda that made her job seem like the greatest opportunity of the century, she thought, and it was thanks to Oliver's presence in the next room that she thought that. Naturally Prometheus used human-projectors to indoctrinate their incoming workforce.

She was also supposed to stay up-to-date on the contents of Oliver's file, but she had long since discounted that information as irrelevant to the little boy in her charge.

V

And, of course, there was that issue of a weekly report, but Crystal had already explained how to accomplish that one.

"You just insert your student's name into a template: 'Lucy is progressing with her studies. She has completed all her homework for this week and has been eating well at all her meals.' That's all they really want to know. Make sure to switch the information around a little each week so it doesn't sound like a template, and voila! You have your report done in five minutes, and the rest of the week to stew over how much longer you have to suffer through this job."

"But what if he hasn't done his homework and he's not eating well?" Emily asked.

Crystal eyed her cynically. "So what if he isn't? Reporting it will only make more work for you. The teachers will take care of the homework situation if it ever arises, which it probably won't. Some of these kids are troublemakers, but they all do their homework because they don't want the detentions they'd get otherwise. As for eating habits, whatever. I wouldn't report a lack of appetite unless they're passing out from starvation. Otherwise you'll have to start monitoring everything they eat at every meal and turning in a food diary for them."

"But what if they do pass out from starvation?" Emily asked, increasingly alarmed at the callous attitude that Crystal advocated.

"They get sent to the school nurse, who diagnoses malnutrition or anemia or whatever. You claim that you thought the kid was eating properly and that you never saw him skip a meal. Then the food diaries begin and you hope that your transfer comes soon. I had an anorexic fourteen-year-old as my second assignment, and those food diaries are an absolute pain. And don't look at me like that. I know perfectly well that eating disorders are bad, but she was going to skip meals whether I recorded it or not. Your kid doesn't look like the eating-disorder type, though."

"I'm just worried that he won't adjust well to being here," said Emily wistfully.

"And if you report as much, you'll create more trouble for him, and vicariously for yourself. Any kid who gets labeled with a developmental roadblock has to start sessions with the school's psychiatrist. If you're the one that labels them, they get vindictive in their revenge."

"The plumbing system in the handlers' dorm gets blown up?" Emily guessed.

Crystal grimaced. "Just remember: we're the expendable ones here, especially at Prom-F, since they've got nowhere else to send these kids. Sit back, shut up, and try to make as few waves as possible."

Emily reluctantly took her advice. She'd already drafted Oliver's status report, and the observation sheets she had to fill out for each class were completed for the rest of the week. The two computers in the room were occupied, like always—and she had yet to figure out how those other handlers always arrived ahead of her—so she had only two options left: she could watch NPNN, or she could stare at the walls.

Hence, the window in Oliver's second period observation room was an incredible bonus.

It had a perfect view of the gates and the driveway that led to the school's main building. A morning PE class was stretching on the lawn, and the leaves fluttered in the trees. It was a beautiful summer day.

And the gates were opening.

"Hey, there are some cars coming up the road," she said to no one in particular.

V

Crystal tossed aside the trashy novel she'd been reading on the sofa. "Oh yeah? They must be having another meeting this week. They had one last week, and the week before. My little darling and her brothers really did cause a lot of havoc, and no one seems to know what to do."

Emily's attention snapped to her face. Crystal flashed a smile as she joined her. "Two weeks ago, it was the principals of Prom-A, Prom-B, and Prom-F. Last week, they invited Prom-C and Prom-D. Let's see who we have this week, shall we?"

Four cars rolled up the driveway. The first parked, and Maggie Lloyd hustled out of the driver's seat to open the passenger door nearest the school's staircase.

"That's Genevieve Jones," said Emily with a strange twinge in her heart. Her attention darted to the classroom next door, where Oliver scrawled his notes in a bored posture.

"And Principal Lee," said Crystal. "Principal Gregory Lee, from Prom-B," she clarified for Emily's benefit. "Michelle must be in another car. There's no way he'd come without her."

"Who else got out of the front of the car?" Emily asked; she had returned her gaze to the spectacle as a man trotted up the stairs out of sight.

"Probably Principal Jones's admin assistant. I don't remember his name. He'd have preference over Michelle to ride in the first car, and Maggie has preference to drive the first car since Prom-F is playing host to this ensemble. It's surprising the hierarchy that exists in these academic circles. Here's Principal Carter from Prom-C getting out of the next car."

Emily watched with curiosity as a rotund man heaved himself from the back seat. Oliver had once told her that Rupert Carter didn't get along well with Genevieve Jones. Seeing him for the first time, she wondered if he got along with anyone.

A Rumor of Real Irish Tea

An arrogant sneer was etched into his face, plain evidence that he frequently viewed the world around him with contempt. His thinning hair swept upward into an elaborate comb-over that was grotesquely obvious from her vantage point.

"Is that the Prom-D principal getting out behind him?" she asked as a petite blonde joined him from the confines of the car. It stood to reason: if there was a hierarchy present, Prom-D would come after Prom-C.

"Annemarie Legrand," Crystal said. "I don't know much about her, except that she's top dog at Prom-D. She kind of reminds me of a toy poodle, all fluff and leathery skin."

It was an apt description, so much so that Emily was hard-pressed not to bark a laugh. Principal Legrand's frizzy, unnaturally blond hair was far more youthful than her face or figure, but it complimented her vibrant pink pantsuit. She certainly looked less austere than Genevieve Jones, whose black-clad figure had already disappeared into the building.

"So if all the principals were in the first two cars, who's in the third?" Emily asked.

Crystal shrugged. "Admin assistants, maybe. I think that was Carter's driving the second car, and Legrand's must have been the one in the passenger's seat. Yeah, that's Michelle getting out of the driver's seat of the third," she said, craning her neck to get a better look at a thin, frigid woman. "Can you believe she's only a couple years older than we are? How'd you like to be not-yet-thirty and ready to take over a prestigious place like Prom-B?"

Emily's brows shot up. "Jealous? I wouldn't think you'd want that job."

"I don't," said Crystal flatly, "but that doesn't mean I can't begrudge other people their success."

V

Emily suppressed a rueful laugh. "So the admin assistants are all accounted for. Then who's getting out of that car?"

Michelle from Prom-B had crossed around to open the back door. Beneath the watchful eyes of Emily and Crystal, a broad-shouldered man stood. All they could see of him was salt-and-pepper hair and the army-green uniform that made his posture seem even more rigid than it was.

Crystal whistled, suitably impressed. "Looks like they've called in the military."

"That's not all they've called in," said Emily in a strangled voice. A second person emerged from the back seat, a woman with immaculate poise and a familiar face. "That's Mary Rose Allen."

Shuffling sounded behind them, and four more handlers crowded to the window to get a look. "It is her," one of them said in awe. "Mary Rose Allen? What on earth brought her all the way here from Washington?"

"What if she's here to audit our performance?" said another in abject terror.

"She's here about the runaways, Einstein," said a third. "Prometheus is a division of the GCA, so it's only natural that she'd get called in eventually."

Emily worked her way out of the sudden crowd at the window, happy to let others take her place to gawk at the semi-celebrity. Mary Rose Allen was the White House's Service Czar, the figurehead at the top of the Government-Civilian Alliance who worked directly with the President of the United States. Everyone who pursued higher education knew who she was because her policies determined how far up the academic ladder they could climb. She was one of the most powerful women in the country.

A Rumor of Real Irish Tea

And Emily, having so recently botched the GCA's efforts to recover the West kids, had absolutely no desire to meet her.

"You okay?" Crystal asked as she joined her on the couch. "You look like you've seen a ghost."

"Just the ghost of what was once my future career," Emily said with a wan smile. "Do you think there's any way the students won't find out who's here?"

"Oh, no. They'll be here a couple of days, at least. They were last week, anyway. The news will spread through the ranks by lunchtime. Why does it matter?"

"Because if Oliver finds out that Principal Jones is here, he'll demand to speak with her," said Emily, but that was only half of what concerned her. If Oliver demanded to speak to Principal Jones, Emily would have to go with him. And since Principal Jones was currently in the company of Mary Rose Allen, there was the smallest chance of an encounter. Mary Rose Allen had been the one to request Oliver's help in finding the Wests, or so he had said. It only stood to reason that she knew who he was. Whether she knew the name or face of his idiot handler was another story, and one that Emily had no desire to discover.

"Just because he demands it doesn't mean that they'll let him," said Crystal logically.

"He's on a first-name basis with her. Oh, this is a complete nightmare. Couldn't everything just die down *a little*?"

Crystal seemed mildly sympathetic. "Cheer up. Maybe he won't find out who's here until it's too late."

Since she had said only a breath ago that all the students would know by lunchtime, Emily had a hard time believing this second possibility. A grim expression settled on her face. "It's fine. There's no point in prolonging the agony. I'll tell him myself."

V

Given the choice, she'd much rather rip the bandage off quickly than waste time dreading how it would feel. Her decision made, she spent the rest of the class period steeling her nerves against whatever encounters might come that afternoon.

"Guess who we just saw arriving out the window," she said to Oliver the moment she rejoined him in the hallway outside his class.

He shot a crusty glare up at her. "They finally caught the Wests and dragged them back to prison?"

Emily bit back a cynical laugh. "No. Principal Jones is here."

He stopped short as a strange array of emotions flitted across his face. "I need to talk to her," he said.

"Your next class starts in four minutes," Emily reminded him.

"I need to talk to her *now*."

"Hey!" Emily snagged his shoulder as he started past her. "After third period, okay? She just got here, and Crystal says she'll probably be here until tomorrow. You can wait until lunch."

He looked mutinous at first but then realized she wasn't forbidding the encounter. He jerked away from her grasp. "Fine. We'll go find her at lunch. Genevieve will straighten everything out. You're not expecting me to put in a good word with her for you, are you?" he asked suspiciously.

"I'm pretty sure I'm stuck here regardless," said Emily, "and I know that you have no good words to say about me anyway."

Oliver grunted, a sound of tacit agreement. Which was perfect in her book. The last thing she wanted was someone to bring up her name to Principal Jones. Right now she'd rather be completely forgotten.

Third period raced by, over almost as soon as it began, according to Emily's perspective. With growing dread, she watched Oliver sweep his school things into his bag.

A Rumor of Real Irish Tea

"Forward to my doom," she muttered.

Maybe they would get nowhere near Principal Jones. That many important people would have several layers of protocol and security around them. It wasn't as though Oliver could walk into Principal Gates's office and demand an audience with Genevieve Jones.

"Straight to Principal Gates's office?" she asked when she joined him in the hallway all the same.

To her surprise, he shoved his things into her hands. "I have to use the bathroom first," he said, and he bolted for the nearby lavatory door.

Stay of execution, Emily thought pessimistically. She didn't know whether it was a relief or a burden to have to wait any longer, but she did make a mental note to discourage Oliver from drinking an extra glass of soymilk for breakfast in the future. But he was probably nervous too. His future at Prometheus might ride on this impromptu interview, and he'd had only an hour to prepare his defense.

His third period was near the bay of elevators at the center of the building. Emily watched with idle interest as the other students and their handlers cleared the hallway. They streamed down the nearby stairs to the cafeteria, or to whatever corner they'd chosen for their midday plotting. In half a minute flat, she was alone.

The elevator nearest her chimed and the doors slid open. A man absentmindedly stepped out, his attention fixed on the cell phone in his hand. Suddenly, he stopped and looked up in surprise. "Oh!" he said, and he immediately slipped the phone into his pocket. He glanced around himself. "I think I got off on the wrong floor. How are you, Ms. Brent?"

Her heart dropped into her stomach. "You know my name," she said with a feeble smile. "That's not really a good sign."

V

There was something familiar about his face, but she couldn't quite place him. Right now she wasn't particularly keen on strangers knowing who she was.

"Of course I know your name," he said, much to her surprise. "We met back in New York. It's kind of hard to forget the sacrificial lamb about to be thrown to the wolves."

That familiar something clicked into place. "You're the man in the gray suit," said Emily in sudden recognition.

He glanced quizzically down at his suit, which was quite obviously black.

"No, I mean," Emily floundered, "you were wearing a gray suit that day. You met me at the train station and took me to the airport. I don't think you ever said your name."

An open smile broke across his face. "Oh, I'm—"

"Birchard!" Oliver emerged from the bathroom, his unexpected entrance causing both adults to jump. He had slicked back his hair with a wet comb, which explained what had taken him so long.

"Ben Birchard, at your service," the man said to Emily under his breath.

"Birchard, I need to see Genevieve," Oliver declared as though speaking to his personal slave. Emily had assumed that only handlers were treated that way.

"Not possible at the moment, Oliver," Ben Birchard said without so much as batting an eyelash. "She's having lunch right now, and she'll be in a meeting all afternoon."

Oliver clenched his teeth. "Look here, Birchard. They've gone and enrolled me at Prom-F. Someone needs to correct this absurd mistake, and the sooner, the better."

"Prom-F is a very good school," Birchard replied with a smile, "much better than the primary school I attended."

A Rumor of Real Irish Tea

Oliver screeched in outrage. "I belong at Prom-A!"

Nothing seemed to ruffle the man. "Principal Jones is fully aware of the situation, and she's doing everything in her power to straighten it out," he said diplomatically. "I'll inform her that you would like to speak with her, of course, but I can't make any guarantees. I have no idea how long she'll be in conference with General Stone and Secretary Allen."

Oliver paled. "Mary Rose Allen is here too?" His accusing eyes shifted to Emily. "You didn't say anything about that!"

"I didn't realize you'd care so much," said Emily defensively.

"I would've expected General Stone's presence to be the more astonishing of the two," said Birchard to the wall.

"Who's General Stone?" Oliver asked sharply.

Birchard favored him with a thin smile and turned back to the elevator. "The cafeteria's in the basement, isn't it?" he asked. The doors opened, and he disappeared within.

"I take it that he's Principal Jones's administrative assistant," said Emily in the ensuing silence.

"Never a straight answer out of him," Oliver grumbled. "He's come up in the ranks by being able to say the right things to the right people. Never can tell what he's really thinking, though."

"How old is he?" Emily asked. He didn't look all that much older than she was, now that she considered it, but he had one of those faces that would probably age well.

"Ancient," said Oliver. "He's at least thirty-two."

VI
Forewarned Is Forearmed

JULY 30, 1:50PM MDT, PROM-F

EMILY WAS ABLE to pass a nice lunch without the threat of impending doom hanging over her head. Ben Birchard had been ambiguous enough in his promises to Oliver that she was confident there would be no meeting with Principal Jones. Part of her pitied Oliver, to be brushed off so easily by adults who had catered to him in the past. Her overwhelming sense of a disaster averted squelched that feeling, though.

Her terror renewed when, shortly after fourth period started, a knock tapped lightly on the observation room door and none other than Ben Birchard poked his head inside. He homed in on Emily.

"Do you have a minute?" he said, and he beckoned her out to the hall.

Self-conscious, she ignored the curious eyes of her co-workers as she exited the room. "What is it?" she asked, dread pooling in her stomach.

"Were you in the middle of something? I'm sorry," he said, and the apology seemed sincere.

"No, no," said Emily. "I mean, I'm observing, but—"

A Rumor of Real Irish Tea

Her words cut off when he snorted. "No, sorry," he said, and he made a heroic attempt to suppress his laughter. "You really aren't doing anything, then. No one ever actually observes. Or do you?"

Emily sighed. "What did you need to speak to me about, Mr. Birchard?"

"Sorry," he said again. "You can call me Ben. Or Birchard like Oliver does, but that kind of makes me feel like a butler. 'Mr. Birchard' makes me sound like I'm sixty. It was actually Oliver I wanted to talk to you about. Could you try to dissuade him from demanding a meeting with Principal Jones?"

"I wish," said Emily sourly.

"He doesn't listen to you, I take it," Ben surmised. "He didn't listen to any of his other handlers either, so I thought it was a long-shot. You two have kind of a different rapport than he did with the others, though."

"What does that mean?"

"I don't know. When I saw how you interacted earlier, I got the feeling that he sort of respects you."

She scoffed, unable to entertain such a ridiculous notion. "He routinely tells me what an idiot I am, and I routinely let him. That's the only *rapport* we have."

"Well, that's different," Ben said with a careless shrug.

"He didn't tell his other handlers they were idiots?"

"They didn't let him. Constant power-struggles, as you might imagine. You're really sure you can't dissuade him?" He fixed a wistful gaze on her, childlike in its utter hope. Emily almost wished that she could satisfy his request.

"There's no way. Look, after everything that's happened, I probably deserve to get stuck here. But Oliver . . . he's being punished for something that wasn't his fault. I can't blame him

VI

for wanting to clear everything up and get back home. Prom-A is the only home he's ever known, so it's not fair to displace him like this."

Ben nodded as he considered this. "Unfortunately," he said, choosing his words with great care, "the only way to 'clear everything up' is to bring our four truants back. Between you and me, I think there's little chance that Oliver will return to Prom-A even then, though."

"Why?" asked Emily.

"Because his adventures tracking the Wests may have exposed him to—" He paused and looked surreptitiously around the hallway. Then, angling his body so that his face turned away from the nearest security camera, he finished in a very low voice, "—to some sensitive and dangerous information."

Altair. That had to be what he meant. "He doesn't know anything about any of that," Emily said.

A lopsided smile appeared on his face. "About any of what?"

"I don't know anything about it either," said Emily stubbornly. After Crystal's dire warning, there was no way she would utter that word aloud again, and to Genevieve Jones's personal assistant of all people. "Look, if that's all you wanted to talk to me about—"

"There was one more thing," he said, and he pulled a handheld device from within his suit coat pocket. Emily watched curiously as he tapped a couple of icons on the small screen.

"Well? What is it?" she asked.

"Sorry. I just remembered that their meeting was about to start, and that I was supposed to record it separately for Principal Jones. Care to watch with me?" He held up the screen. It displayed the security feed for a conference room where the distinguished visitors had assembled around an oblong table.

A Rumor of Real Irish Tea

"That was your 'one more thing'?" she asked in disbelief.

"No. My 'one more thing' was that Oliver's immediate future may be decided in this meeting, and that you might want to keep an overnight bag packed and ready. I seem to recall that you were unhappy about not having even a toothbrush with you the last time, so I thought I'd give you fair warning."

He started to amble up the hallway toward the elevators, but Emily lunged to catch his elbow. "They're sending us out again?" she asked in sudden panic.

Ben remained nonchalant. "They may have no other choice. They need a null-projector. Quincy's abilities are too localized, and Cedric is too young to be approved for any time away from Prometheus. Trust me—they've considered any number of alternatives. I'm all for long-distance snipers with tranquilizer darts, but then there's the problem of isolating the kids away from the public in order to do the deed. Civilians tend to panic when they see a six- and nine-year-old shot in broad daylight, even if it is only with a tranquilizer."

"I should think so," said Emily. "So their only option is to have Oliver track down the Wests again?"

"It's not a matter of tracking. They're in Phoenix. We just can't get anywhere near them."

Disbelief snaked through her. "In Phoenix? What on earth are they doing in *Phoenix*?"

"They went to the zoo on Monday," he said. "We had a couple men following them, but they ended up gawking at the giraffes until the place closed. The last thing they remembered was Honey shooing a group of people away while Happy showed them all a beatific smile. Those were their exact words." He finished with a sage tilt of his head.

Having experienced Honey's trancelike abilities, Emily could

VI

only think that the men got off easy. "If you know they're there, surely you can get to them at night, when they're asleep," she argued.

"Yeah, if we find where they're staying for the night and feel up to braving the murder of crows that guard them. That bird of Hawk's collects friends to help him with the lookout. After the disaster in Vegas, we really don't want to trigger the bird-alarm unless we know for certain we can get to the kids before they run away. It's all very frustrating, I know, but because they're children, we have to be able to secure them in as unsuspicious a manner as possible. If they were adults, it would be a piece of cake. We'd just send in a team and arrest them."

"But," said Emily, "the general public has seen the news reports. They know that Maddie and Alex North are missing, so there shouldn't be too much damage control in recovering them that way."

He shook his head, though. "The general public knows that two children are missing. They're not looking for four, and when you go in and ambush four, the original story starts to unravel. If that happens, people start to question what's going on, and then there are inquiries made into things that don't need to be inquired upon, and everything takes forever to clear. Do you have any idea how many conspiracy theories there are in this country?"

"A lot," she conceded.

"A lot," Ben confirmed. "The last thing this government wants is for its people to lose trust in it, and the best way to prevent that is through information control. Tell them what they need to know in the most effective means to bring about your desired ends."

Emily rolled her eyes. "How very trustworthy."

"Are you questioning your government?" Ben asked in a controlled voice.

A Rumor of Real Irish Tea

Even though a hint of humor glimmered in his eyes, her answer was immediate. "No. Not at all."

He smiled, but it seemed extremely practiced. "Good. Now, if you'll excuse me, I really do have to keep an eye on this." He raised the screen, where the surveillance footage still played.

"And I . . . have to get back to observing," said Emily, feeling more than awkward that she had waylaid him for so long.

"It was nice talking to you," said Ben with a polite tip of his head, and he strolled away.

"Yeah," Emily mumbled. He turned to take the stairs rather than the elevator this time. She wasn't sure what to make of him. He had been kind enough to give her fair warning, but why? Was it out of the goodness of his heart? Had he been commanded by someone higher up the ladder? From what he had said, Oliver's involvement wasn't even officially decided yet.

"I don't want to go back out on the road," she said to the empty hallway. She knew which pair of pants she would *not* be taking with her, though.

VII
An Afternoon at the Movies

JULY 30, 2:15PM MST, PHOENIX

"Do you think we're being followed?" Hummer asked.

"Of course we're being followed," said Hawk. "We're always being followed by this time of day."

On impulse, Honey called out to the crowd around them, "How many of you work for the GCA, raise your hands!"

Three hands shot up.

"Slightly more than usual," she said to herself. Then, "Everyone else, go away. You three, follow us. Hummer, get the duct tape."

"Maybe we should think about moving to a new city," Hummer said as he pulled the roll from his backpack.

"But we've already invested so much in this one," Honey pragmatically replied. "Happy, can you try thinking about how much you hate the GCA? I'd like to see how well these guys cooperate when they're immersed in self-loathing."

"And we begin Honey's unethical sociology experiments again," Hummer whispered under his breath to Hawk

"Where are we going to take them?" Hawk asked Honey. "You can't interrogate these filthy, disgusting scumbags here on the street, especially if you're planning on using the duct tape.

A Rumor of Real Irish Tea

Happy—" He shifted abruptly to his youngest brother in wonder. "You really hate the GCA, don't you?"

Happy's face was set in a critical stare upon the three agents, but he took the time to nod a short yes.

"We need to get off the streets," Hummer said with a nervous glance around the shopping center. The other pedestrians were turning malevolent glares upon the GCA agents, and a general air of restlessness pervaded the area. The sooner they moved out of the public eye, the sooner he could exact his revenge.

Or Happy's revenge. He wasn't exactly sure which one it was.

"There's a movie theater over there," said Honey. "You three, get out your money. You're buying us tickets to the matinee showing of *Princess Pretty Goes to Sparkleville*. And you're springing for popcorn."

"Can't someone else choose the movie?" Hummer complained to no one in particular. "I don't see why we have to be tortured too."

There weren't many choices, though. The afternoon shows were either geared toward indoctrinating three-year-olds (as was the case with *Princess Pretty Goes to Sparkleville*), or else they were aimed for older audiences. Children in the Wests' age group were in school until five o'clock, so there was no point in showing films crafted for their demographic.

The movie had already started by the time they made it through ticketing and concessions. Thanks to Happy's intense focus, the GCA agents were wallowing in a puddle of self-contempt. They filed into a sparsely populated theater, where only a handful of toddlers and their parents or nannies watched the computer-animated princess lecture her animal friends about how to recycle their sparkles properly. No one paid the newcomers any heed as Honey directed her captives to the back row, two seats apart. She collected their wallets and cell phones.

VII

Hummer followed behind with his duct tape and secured their hands to the armrests.

"We should take their shoes, too," Honey said thoughtfully.

"Why?" asked Hawk.

"Because it's inconvenient for them," she said. "And because I saw a thrift store a street over that could probably use the donations."

It was a good enough answer for him. He followed behind Hummer and removed the shoes of each agent. None of them seemed to notice or care, too intent upon hating himself.

Honey began her interrogation of the first. "Were you all working together?"

"Together?" he repeated stupidly.

"Did you know that these two men were also following us?" she asked. "Were the three of you working together?"

"I didn't know," said the man. "They didn't tell me much of anything."

"Yeah, they really don't. That's because they're evil."

He nodded, feeling the brunt of her words and Happy's hostility combined.

She continued. "Do you have a partner?"

"No. I'm just a peon. I don't know why they sent me when I'm so far down the chain of command. The GCA really is evil, awful, terrible—"

"Who do you report to?" Honey asked. "And where?"

"Agent Knox at the Central Phoenix office. A call came in this morning and he ordered me into a car. They dropped me off and told me to follow you. That's all. I'm just a technician. I hate my life so much."

"That story's getting very familiar," said Hawk to Hummer quietly.

A Rumor of Real Irish Tea

"They're probably trying to establish two layers of surveillance," Hummer replied. "They've got these low-level guys they send up close because they know we'll find them. The higher-level guys probably track or follow at a distance. Where's Revere?"

"I left him outside," Hawk said. "No one likes a bird in a movie theater."

"You should see if he can scare up some friends and fan out across the area to look for government sedans. The last thing we want is for someone to follow us home because we thought we'd already gotten rid of all our shadows."

Hawk chewed thoughtfully on his lower lip. "I'll tell him, but wide-range surveillance is difficult with birds. They don't always know what they're looking for."

"What're you saying?" asked Hummer.

"We should probably take a roundabout route to our place tonight," Hawk answered. "More roundabout than usual, I mean, just to be sure we're not followed."

"And the sooner the better," Honey said. "These idiots can't be anything more than decoys." She had continued her interrogations but saw no reason to delve any further. "Hey, you," she suddenly said to the third man, "poke yourself in the eye."

The man instinctively tried to obey, but his hands were, of course, duct-taped firmly to the armrest of his chair. Desperate to comply, he lowered his head to meet a raised finger. "Ow!" he cried.

"I love doing that," said Honey as she rifled through the three wallets. "They're not even carrying much cash anymore," she said with a scowl, and she turned again to her captives. "You three all need to poke yourselves in the eye as punishment."

"Come on." Hawk pulled her by the sleeve to the door. Hummer and Happy filed behind. They paused just outside the

VII

theater so that Honey could dump the pilfered wallets into the trashcan there.

"Do you think they've got tracking devices on that cash?" Hummer asked. "I mean, we're kind of getting a modus operandi here."

Honey sighed. "Who wants malted milk balls?" Without waiting for a response, she headed away toward the concession stand. Happy trotted eagerly behind her.

Hummer took the opportunity to pull Hawk off to one side. "It may be time to consider some drastic measures," he said in a low voice. "We're not getting anywhere in our search for Altair, and the GCA is slowly, systematically pinning down our movements. It's only a matter of time before they come rushing in to get us. I'm kind of surprised they haven't done it already."

"Happy," said Hawk shortly. Upon seeing Hummer's perplexed expression, he elaborated. "They can't rush in yet because they have nothing to neutralize Happy right now. They don't need all of their agents descending into utter panic when they get close to him—and if we were surrounded by GCA agents, you can bet Happy would be panicking."

"Do we even know how far his projections can extend?" Hummer asked.

"No. It seems to depend on how strong he's feeling any given emotion at any one moment. He does a good job controlling it, though, considering how young he still is. So what drastic measures did you have in mind?"

"I don't know. We could ambush a GCA office. What?" he asked when Hawk looked at him like he had gone absolutely insane. "If they're not expecting it, it could work. We'd do a quick job—find out if they have any information on Altair or Mom and Dad, and then get back out. Between Honey and

Happy, we could have the whole office at our mercy. After we get what we need, we create a diversion and steal a vehicle to escape."

"How long have you been plotting this?" Hawk asked suspiciously.

Hummer shifted from one foot to the other. "A couple weeks, maybe. Hey, I need *something* to do on those days when we hole up for hours on end. I already memorized all the local GCA addresses, and I was even able to get some of the building schematics off the internet when we were at the library last week. I've already figured out two or three different routes in and out. I really don't think it would be too difficult."

"Aside from the whole danger-of-getting-caught part," said Hawk. "But why not risk having us all thrown back into the government's clutches on the off-chance that we might get a good lead?"

"How are we getting a good lead?" asked Honey, who rejoined the conversation in time to hear that last phrase. She and Happy both looked between their older brothers expectantly.

Hawk answered before he considered the wisdom of doing so. "Hummer wants to ambush one of the GCA's branch offices."

"I'm game," said Honey, much to his dismay. "I said we should do that weeks ago."

"And I said weeks ago that we weren't going to take those kinds of risks," Hawk replied.

She waved a flippant hand. "Desperate times call for desperate measures. We've been free almost a whole month, and we're no better off now than we were when we started. It's time to start considering risks."

"Whatever we decide, everyone has to agree," said Hawk, and he looked around at their faces one by one. Each in turn

VII

nodded. "And it has to be planned out. We don't run headlong into a situation we can't get ourselves out of. Understood?"

"I hate the GCA," said Happy suddenly. "I want to ambush them."

"So do I," said his three siblings in unison.

"Not fair, Happy," said Hawk a moment later when he recovered his wits. Even without his youngest brother's strong feelings on the matter, though, he suspected they would have come to this decision eventually.

Eventually was just supposed to be a whole lot farther off than today.

VIII
Spaghetti and Stars

JULY 30, 6:13PM MDT, PROM-F

It took every last ounce of Emily's patience to deal with Oliver that afternoon. He fixated on meeting with Genevieve Jones, and when she warned him that it probably wouldn't happen, he only became more determined. At dinnertime, he demanded that they ferret out Birchard wherever he was hiding so that he could tell Oliver where Genevieve was staying for the night.

To Emily's astonishment, they found Birchard with no trouble at all. He was loitering in the hall just beyond Principal Gates's office talking to Principal Lee's administrative assistant, Michelle. Her icy exterior had disappeared, but it returned when Oliver unceremoniously interrupted their conversation.

"Birchard," he said, apathetic to the discussion he had just intruded upon, "when is Genevieve going to see me?"

"Tomorrow before she leaves, I suspect," said Ben, and he arched his brows at Emily as though to inquire whether she'd even tried to dissuade the boy.

"What time is she scheduled to go?" Oliver asked, oblivious to this nuance.

VIII

"Noon-ish."

"And she *will* see me?"

Michelle broke into their conversation. "Principal Jones is a busy woman, little boy, and a child your age should address her by her proper title, not her first name."

"Principal Jones is tolerant of some of the better students," Ben told her. "It helps foster a good camaraderie among them."

"Really?" she said, her iciness melting again as she spoke to him. "It's so informal. Principal Lee would never let any of his students call him Gregory. I don't even dare call him Gregory." And then she laughed, a forced, tittering sound.

Emily thought she might puke at the obvious flirtation. "Oliver, you've got your answer," she said. He was glaring daggers at Michelle, and it was best to extract him from the situation. "You'll see Principal Jones tomorrow."

"He didn't say so for sure," Oliver replied. "Yes, Birchard, I'm perfectly aware of how you twist words around so that you can weasel out of giving a concrete answer."

"Caught red-handed," Ben said to Michelle, who foolishly laughed again.

"Did you even tell her I wanted to see her?" Oliver asked.

"Yes, I did. I don't have any control over whether she actually agrees to meet with you, though. Right now she's having dinner with Principal Gates and General Stone."

"Not with Secretary Allen?" Oliver asked.

"Secretary Allen has already left for the airport," Michelle said in a superior voice. "She's a very busy woman. Honestly," she added to Ben, "the way information travels through these schools is incredible. Secretary Allen was here for only a few hours, she saw no one but the administrators, yet all the children somehow know about her being here. Of course, the handlers can be such terrible gossips." She slid a critical glance toward Emily, who instinctively recoiled.

What had she done to deserve such an unprovoked attack?

She was even more surprised, though, when Oliver came to her defense. "Birchard told me she was here," he said. "Maybe he's the terrible gossip."

"Caught red-handed again," Ben said with a mild laugh. "I was the one to tell him, Michelle. You can't jump to conclusions about perfectly respectable handlers."

Michelle fixed a pointed stare on Emily. "You're the one that Honey West tied up with duct tape, aren't you? You were like putty in her hands."

Embarrassment flooded Emily from head to toe. "I—"

"Didn't Honey West once make you and a bunch of other administrators eat a handful of earthworms each?" Oliver abruptly asked. Michelle's face turned a mottled shade of purple. Encouraged, Oliver elaborated. "She got them from the school gardener, his composting box, wasn't that right? And there was a little song you had to sing while you chewed them—how did it go? 'Nobody likes me, everybody hates me . . .' Kinda hard to sing with a mouthful, I'd think."

Michelle suppressed a gag.

"So you'd know firsthand how strong Honey West's projections are," Oliver continued as though oblivious to the memories he was stirring up. "It seems odd that you'd single out someone else for scrutiny when you've experienced the same thing. But then, I'm just a *little boy*, so what do I know?"

"I hadn't heard that story," said Ben to Michelle with compassion. "That's really awful." The remark heightened her embarrassment instead of alleviating it.

Oliver clicked his tongue against his teeth in mock regret. "I

VIII

guess I shouldn't have mentioned any of that in front of such a terrible gossip. Try to keep that story under your hat, Birchard. Some people might think it makes Prom-B's admins look undignified. Emily, I think we're done here." He spun and headed down the hallway.

Emily ventured a glance at the pair before she followed. Michelle was trying to kindle some ego-saving outrage. Ben, on the other hand, seemed entertained. Emily was grateful that Oliver had already decided on a hasty retreat.

"How did you know that thing about the earthworms?" she whispered as she caught up with him. "Do the stories from one campus spread to another?"

"It was in Honey's file," he said with a sidelong glance, "in the discipline section. It happened last May. She had detention for a week afterward. I was only guessing that Michelle was one of the admins involved, though."

Emily shuddered. "I think I may have gotten off lucky with the duct tape. Why would she do something like that? Just a prank?"

"Pranks are for handlers," Oliver said. "You don't attack the admins unless you have a real reason. The punishment isn't worth it otherwise. And I don't know why she did it," he added before Emily could ask again. "It wasn't noted in the file, and it happened after the dates we were really interested in. Maybe it was payback for whatever that job was they had her do back in March. Maybe she had some other beef she wanted to get even for. Whatever it was, seven admins got a handful of thick, juicy earthworms to chew up and swallow."

Emily shuddered again. "I don't think I'm hungry anymore."

"You sure?" Oliver asked wryly. "I'm pretty sure spaghetti was on the menu for tonight."

A Rumor of Real Irish Tea

To her utmost dismay, he wasn't kidding. Oliver made further show of slurping his noodles, which had Emily gagging and him trying hard not to laugh at her.

She was both relieved and sorry to part with him at the dorms—relieved because he couldn't make gross noises at her, and sorry because that had been the most normal interaction they'd ever had. She'd seen glimmers of a normal little boy—a *funny*, normal little boy—rather than the intellectual snob he usually acted.

Children retired to their rooms by eight o'clock, though, an hour before bedtime to finish up any homework or reading assignments. Handlers could socialize in their half of the dormitory, but the majority seemed to prefer their solitude, Emily among them.

Her room was still a mess of boxes, even though she had started to unpack. Most of her clothes were in the closet now, and her books were ready to be stacked on the provided bookshelf. Several of the boxes held her kitchen supplies, though, useless in this single dorm. The handlers shared a small kitchenette, but it was fully stocked with dishes and cooking ware. Emily wished the government movers who had boxed all of her things had left that particular section of her tiny apartment behind for its next tenant. Prom-F was too far removed from civilization to donate the lot to a thrift store, and she could only fit so much beneath her bed.

The first thing she wanted to do tonight, however, was pack her overnight bag. Ben's warning had replayed itself in her head all afternoon. If they wanted Oliver, she wouldn't head out so empty-handed this time around.

She was in the midst of sorting between her clothes—what would she hate the least if she had to wear it multiple times?—when a knock on the door interrupted her. Crystal sometimes

VIII

visited in the evenings, so Emily fully expected her to be on the other side of the door. She was wrong.

"Hello," said Ben with a cheerful smile.

"Hi," said Emily, utterly confused.

"I came to see if you wanted to catch some fresh air with me."

She looked suspiciously up the hallway one direction and then down the other. Nothing seemed out of the ordinary.

"Come on," said Ben. "I'll make it worth your while, I promise." He pulled a brown bag out from behind his back and waved it enticingly.

Emily stepped out of her room and shut the door behind her. "Am I going to get scolded for something?"

"Is there something you should be scolded for?" he asked.

"Look, I tried to talk Oliver out of pushing for a meeting with Principal Jones, but like I told you, he doesn't listen to a word I say. What he wants to do, he does."

"Why is it that you see a brown paper bag and think that I've come to scold you?" Ben asked, amused. "I brought you something to eat."

Her expression flattened. "Is it worms?"

"No."

"Spaghetti that looks like worms?"

He tried hard not to laugh. "It's a sandwich. I noticed you didn't eat much of anything for dinner."

Her suspicions spiked. "Noticed? How?"

"The school is replete with surveillance cameras," said Ben, "and before you accuse me of stalking, I'll have you know that I was under orders to watch."

"Under orders?" Emily echoed.

Ben tipped his head toward the exit. "I'll tell you all about it. Come on."

A Rumor of Real Irish Tea

She felt like the foolish girl at the start of an old horror movie as she allowed this near stranger to lead her away from her dorm room. Only when he turned up at the stairwell instead of down did she think to question where he was taking her, though.

"Where are we going?"

"To the roof. I have the access code. There's a nice view of the campus—at Prom-A there is, anyway. The skyline here will be different, but the campus below should be roughly the same."

"Is the access code roughly the same too?" Emily asked impertinently.

"No. I thought ahead and got this one," said Ben. "Come on."

She followed him up the stairs, questioning all the way whether this was such a good idea or not. If he really did have a sandwich in that bag, though, she'd be eternally grateful. Now that Oliver's spaghetti-infested plate and worm-slurping noises were gone, she was hungry again.

They climbed three stories. Ben punched a code into the door at the top of the stairs, and the lock clicked open. "Just in time to catch the last of the sunset," he said as he motioned her outdoors. "Thank you, daylight savings."

The western horizon was stained with crimson-orange that fast faded to purple and midnight blue. Overhead, the Milky Way spread across the sky. "There are hardly any stars in New York," said Emily as she looked up in appreciation.

"They're trying to crack down on light pollution, but with a city that large it's next to impossible. Out here in the sticks Prom-F is the only thing producing any light at all, and it's all carefully shielded. Here's your sandwich." He handed her the paper bag.

Emily took it from him. "Thanks. So what did you want to explain, and why did it need to be on the roof?"

"It didn't need to be on the roof," Ben said. "I just like it up here. It's a nice view, and there's excellent cell reception. Check your phone if you don't believe me."

She had been in the process of opening the brown bag, but one hand flew to her pocket in alarm. "I left it back in my room," she said in panic. "I should go back and—"

"It's fine, you're off-duty," Ben said calmly. "I was only giving a stupid example of why the rooftop is great, not testing to see whether you were diligent in carrying around your phone."

She heaved a sigh of relief and returned her attention to the bag. She fished out what looked like turkey on rye and noted with growing excitement the presence of alfalfa sprouts and tomatoes nestled in among the lettuce leaves. "So what are we here to talk about? Why were you ordered to watch surveillance of the cafeteria?"

"I was instructed to watch surveillance of you and Oliver," said Ben. "Principal Jones wanted my assessment of whether to send the two of you down to Phoenix to deal with the Wests."

Emily's nerves stood on edge. "What did you tell her?"

"I haven't told her anything yet. They're making their final decision tomorrow. The truth is . . . well, she wanted me to assess whether you're still loyal to Prometheus."

Her jaw dropped.

"Yes," said Ben mildly, "I imagined you would have that sort of a reaction. Look, the GCA and Prometheus in particular take security breaches very seriously. This is just standard procedure when we're looking to use someone who has already experienced a lapse."

"So you're still trying to figure out whether I intentionally got myself bound and gagged by a bunch of children?" Emily asked, sarcasm thick on her voice. "I thought that's what those three weeks of confinement were for."

A Rumor of Real Irish Tea

"Oh, no," he said. "No one thinks you did that on purpose, or that you intentionally disclosed anything to them. You're not the only one to get the duct-tape treatment from the Wests either, if that makes you feel any better. That seems to be their favored method of confining people."

"Then what's this about assessing my loyalty?" Emily asked, confused.

He answered her very carefully. "Employees who run afoul of their employers' policies—especially those who are not really at fault when they run afoul—have a tendency to become embittered. Sometimes, the experience opens them up to thoughts of treachery or vengeance, especially if they are aware of one of their employers' . . . shall we say *competitors*?"

He was talking about Altair again. He was doing it in a roundabout manner, but he was doing it nonetheless. "I would never do something like that," said Emily firmly.

Ben nodded. "I know. You're extremely honest. It's a rare trait these days. What's more, you've been conditioned towards obedience to your superiors, according to your personnel file. There's not a treacherous bone in your body."

"My personnel file says I'm obedient?" Emily asked. It didn't surprise her that he had read it. Crystal had said the admin assistants had access to basically every piece of information within the Prometheus Institute's system.

"You scored high for obedience on your personality assessment—the one you took two years ago when you first applied for a Prometheus internship. Most people don't realize that they test for that, but it's an extremely important characteristic to have in your position. Handlers aren't exactly the top of the food chain around here, as I'm sure you've noticed."

"Does anyone call them 'child-life counselors'? I'm just curious,

VIII

because that's what the position was billed as, and I haven't heard anyone actually use it since I stepped foot on Prometheus soil."

He smiled. "It's a nice euphemism for recruitment. It doesn't have much use beyond that. The students have such a hostile view of their 'child-life counselors' that not much counseling occurs. At some point—fairly early on, I think—the term 'handler' was applied and stuck."

"Which is why it's important for us to be obedient," said Emily. "So why are you telling me all of this?"

"I told you I was instructed to assess you."

"Somehow, I doubt that meant *telling* me as much."

It was a valid accusation, but he dismissed it with a shrug. "Principal Jones doesn't usually specify *how* I'm supposed to do my job. She tells me what she wants done and lets me pick my own methods of accomplishing it. And after our little conversation just now, I can report to her with absolute certainty that you have no affiliations with Altair."

Emily hissed at that word and looked instinctively around the darkened roof.

"It's over there," Ben said helpfully, but when she looked, she discovered that he was pointing not to a security camera but to a bright star in the night sky. "Altair, part of the Summer Triangle. It's perfectly visible this time of the year."

"I was warned not to talk about it," Emily said nervously. "I don't want to know anything more than I already do, which is nothing."

Ben nodded. "Understandable. They're quite a troublesome organization."

"I think I should go back to my room," said Emily. She felt like an animal he was trying to cage, like she was being forced into a situation that would compromise her no matter what she did.

A Rumor of Real Irish Tea

Unfazed by her decision, he nodded toward the exit. "The door should be open. Enjoy your sandwich."

Emily bolted, brown bag clutched in her hands. Before she slipped into the safety of the building, though, she paused. "So they really are sending Oliver out again?"

His back was to her, but he looked over his shoulder with a pleasant smile. "Final decision tomorrow. Any other questions?"

"Are you a human-projector?" she blurted. He wasn't the same as Honey West, but he had such a way of manipulating conversations that her nerves practically sang a warning.

The smile cracked into a grin, though. "Me? No. I'm completely one-hundred-percent normal. At least, that's what my personnel file says. I'm flattered you asked, though. Good night."

"Good night," Emily mumbled, and she shut the stairwell door behind her.

What had that all been about? Why did he need to bring up Altair by name? It must have been his method of assessing. If Principal Jones didn't question what he did, he was free to use whatever means he saw fit, even if it meant bringing up a taboo subject.

"A troublesome organization," she muttered, disgruntled. "I could've lived the rest of my life without having to know that little detail."

IX
The Shadow Campus

JULY 30, 8:23PM MDT, PROM-F

GOING ALMOST A full month without a roommate had done no favors for Oliver. He had grown accustomed to solitude, to quiet nights of reflection where he didn't have to worry about the existence of another soul. He knew that returning to his former habits would require some adjustment. Unfortunately, he had assumed he would return to Prom-A and the same annoying roommate he had left behind.

Prom-F was no Prom-A, and his current roommate was nothing like his former one. Tyler had no more inclination to talk with Oliver than Oliver did with Tyler, which infuriated him when he thought about it. They had exchanged no more than two or three curt sentences since his arrival. Oliver was an outsider, someone not worth engaging in conversation.

Not that he cared. Prom-F was filled with idiots and delinquents who could only in their wildest dreams ever aspire to the high achievements of Prom-A students. Prom-A was an escalator straight to one's ivy-league university of choice, all expenses paid. Prom-A produced brilliant doctors and lawyers, skilled artists, and savvy politicians.

A Rumor of Real Irish Tea

What did Prom-F produce? Nothing. Prom-A had a whole list of prestigious graduates. Prom-B and Prom-C were the same, though not to the same degree. Even Prom-D sometimes produced someone noteworthy. No one distinguished ever came from the Prometheus-F campus.

And yet, the Prom-F kids never seemed to know their place. They had these inflated attitudes, as though they had scores of Nobel laureates among their alumni and were about to start mass production on a cure for cancer out of their biology lab. It had been that way at last year's multi-campus exhibition, the rag-tag bunch at Prom-F thrusting out their chests and acting as though they owned the place.

Which, technically, they did, but they should have had the common sense to defer to their superiors from the other campuses.

The exposition had lasted a week, and the Prom-A and Prom-B kids had cleaned house for the awards in almost every category. Even in the face of numerous defeats, though, the Prom-F kids had maintained their pride. When Hummer West won the mechanics exposition (which, had it been at any other school he couldn't even have entered because he wasn't old enough to travel from Prom-F, Oliver thought bitterly), his classmates nearly exploded with triumph. One lousy award, and they acted like they had swept the competition.

Oliver had let his entire school down when he came in second. The Prom-A kids shook their heads in disappointment, and the Prom-F kids looked down on him. In fact, the Prom-F kids—and his new roommate in particular—*still* looked down on him.

"Do you really have to tap your pencil like that?" Tyler asked.

Oliver ceased the motion, previously unaware that he had been doing it, but then he realized that he didn't have to cater to a Prom-F flunky. "It helps me think," he said, starting it up again.

IX

"Does having your chair yanked out from under you help you think, too? 'Cause I can help with that."

Oliver turned a sour glare upon the boy across the room. Their desks faced opposite walls, and on the two nights before this they had said not a single word to one another as they each completed their homework. Tyler was a year older and on a different track of courses than Oliver, so they had no interaction during the daytime unless they happened across one another in the cafeteria or the shared boy's room at the end of the hall.

"What is your problem?" Oliver asked. "I mean, aside from the obvious brain damage that landed you here at Prom-F to begin with."

"My problem is getting stuck with a namby-pamby Prom-A discard for a roommate," Tyler retorted with equal venom. "And a null-projector to boot," he added in complete disgust.

"I didn't ask to be shuffled in with the clown brigade," said Oliver. He didn't mind being called namby-pamby because that was an obvious lie, but "Prom-A discard" had struck a nerve.

"Yeah, well, the least you could do is keep your stupid pencil quiet now that you are here. It was my room first."

"Sorry to intrude upon your solitude," Oliver sneered.

"Best two weeks of my life," Tyler said.

The number gave Oliver pause. "Only two?" he asked in confusion.

Tyler's face twisted in contempt. "They didn't switch room assignments until after they had lifted the lockdown. I *thought* I was getting my own room, which is practically unheard of."

Oliver's brows shot up. "They only lifted the lockdown two weeks ago?"

A snort escaped his roommate's nostrils. "Took 'em almost that long to replace all the circuitry that was fried by Hummer's

EMP, and then they had to make sure the whole system was working right before they set us loose."

"And you just stayed in your dorms the whole time?"

"They let us out for breakfast, lunch, and dinner in small groups, and on periodic bathroom breaks throughout the day. We had homework assignments to keep us busy the rest of the time. You think there's something funny about a whole school of kids being treated like they're criminals in a prison?"

He hadn't realized he was smiling. It must have been from a sense of shared suffering. Faint though the expression was, Oliver wiped it from his face. "No. I mean, Prom-F is kind of like a prison anyway, but it's nice that they let you out for meals. Try spending three weeks in a GCA confinement cell with nothing but pre-packaged vending machine food brought to you at intervals."

"What'd you do for a toilet?" Tyler asked with grudging interest.

"There was one in the room," Oliver said.

"Gross. Like you really were in prison. Man, Hawk and Hummer must have gotten you good."

"Their sister got my handler," he said. No sense in admitting that Hawk had cast aspersions on his loyalty to Prometheus and the GCA. That was all hogwash anyway.

Tyler grunted, and a particle of respect gleamed in his eyes. It was gone just as soon as he remembered he was speaking with the enemy. "Yeah, well, this may be a step up for you, but that doesn't mean anyone's going to throw you a welcome party."

"A step *up*?" Oliver echoed with utter disdain. "I'd choose eternal confinement with a bucket for a toilet over Prom-F any day of the week."

"Shut up," said Tyler. "No one's that stupid."

"Except the entire student body of Prom-F."

IX

"Shut up. And if you start tapping that pencil again, I swear I'll break it in half and shove both pieces up your nose."

"Ooh, violence. How very superior of you."

Tyler started menacingly, and Oliver recoiled, even though there was a good six feet between them.

"Wuss," said Tyler.

"Delinquent," said Oliver.

They both returned to their homework. Several minutes of stubborn silence passed before Tyler spoke up again, belligerence thick on his voice.

"So what's it like to be the administrators' lackey? Do they give you lots of treats for doing their bidding?"

"Oh, yeah. Loads of 'em," said Oliver sarcastically. "They put me in solitary confinement for three weeks, they transfer me to the armpit of the Institute, they stick me with an utter Neanderthal for a roommate. There are so many treats I can't even count 'em!"

Tyler shot him a dirty look. "That was after you failed. What about when you succeeded? I heard they've used you to restrain projectors a dozen times before this."

"Not a dozen," said Oliver self-consciously. "Most projectors know not to act up, so it's only the idiot few that I've had to deal with. And why are you so interested?"

"I guess I'm just curious what would make a kid betray his own to join forces with the enemy," Tyler said, and he glared at Oliver critically.

The accusation rankled, even though it came from a Prom-F ninny. "You're acting like I had some sort of choice in the matter," Oliver said. "Do you honestly think they ask my opinion? 'Hey, Oliver, we're having this situation down at Prom-D. What do you think about maybe lending a helping hand?' Yeah, right. They come in, tell me to pack my bag, and give me half an hour to get ready, if I'm lucky. And I can't help it if my very presence restrains projectors. I never asked to be a null-projector either."

In the wake of this tirade, silence descended between them again. Oliver was annoyed that he had said so much already, and Tyler seemed too stunned to respond. Instead, he only stared, his eyes wide and round.

"Sorry," he mumbled at last, and he turned back to his schoolwork.

"This is idiotic," said Oliver. "My one consolation is that when I'm an adult and in charge, I can slap all of these administrators in a nursing home and throw away the key. But even *that* is meaningless if I get stuck here at Prom-F permanently. No one of importance comes from Prom-F! It might as well be called Prom-Oaf!"

"No one comes from Prom-F at all, you moron," Tyler muttered, so low that Oliver barely heard it.

"What was that?" he said sharply.

Tyler hissed his reply across the room, as though he was wary of being overheard by outsiders. "I said, no one comes from Prom-F at all. There's no record of anyone past graduation. They disappear."

"That's absurd," said Oliver, but a strange quiver ran through him. Quincy had said something similar.

"It's the truth," Tyler replied. "The rumor was floating around for a while. Every year a handful of kids turn eighteen and supposedly graduate, but no one knows where they go. They never write their friends here like they always promise, and they're not in the Prometheus system after that, either."

"Okay, now I know you're lying," Oliver said. "Once you're in you're always in. If everyone really disappeared after graduation, you'd all be climbing the walls to get out of here."

IX

Tyler shook his head. "Before Hawk and Hummer, no one believed it was possible. We're out in the middle of nowhere, if you hadn't noticed. Some of the older students said that there was one kid a few years ago who tried to run away while he was on a field trip. They caught him in under two hours, but he didn't come back to Prom-F. 'Transferred,' some of the admins said. 'Expelled,' some others said. Like anyone is ever transferred or expelled from Prom-F. Where would they transfer them to? Prom-A?"

"It's just a story. You don't even know it's true, and it probably isn't."

"Every kid here has a theory about what happens after graduation," Tyler said. "Just ask around, if they'll even talk to you. Some think the graduates are turned loose for manual labor, some think they're experimented on by a secret division of the military, but most people think they're sent to Prometheus's shadow campus."

Now Oliver had heard everything. "The shadow campus?" he echoed in complete skepticism. "Really?"

"Prom-E," said his roommate with a sober nod. "It's not on any maps or connected into any databases. It's a complete void."

"That's because it doesn't exist. There is no Prom-E."

Tyler frowned. "What kind of sense does that make? They just skip a letter in the alphabet when they're building campuses?"

"It corresponds to the old-school grading system," Oliver said with long-suffering. How could his roommate be this thick? "It's still used in a ton of universities across the country. Any imbecile with half a brain knows that."

"That's a convenient explanation," Tyler said.

"There is no Prom-E," Oliver insisted.

"Or maybe you know there is, and you're in on the secret."

A Rumor of Real Irish Tea

That was the last straw. "Great. Just great," he said to the ceiling, since it seemed to be the only sane object he could talk to. "Not only is my roommate a complete moron, but he's also a nutcase conspiracy freak. Can this get any worse?"

X
Of Ducks and Geese

JULY 31, 7:09AM MST, PHOENIX

"Now, if they're anything like other government offices, they're required to run end-of-the-month accounting reports today," Hummer said. "It's a lot of time-consuming paperwork, and there should be a whole department dedicated to getting it finished before the end of the day."

"How do you know how other government offices run?" Honey asked.

He stiffened, as though realizing he had disclosed more information than he intended. "I read when I'm bored," he said after a moment's hesitation, "even if the only thing to read is a procedural manual that one of the admins accidentally left lying around." Defensively he added, "You never know what kind of information might come in handy someday."

"No one's going to make fun of you for reading, Hummer," said Hawk, "and the information has come in handy a number of times over the last couple months. We orchestrated our escape based on that manual."

They were crammed onto a city bus with a slew of commuters and students. There had been standing room only when they got on, but Honey's winsome smile had earned them a couple of seats near the front, courtesy of a pair of office workers. Hawk tried to suppress the flutter of nerves in his stomach; when he thought of everything that could go wrong with this plan, he felt positively sick.

"It's the next stop," said Hummer, who had taken the lead on this venture. "Does everyone remember what they're doing?"

"Yes," said Honey and Happy together.

"Kind of hard to forget, what with how many times we went over it," said Hawk. He stooped to peer out the window. Revere was gliding alongside them, easily keeping pace with the slow-moving bus. The raven didn't understand why they were putting themselves in danger, and he certainly didn't agree with the idea, but he had come along anyway, faithful to the end.

"All right," said Hummer, and he pulled the cord to signal the bus to stop.

It lumbered to the curb, and the four children threaded their way through the aisle and out the door. They hopped down to the busy sidewalk and immediately turned north.

"The office doesn't open to the public until eight, so it'll be understaffed," said Hummer, repeating for the umpteenth time information that they had all learned by heart. Even though his words were nothing new, his voice gave them something to concentrate on as they walked. "The accounting department should be there already—they have to finish their reports by five o'clock eastern time, and thanks to daylight savings, that's three hours ahead of here. They should've started an hour ago, if they're holding to protocol. The main entrance will still be locked with a security guard on duty. Any arriving employees will come through the entrance down in the parking garage. With any luck,

X

Honey's distraction will go into effect any minute now. Are we ready? Any final questions before we start?"

"Let's just get into position," said Honey.

"You seem to be forgetting something you were supposed to do first," Hummer retorted.

Annoyance flashed across her face. "I didn't forget." She called out to a nearby pedestrian. "Hey, Mister! Can I have your cell phone? Pretty please?"

The man, in mid-conversation, instantly stopped and handed over the phone.

"Thanks! Bye-bye!" Honey said, and he rightly took this as cue to walk on. Honey spoke into the phone. "He had to go. He'll call you back later, I promise." Then, she hung up on the person and handed the device to Hummer. "Program it, quick."

It took a moment for Hummer to orient himself to the cell phone's layout. "We should've done this on the bus," he murmured as he typed a couple numbers into the contacts list.

"You don't steal things on a bus," Honey said. "You don't steal things anywhere you're trapped with a large group of people. If the projection wears off before you can get away, they raise a stink and then you have to play cleanup. It's too messy."

"I'm both relieved and disturbed that you've thought it out that far," said Hummer.

Honey stiffened, defensive. "My projections aren't like Happy's or Hawk's. I have to keep talking to mesmerize my victims, or it wears off in a couple of minutes."

"I don't consider Revere or any other bird to be my victim," Hawk said. He had been looking around absentmindedly, but the comment proved that he was still listening to their conversation.

Honey huffed. "Maybe not, but you still have a mental projection, like Happy's. Mine is all verbal."

A Rumor of Real Irish Tea

"Good thing you like talking," said Hummer sarcastically. She kicked him in the shin.

"Ow! Honey!"

"Are you done, or what? We've got to get this party started, or someone around here is going to recognize me and Happy, and my little distraction from earlier won't be worth a thing."

"Looks like your distraction was effective," said Hawk. "A pigeon across the street says there's a car coming out of the garage." The foursome instinctively backed up to the nearest wall. Ten feet down the sidewalk, a black sedan rolled out of the opening to an underground garage and maneuvered into traffic, lights flashing in its windows to signal cars in front of it to get out of the way. The sluggish cars ahead pulled off to one side and the sedan picked up speed.

Hummer had taken into consideration the location of their bus stop in relation to the GCA office. The sedan was headed in the opposite direction, and with enough urgency that the Wests were confident that no one was looking in the rearview mirror. Still, they remained positioned against the wall, mostly shielded by an unsteady stream of pedestrians.

"Here comes the second one," said Hawk, and another sedan emerged.

"High-level agents distributing their pawns," said Honey with a smirk. "It wouldn't do to send them all out at the exact same time, or they might know there are others out there with them."

"Information control at its finest," Hummer agreed. From the collection of agents they had encountered, interrogated, and disposed of over the last few days, it had become apparent that the GCA was sending out their most expendable people and telling them next to nothing, either about their mission or about one another. In order to maintain that level of ignorance in their peons, though, the higher-level agents had to be doing some pretty systematic management of their resources.

The four children watched as the second sedan turned the same direction on the street as the first, but then it made a right at the nearest light instead of going straight through.

"It's nice to see that they position them in different parts of the area too," Hummer said. "I kind of feel bad for that waffle house they're going to stake out."

"Why?" asked Honey. "If the low-level agents are told to blend into their surroundings, they'll go inside and order something. The waffle house gets some extra customers, and the agents get some breakfast on the GCA's dime. Everyone's a winner here."

"Two is probably the max they'll send from any one office, don't you think?" Hawk asked. "There are four GCA offices within a ten-mile radius of that waffle house, and they'll probably pull resources from all of them. You'd think after a while they'd start running out of pawns to send."

Hummer grunted. "The GCA has an overabundance of pawns. Let's go now before this branch starts getting its supplies replenished for the day. Happy, make sure you stay with Honey, okay?" He handed the pilfered cell phone back to Honey, and they stepped away from the wall.

Hawk whistled a call to Revere, who flapped off the branch of a nearby tree to perch on the surveillance camera positioned in front of the parking garage's entrance. As the children came into its sight, the bird lowered one wing to cover the lens. They crossed not into the garage but toward the main entrance.

"Make the call, Honey," Hummer said.

Honey already had the phone to her ear. "Hello, accounting department? Can you transfer me to the security desk in the front lobby?" A couple breaths passed, and then a new voice picked up on the other end. "Hi," said Honey. "I'm coming in through the front door. Could you please unlock it for me right now?"

They watched through the broad windows as the guard at the desk put down the phone and obediently crossed to the door.

"Let's hope that projection lasts long enough," Hummer said as they all started forward.

"There's usually at least thirty seconds after I make a command before anyone thinks to question it, unless they're conditioned," said Honey studiously. "Let's hope he isn't."

Luck seemed to be on their side, for the guard swung open the door. "Thank you," Honey said as she and her brothers slipped inside. "Could you give me your gun, please? And make sure to lock the door behind you."

He complied on both counts, but Hummer immediately confiscated the weapon from her.

"It's only a stun gun," Honey complained.

"I still wouldn't trust you with it," he said, and he tucked it into his pocket.

She made a face but didn't press the issue—a great show of restraint on her part, since she could have the gun back from Hummer with a simple request. She turned her attention to the guard instead. "Thanks for helping us out. Forget we were here and go back to work, okay?"

"Okay," he said with a cheerful salute.

Hummer, meanwhile, skirted behind the guard's desk to look at a layout of the building there. "Got it," he said. "Elevators are this way. Accounting's on the third floor. Let's go, chop chop."

Together they filed into a waiting car, and Hawk hit the button for the third floor. "Here's where we find out whether they're guarding the home nest or not," he said, and his nervous gaze traveled up to the security camera in the corner.

Next to him, Honey put one finger beneath her left eye and pulled the skin there, making a face for the camera's viewing pleasure. The elevator chimed for the third floor, and the doors slid open. The hallway was empty, but voices traveled from beyond an open door marked "Accounting."

"C'mon," said Hummer. "Honey first. You know what to do."

She bolted into the room with Happy right behind her. "Good morning, everyone! I need the supervisor here to come stand with me, and everyone else needs to come play with my little brother. What are they going to play, Happy?"

"Duck-duck-goose!" he cheerfully replied. "I'm first!"

Hawk and Hummer entered the room to discover five workers eagerly clearing away chairs and nudging desks so that they had enough room for everyone to sit in a circle. Honey stood between a couple computers with their supervisor.

"Have you already hooked into the GCA's main network?" she asked.

"Not yet," the supervisor said. "We just finished running our first report." He shifted bewildered eyes over to where his underlings patiently awaited Happy's pat on the head. Apparently he could tell there was something off, but that nagging feeling wasn't enough of a defense against two high-level human-projectors.

"Good," said Honey. "You'll be back at work in no time at all. I just need you to key in clearance to the main system on these two computers here, and then you can join the game, okay?"

The puzzled furrow between his brows smoothed out as he typed a ten-key password into the prompt on first one screen and then the other. The GCA's welcome page flashed up in response.

"Done," he said proudly.

"Goose!" cried Happy from the circle, and he shrieked like

mad as the worker chased him around back to his place. The supervisor went to join the fun as the next round began.

Hawk and Hummer had already slipped into the empty seats. "You know what you're doing?" Honey asked.

"It's not the first time we've cracked the main system," Hummer said as he began to type. "We did it a couple times back at Prom-F to prep for our escape."

"In only five minutes?"

"If you're going to talk, say something useful."

"Type faster," she said sarcastically, and then she left them to watch the hallway.

Hummer brought up a search engine on his screen, while Hawk tapped into the surveillance database and keyed into their location.

"Looks like we've got newcomers at the parking garage door," said Hawk. "They don't look like they're on alert yet. What else is on this floor?"

"It's administrative," said Hummer as his fingers flew across the keyboard. "No one else should be here yet. There's next to nothing here on Altair, Hawk."

"Next to nothing is still something. We don't need the mother lode. We just need a lead. Copy it."

Hummer plugged a portable drive into the computer's casing. "All of these files are pretty old—ten, twenty years. It's a wonder they even still exist."

"The GCA doesn't get rid of anything. And in a digital age, why should they? It's not like these are file boxes taking up space in a warehouse." Hawk's gaze shifted between Hummer's screen and his own, which was split between four different camera views. Searching for Altair on the main network would surely trigger an alarm, which made their time now all the more precious. As few files as Hummer had to work with, it seemed to take forever to save them. Every movement on Hawk's screen made his pulse spike.

"We've got agents at the elevators," he announced, his heart almost leaping out of his throat.

"Just a second more," said Hummer.

"They know we're here," Hawk said. "They'll be covering the stairs before we can get out."

"Then we use Plan C."

"There was no Plan C. What's Plan C?"

"Line 'em up and zap 'em with the stun gun," said Hummer.

"Stay calm," Honey said. In front of her, the duck-duck-goose game had become frenzied under influence of Happy's increased nervousness. Her command brought everything back to a quieter atmosphere.

"We've got maybe thirty seconds before they have us cornered in this office," Hawk said, "and there are five agents coming up the stairwell."

"That's it," said Hummer at long last. He ripped out the drive again and slapped it into Hawk's waiting hand. "Honey, wrap it up. We've got to go."

"Okay, people!" called Honey to the group. "New game! It's time to trash the office! Whoever's able to get a computer through the window first gets ten extra bonus points! Go!"

Hawk snagged Happy by the arm on his way out the door, with Hummer and Honey close behind. "Five guys in the stairs," he said to Honey. "Work your magic."

"Happy, back me up here," Honey said with an anxious little tremor in her voice. The pressure was getting to her more than she wanted to admit.

They slammed open the door to the stairs as a man rounded

A Rumor of Real Irish Tea

the landing on the flight below. "GCA workers stand against the wall and throw your weapons to the ground!" Honey shouted down the shaft.

The nearest man complied. Below, the pounding footsteps lessened but didn't entirely stop.

"Against the wall!" Happy yelled in desperate fury. This time, only the four children's footsteps echoed as they raced down the stairs. At the rear of their line, Hummer extracted the stun gun from his pocket and jabbed it at the first man they passed. He slumped against the ground, unconscious.

"Four more to go," Hummer muttered.

They made it down two flights and past four men when they heard the door fly open back on the third floor. Shouts ricocheted into the stairwell.

"Get against the wall and stay still!" Happy called up before his sister had the chance.

"Honey, there's no time to hot-wire," said Hummer. "Ask this last guy if he has any car keys."

She paused in her descent halfway down the next flight. "Give 'im your car keys," she said.

The man fished a set from his pocket. Hummer repaid him by thrusting the stun gun into his shoulder. "To the garage!" he called.

As they burst through the last stairwell door into the parking garage, Revere let out a shrill call from near the exit. Hummer hit the unlock button on the keychain, and a black sedan on the middle row chirped. "Get inside! We're cutting it awful close!"

As the three younger kids piled in, Hawk extracted the portable drive from his pocket and threw it to a circling Revere. The raven caught the object with ease and glided out of the garage into the bright morning sunlight. Hawk climbed into the

X

back seat with Honey and Happy, and the car sparked to life with Hummer in the front.

"And away we go," he cried, and he peeled out of the parking space, up the row, and straight through the restrictive arm that blocked unlawful entry to the lot. Lights flashing, he cut into traffic and careened around the corner, clipping a mailbox and narrowly avoiding a couple of pedestrians.

"Never again," said Hawk. "Never, never again."

Beside him, Honey placed a protective arm around a jittery Happy but lifted her eyes in skepticism. "You say that now, but we all know you'll change your mind if the need arises."

"Never again," he repeated firmly.

"Goose!" said Happy with a punch-drunk laugh.

XI
A Meeting of Minds

JULY 31, 9:04AM MDT, PROM-F

Classes at prom-f started at exactly 9:05 every morning, Monday through Saturday. Emily thought this was a rather odd time, especially at a school where the entire student body lived on campus instead of getting bused in or dropped off. Whatever the logistical or managerial reason for this scheduling, it was beyond her understanding. On a morning like this, though, when Oliver dragged his feet at every turn, she was grateful for the five-minute grace period.

He was not a morning person. She'd learned that fairly early on in their time together. Even with the rigid nine o'clock bedtime that the Prometheus Institute mandated for their students, Oliver still had trouble waking up. The hour they were allotted for breakfast gave him some wiggle room, but this morning, he woke up late and moved at a snail's pace. It was a dangerous combination that had a dinner-detention riding on the line if he missed the bell for his first class.

Emily prodded him. "Hurry, hurry." The corridor was all but empty, except for a few stragglers and their handlers. "You've got less than a minute before the bell."

XI

"The classroom's just around the corner," Oliver said grumpily, "and I still have forty-three seconds." Nevertheless, he did pick up his pace, much to her relief.

As they rounded the last corner, though, a new obstacle appeared in their path: Ben Birchard stood nonchalantly next to the classroom door. Emily's heart sank. She'd had quite enough of his presence after last night's conversation.

Interestingly enough, Oliver shared her sentiments. "Stand aside, Birchard," he said as he tried to skirt majestically past the man. "I'm about to be right on time for my class."

"Think again," Ben replied, and he fluidly redirected Oliver by the shoulders.

"What're you doing?" Oliver cried. The school bell pealed across the intercom, signaling that he was officially late.

"You harass me about setting up a meeting with Principal Jones, and then you yell at me when I come to deliver?" Ben asked. "How ungrateful can you get?"

Oliver's breath quickened. "She's going to meet with me?"

"Yes," he said. "Probably."

That tacked-on qualifier caused both Oliver and Emily to stare in open disillusionment.

"There's a very good chance of it," said Ben, seeming not to notice their frowns, "but she won't have a lot of time, so rather than pulling you from class when that time comes, I've excused you. Your teachers have been kind enough to provide a list of your assignments, so it'll be self-study for you this morning, just how you like it. Come this way."

Emily would have complained further, but Oliver fairly *bounced* with suppressed glee. Of course he'd prefer a morning of self-study over attending class. What kid wouldn't? The meeting with Principal Jones didn't even factor into the equation.

A Rumor of Real Irish Tea

If he was fine with this arrangement, then she had no cause to object. She was only going to spend the class period gossiping with Crystal anyway.

She followed Oliver and Ben down the hallway to the elevator, which immediately opened. How was it always ready when Ben Birchard was involved? Did he have some sort of administrative access to the system, something that would allow him to summon an elevator car whenever he wanted, like how law enforcement officials could change traffic lights at will?

She decided against asking this aloud. Ben would undoubtedly deny it, and Oliver would probably call her an idiot for speaking.

Once they all filed in, Ben hit the button for the second floor. "Principal Jones is in a meeting with the other Prometheus principals. *If* she has time to meet with you, it will be when that meeting has adjourned. That could be anywhere between nine-thirty and noon."

The doors opened to the campus's administrative offices. "Now it's *if* she has time to meet with him?" Emily asked archly.

"It was always *if*," Ben said. "I can't absolutely guarantee her schedule unless she tells me to, and she was, unfortunately, a bit vague this morning when I spoke to her."

Oliver immediately picked up on his verbiage. "You didn't speak to her about it until this morning?"

Ben rolled his eyes toward the ceiling. "When I spoke to her *again* about it." He gestured to an open door. "You can both wait in here. It's the office they've lent to Principal Jones and me for the duration of our visit."

Emily followed Oliver inside, taking a quick evaluation of the office as she did. It was large enough to fit two executive-style desks in the back half of the room and still have a more casual

XI

space in the front. Two thick-padded chairs faced a short sofa in one corner, with a low coffee table between them.

She was impressed. "They give an office like this to all the visiting principals?" Did the room stand empty waiting for someone of importance to show up? And how many more were there like it on this floor?

"Principal Jones always requests an office," Ben said. "Principal Lee does as well. Carter and Legrand prefer to work from their allotted quarters. I'm not sure where General Stone is working."

"He's not a principal," Oliver said as he flopped into one of the padded chairs.

Ben simply arched his brows, otherwise ignoring the remark entirely. "Make yourselves comfortable. I'm supposed to be observing the principals' meeting, but I took a break to fetch you here. With any luck I haven't missed anything important." He punctuated this with a wry laugh.

Emily assumed that he would leave the office, but instead he sat at one of the desks. The computer screen flashed to life to reveal a familiar surveillance feed as Birchard fitted a pair of headphones over his ears. Silence descended upon the room.

She had nothing to do. Crystal had said something about loaning her a novel to read today, but of course she hadn't seen her at breakfast. She only had her weekly report journal and Oliver's file. A glance around the room showed how bare it was: no books, no magazines, not even a pamphlet. Ben sat at one of only two computers, and since she assumed the second had been provided for Principal Jones, she dared not even ask whether she could use it. With growing discontent she settled on the couch and belatedly recalled how much she hated the couches here.

Oliver shot her a glare that commanded her to behave herself. Ever obedient, Emily schooled away her annoyance.

A Rumor of Real Irish Tea

Three weeks in a holding cell had given her plenty of practice on how to endure the next who-knew-how-many hours.

Soon, her eyes focused over Ben's shoulder to what she could see on the computer screen. The security feed was from the same angle as the one he had briefly shown her the day before in the hallway. Emily could make out some of the figures around the table—three of them she had only seen from above anyway, so it wasn't hard to recognize Principal Carter's hideous comb-over or Principal Legrand's frizzy blond hair. The others were blocked from her view until Ben leaned back in his chair and put his feet up on the desk, thereby exposing the full screen.

Principal Gates was next to Principal Legrand, and Principals Lee and Jones were on the other side of the oblong table. Emily recognized General Stone's salt-and-pepper hair cut at the table's head. It made sense to let the military man run the meeting.

The two visible corners of the room had occupants as well. Maggie sat in one and Michelle in the other, and each tapped away at a keyboard in front of them—a laptop for Michelle, and a stenography machine for Maggie. Either Principal Gates was extremely old-school, or else Prom-F's budget was utter crap compared to the other schools.

"Psst!"

Her attention shifted away from the screen to the source of this noise, a rather annoyed Oliver. He scowled at her, and then glanced quickly over his shoulder, as if to ask, "What on earth are you staring at?"

She tipped her chin, mutely prodding him to turn and look for himself.

Reluctantly he did. The scowl deepened as he pinned his gaze back on her. Emily expected him to make some sarcastic

XI

comment about how nosy she was. Instead, he picked up his notebook and moved to sit next to her on the couch.

His eyes narrowed in a challenging "What of it?" glare.

Emily shook herself from her stupor and returned her gaze to the computer screen. There really was nothing of interest with the sound off, and yet her eyes remained glued there, watching and waiting. Oliver was the same, though he tried to be more subtle about it. Every five seconds or so, he'd at least glance down at his schoolwork.

A loud ringing cracked the silent atmosphere. Emily and Oliver jumped and averted their eyes. Ben tore off the headphones and stood to retrieve his cell phone from his pocket.

"Ben Birchard," he said shortly, then he paused to listen to the voice on the other side. A number of emotions crossed his face: shock, disbelief, and a brief flash of humor, among others.

"I—I'm sorry," he said after a moment, as though having trouble finding the correct thing to say. "Could you ... could you *repeat* that?" And then, with an apologetic wave toward Emily and Oliver, he strolled out the open door into the hallway beyond. His voice floated in as he retreated up the corridor. "You're serious? Yes, I know it's hardly something to joke about. Yes, I'll tell her immediately. Thank you for calling."

There was a slight pause, followed by a knock on a door. Emily exchanged a bewildered glance with Oliver, but then movement in the corner of her eye caught her attention.

"Look!" she hissed, and she pointed at the computer screen. Ben had joined the meeting.

Oliver launched out of his seat, scrambling to the computer. He unceremoniously disconnected the headphones.

"... just called to my attention," Ben was saying. "Again, I do apologize for the intrusion."

A Rumor of Real Irish Tea

Principal Jones had already stood from her seat. "Please excuse me," she said to her colleagues. "This should only take a minute." Then, she and Ben stepped outside the room.

"Oliver!" Emily whispered with an anxious glance at the door. "Connect the headphones again! What if they come back here?"

"Check the door," he said, his eyes still glued to the screen.

Emily hesitated only briefly before complying. A cautious peek out the door into the hallway showed her Ben Birchard and Genevieve Jones a stone's throw down the corridor, just outside of what was presumably the conference room on the computer screen. He was speaking to her in a low voice. She did a double-take and then pinned him with a stare.

From the computer speakers, which Oliver had blissfully turned down, the conversation from the conference room continued.

"If it's Birchard, something important has happened," said Principal Gates. "He always seems to know everything that happens before anyone else, but he wouldn't intrude like that if it wasn't something major."

"I wonder what little incident has caught his attention this time," said a woman. Emily reasoned that it must be Prom-D's Annemarie Legrand. Out in the hallway, Ben spoke with animated gestures.

No idea, he seemed say. *I don't know anything more than I've just told you.*

"Let's hope it's nothing like the incident that brought us here," said a man on the computer screen.

Principal Jones shook her head, and then abruptly swung the conference room door inward. Emily could have sworn that Ben glanced her direction before he followed his boss inside. She cringed away from the door and returned her attention to the computer screen alone.

XI

"My deepest apologies," Principal Jones said to the others as she took her seat again. "Sit down, Birchard."

"Some sort of trouble?" Principal Lee asked as Ben took a chair midway between Maggie and Michelle.

"Oh, quite a lot of it," replied Principal Jones, "but I'd rather not say anything until the report's been confirmed. Which it will be soon if it has any substance. Now where were we before this unfortunate interruption?"

"We were discussing our options for a null-projector to neutralize the younger Wests," said General Stone. "For the fifth time since yesterday," he added, and there was a note of impatience in his voice.

Emily should have made Oliver restore the sound to the headphones and return to his seat. Morally and ethically neither of them should have eavesdropped on this meeting. It was difficult to put into practice what she agreed with in theory, though, especially since the subject at hand had to do with Oliver's fate. As Oliver's fate was tied to her own, she guiltily held her peace.

"I still maintain that Cedric is too young to be sent away from the safety of the Prometheus campuses," Principal Carter said disagreeably. "Send him from one campus to another for on-site jobs, fine, but set him out in the world? He's only seven."

"You're just worried he'll end up here with the other two," Principal Legrand said. "Then you'd have nothing but a few low-level projectors to brag about."

"Which is more than you've got at Prom-D," he sneered.

"Enough," General Stone interjected. At a single word he captured the attention of the whole room. "Now is hardly the time to indulge in friendly rivalries. We have a situation that has gone on far too long. I'm inclined to agree with Principal Carter.

Cedric is too young and too impressionable to be handed the task of retrieving the truants. He might identify more with them than with us."

"His null-projection is still hit-or-miss, too," said Principal Lee in a flat voice. "With a projector like Happy West, we can't take any chances."

"They're worried about *Happy*?" Emily hissed to Oliver. "*Honey's* the menace."

Oliver irritably shushed her.

"However you look at it, Oliver is still the best fit for the job," said Principal Jones. "Quincy is too old and the focus of her null-projection is too narrow."

"Don't forget that she was friends with Hawk and Hummer," Principal Gates said. "According to her last handler's reports, she wouldn't *want* to catch them."

"Since when does anything these children *want* come into play here?" General Stone asked in an icy voice. "Our job is to use the resources we have at our disposal to recover the ones that we've lost."

"Then why aren't we using any of the nulls under your authority?" Principal Legrand asked peevishly. "You have more than any of us, and yet you hoard them."

"Mine are all security risks, as well you know," General Stone said. "They're an absolute last resort."

"Which we're fast coming to," said Principal Jones.

Everyone glanced suspiciously at her. "Something you'd like to share, Genevieve?" Principal Carter asked, a nasty catch to his voice.

Before she could reply, a phone rang. General Stone extracted a small black cell from his pocket and answered it. "This is General Stone," he said rigidly.

XI

"That'll probably be it," Principal Jones told her colleagues. They all turned to watch with interest. Emily and Oliver, too, kept their attention riveted on the stern military man.

General Stone's face hardened into an unreadable mask as he listened to the voice on the other end. Two minutes passed in complete silence. At long last, "Understood," he said curtly, and he ended the call. The cell phone was carefully placed back into his pocket. Then, with a sweeping glance at the other occupants of the table, he announced, "Your truants just ambushed a GCA office in Central Phoenix. They stole a series of files from the main computer system and drove off in a government car."

"They got *away*?" cried Principal Carter.

"If they're in a company car, they should be easy enough to catch," said Principal Lee. "The GPS will tell us their exact location."

"The car's already been recovered," said General Stone, his voice hard, "along with its driver, a bewildered paralegal who couldn't remember anything beyond her morning walk to work and an incredible urge to eat breakfast at a local waffle house. That's where she was headed when they pulled her over. Incidentally," he added, "that same waffle house figured in several reports to our national hotline this morning: little Maddie and Alex North were seen eating breakfast there by no less than eight concerned citizens, only fifteen minutes before the ambush. The drive-time with morning traffic is at least that long."

"How . . . ?" began Principal Gates.

General Stone slammed his palms down on the table. "They know we're using the hotline to track their movements. They turned it around on us with false reports and used it to empty that office of its off-hours agents."

"How did they get into the main computer system?" asked Principal Jones. She alone of all of them had maintained her composure throughout the whole. The content of Ben Birchard's mysterious call was no longer so mysterious.

"Through the accounting department," said General Stone slowly, so as to regain control of his emotions. "The supervisor was issued passwords so that they could file their month-end reports, per protocol. These *children*"—he pronounced that word with utmost contempt—"exploited our system for their own purposes. We're lucky that they didn't cause more damage than they did. We're lucky that they didn't have any more time than they did. They are an absolute menace, and we cannot waste any more time in reining them back in."

The five principals exchanged nervous glances.

"Thus far," General Stone said, "the GCA has been content to take a passive approach to recovering these children, as though they had all the time in the world to quietly slip a noose around the bull's neck and pull it tight. I was against that. I have said before and I'll say it again now: we need to be more aggressive. Our number one priority is to get these children off the streets and away from the public eye before they can cause any more damage."

"We send Oliver, then," said Principal Jones.

"Agreed," said Principal Lee. "The only way you're going to get close enough for a full assault is if you neutralize the projections from Honey and Happy. Honey's easy enough: give the men earplugs and you're done. For Happy, you need a high-level null projector. Oliver's your only choice."

"Hmm," said General Stone absentmindedly. "The girl, what's her name?"

Principal Gates leaned forward. "Quincy? Her null-projection is only a few feet, too narrow to be of any use in an aggressive assault."

XI

"But you said she was friends with the older boys. We may be able to use her."

"You're going to choose Quincy over Oliver?" Principal Carter asked in disbelief.

General Stone leveled a hard stare at him. "I didn't realize I had to choose."

"You're taking them *both*?" said Principal Jones, finally moved from her superior calm.

"Yes," he said. "Quincy, and Oliver, and . . . you." Astonished silence enveloped the room as he turned and pointed directly at none other than Ben Birchard.

Ben squeaked. "*Me*?"

"If I'm not mistaken, you knew about this little ambush before even I did," General Stone said. "From what I've heard, you've got your finger on the pulse of everything that happens in the Prometheus network and the GCA. I can put a man of your resources to good use. Congratulations," he added dryly. "You've just been promoted. You're no longer Principal Jones's assistant—you're mine."

Ben didn't look at all pleased by this announcement. His wary eyes shifted almost hopefully in Genevieve's direction, but her unmoving posture testified that there was nothing she could do.

General Stone didn't seem to care one way or the other. "Carter," he said, and the Prometheus-C principal jumped. "Contact your people at NPNN and have them release the story we discussed yesterday."

Principal Carter's head bobbed in mute, terrified agreement. Emily wondered what story they were talking about, but since it was about to broadcast on NPNN, she'd find out soon enough. NPNN was the only channel the GCA offices ever showed, and that was where she would spend the next several days—or weeks—if this excursion was anything like the last one.

"No more tiptoeing around these little monsters," said General Stone, and the steeliness of his voice showed that he meant every last word. "We do it my way, and we'll have it sewn up in a matter of days."

"That's what they said the last time," Emily muttered under her breath. Next to her, Oliver grunted.

The headphones were quickly reconnected and both Emily and Oliver retreated back to the couch before Ben returned. They looked up innocently when he entered from the hallway. His expression was deadpan, but Emily had the sneaking suspicion that they hadn't fooled him at all.

He said not a word to either of them. Instead, he crossed to his desk, where he typed a couple of words into a prompt and closed the surveillance window.

From the hall sounded the austere click of heels against the tile floor. Every ominous tap had Emily sitting up a fraction of an inch taller, as though her doom approached in a pair of expensive designer pumps.

Genevieve Jones crossed the threshold, as severe up close as she had sounded through the computer's speakers. Everything about her was neat as a pin, from her crease-free business suit to her perfectly smoothed hair in its immaculately arranged chignon. To someone such as Emily, she was both awe-inspiring and terrifying.

Luckily, she had no attention to spare for an insignificant handler. "Oliver," she said to her former student, a subdued warmth to her voice, "I trust you've been well since we last met?"

Oliver glowered. "How could I be well when they've enrolled me here at Prom-F? Is this my punishment for trying to help?"

XI

"The situation is atypical," said Principal Jones, but Emily noticed that she made no attempts at an apology. "You were transferred to Prom-F in order to assist in the recovery of our four truants. Since the Wests are still out there, your records are still here."

"So once the Wests are caught and brought back, I'll get transferred back to Prom-A?" Oliver asked.

"That's right," said Principal Jones a little too easily. Was she telling the truth, or only saying what Oliver wanted to hear? "They've decided to give you a second chance, Oliver. You're being sent out again, to Phoenix this time. We need you to do your very best, do you understand?"

He nodded.

"Good. And you'll be glad to hear that you're not going alone this time."

He didn't go alone last time, Emily thought in annoyance.

"Who else is coming?" Oliver asked, his grudging curiosity so well feigned that Emily would have sworn it was genuine if she didn't know better.

"They're sending Quincy along too. You two will need to work together and do everything the grown-ups ask. You do understand that, don't you? The only way I can get your records transferred back to Prom-A is if you cooperate and bring the Wests home."

"Understood," said Oliver.

Principal Jones smiled a very controlled smile. "I'm sending Birchard with you as well," she said, as though the addition of her personal assistant had been her idea. "He'll report your progress directly back to me, and we'll see what we can do to get this mess cleared up. Now, you have twenty minutes to pack your bag. Is that enough time?"

"I'll do it in ten," said Oliver, and he snapped his notebook shut. "Thanks, Genevieve." He passed her to the hallway.

Emily followed, but, to her astonishment, Principal Jones caught her by the sleeve.

"A second chance like this is extremely rare," the austere woman said in a low, ominous voice. "See that you don't squander it, Ms. Brent."

"I won't," Emily whispered. "Thank you." Upon the release of her sleeve, she fled from the office.

Oliver had actually paused halfway down the hall to wait for her. "What's wrong with you?" he asked.

"I'm fine," said Emily, desperately trying to smooth her frayed nerves. "Let's hurry to get your bag packed."

His nose lifted in a sneer. "Worry about your own. It was your lack of preparation last time that got us into so much trouble."

She opened her mouth to make a sharp retort—it wasn't her fault she'd been dragged away without any advance notice—but then she realized that the words would be wasted. Oliver knew all the details of their previous excursion. For whatever reason, he was needling her. Perhaps it was a childish attempt to settle his own frayed nerves.

"This time will be different," she promised, her voice quiet.

"It has to be," said Oliver with a solemn frown. "My future depends on it."

XII
Real Irish Tea

JULY 31, 9:35AM MST, PHOENIX

"Is this safe house still safe?" Happy asked with a wary look up and down the quiet residential street.

"None of the local birds have noticed anything out of the ordinary," Hawk said. "That's about all we can ask at the moment."

"Do you think Hummer and Honey got here okay?"

"If they're not here yet, they will be soon," he said reassuringly, even though he wasn't certain he spoke the truth. That was the part of the plan he disliked the most, where they ditched the car and split up. But Hummer had insisted that two groups of two children were less obvious than one group of four. They would draw less attention, especially since the general public was being programmed to look for Maddie and Alex North together, not separately.

"What about Revere?" asked Happy.

Hawk pointed to a scraggly tree outside their rental house. "He's already here. Should I have him go look for Hummer and Honey?"

The six-year-old considered this question but made no

definitive response. Revere, on the other hand, caught sight of his young master; he raised one claw to remove a black object from his beak so that he could give a loud, hearty caw in greeting.

"Hello yourself," said Hawk as he approached. He held out his hand, and the bird dropped the portable drive onto his outstretched palm. "Shall we go inside?" Revere fluttered to the door. "Happy, do you have the key?"

Happy pulled on a string around his neck, tucked beneath his shirt. The silver house key dangled from its length, a copy of the original that Hummer carried. Happy had been thrilled to act as its bearer. He jogged forward now and inserted it into the door lock. The door creaked inward on squeaky hinges.

It was the first house they had rented, and they had only stayed here one night, more than two weeks ago. They had walked by it yesterday evening to scope out whether it would be a safe place to return to after this morning's adventures. If the GCA minions had discovered it, logically it would be staked out with agents. Instead, it stood empty and the surrounding neighborhood was peaceful and quiet.

Hawk shut the door and locked it behind him. "Hummer? Honey?" he called, but he received no answer. Happy looked up at him in concern. "Their route was a little longer," Hawk told him, not wanting to nourish that small panic that was welling up in both of them. "You can watch out the front window for them as long as you don't touch the curtains."

He gestured to the sheer white panels that covered a bay window in the room next to the entryway. The curtains, light fixtures, and kitchen appliances had come with the rental, as was standard, but there was no other furniture. Happy obediently stood two feet back, his eyes fixed on the street outside.

XII

Revere rubbed his beak against the carpet and then flapped upward to perch on the ceiling fan. "Don't get too comfortable," Hawk warned him. "You may have to head back out and sweep the area for the others."

The raven cawed and began to preen himself.

Hawk, meanwhile, turned the drive over in his hands, contemplating its contents. He and Hummer had each accessed the GCA's main computer system back at Prom-F half a dozen times in search of any mention of their parents. It had been a sort of game, not just among them but among the student body in general, to orchestrate some means of accessing an administrator's work station. Practically everyone had something they wanted to look up, and many of the lesser pranks they played were done with the intent of getting sent to the principal so that they could gain access to a computer in one of the administration offices. The pranks usually involved a nasty mess and a handler that needed a lavatory to clean up.

He smiled faintly at the memories. Those brief searches had been almost fruitless, except to familiarize them with the main system itself. Most of the Prom-F administrators didn't have clearance high enough to access any sensitive files. Principal Gates did, but accessing his computer when he was logged on was next to impossible. Unlike many of his underlings, he actually logged off whenever he left his office.

Hawk seriously doubted that the accounting department in the Central Phoenix branch of the GCA had clearance any higher than that of the Prom-F administrators. Back at Prom-F, he and Hummer had been looking for any information on their parents, though. Now they had another search term. There had been little of value on James and Sara West. Would the information on Altair be worth the risks they'd taken to get it?

A Rumor of Real Irish Tea

He would have to wait until Hummer and Honey got back to find out.

By splitting up, they reduced the risk of everyone getting caught. By sending the stolen information ahead with Revere, they helped ensure that one of them would get to look over its contents. Hummer had their best means of looking at it packed among his things, though: a five-year-old laptop they'd acquired in a pawn shop the week before, probably for less than the owner had paid for it, thanks to Honey's brilliant (and completely unfair) negotiation skills. It ran sluggishly and had only a bare number of programs, but it would be good enough. If Hummer didn't return—which he would, Hawk thought adamantly—the only other option would be a computer lab, either in a public school or a library.

Hawk didn't want to take that option, but a glance out the window showed him an empty street beyond. There was no sign of his little brother and sister.

His nerves were more on end than he realized. A noise at the back of the house made him jump, and he called a warning to Happy as he went to investigate. "Stay here! Keep watching!"

The noise had come from the back door, situated in the kitchen. The handle jiggled and turned just as Hawk slid into the room.

"Oh, good," said Hummer, poking his head inside. "You're already here. C'mon, Honey." He turned and beckoned behind him.

Hawk watched through the window as his sister emerged from some bushes by the back fence. "The front door wasn't good enough for you?" he asked.

Hummer grunted. "We thought it better not to hazard someone seeing two pairs of kids on the street only a few minutes apart. Why? Were you worried?"

XII

"Happy was," said Hawk.

The six-year-old appeared from the front room and threw his arms around his sister with a joyous squeal.

Hummer's face broke out into a grin. "Well, if Happy was, you were too. Sorry. We came as quick as we dared."

"Any trouble?"

"No. You?"

"None that I saw."

"Did Revere get here all right?"

Hawk held up the portable drive. "I told you he would."

"You can't blame me for having my doubts," Hummer said as he swiped the object. "We just entrusted everything we risked ourselves for to a bird. He'd only seen this house twice."

"He's a smart bird," said Hawk. From the front room, Revere cawed.

"Come on," Hummer said, amused. "Let's go find out what we got."

Together the four marched into the back bedroom. Hummer quickly extracted the thin computer and plugged it into an electrical outlet.

"Is anyone else hungry?" Honey asked. "All those references to waffles this morning kicked up my appetite."

"We don't have waffles, and we have no way of getting them," said Hawk. "And no, we're not going to go buy some. After this morning's escapade, I think it's best we lay low for the rest of the day."

Honey pettishly crossed her arms. "I didn't say we had to have waffles. I just said talking about them made me hungry. I've got . . . let's see . . ." She dug through her backpack as she listed off the contents. "Graham crackers, a box of malted milk balls, and . . . Oh! There's the rest of our popcorn from yesterday."

A Rumor of Real Irish Tea

"You saved that?" Hummer asked.

"I thought Revere might like it," Honey said.

The raven, on alert when food was involved, hopped into the room with an eager little cackle. Honey extracted the crushed theater tub and set it on the floor for his eating pleasure.

"I also have a couple more candy bars from the concessions stand and a half a box of granola bars," she said. "Oh, and two apples here at the bottom."

"I'll have one of those," said Hawk, "or split it if someone else wants half."

"Hummer's got the knife," Honey said as she slapped the apple into his outstretched hand. "Happy, you want to split an apple with Hawk?"

Happy was busy watching Revere extract the contents of the popcorn tub, enthralled by the bird as always. He nodded absentmindedly. Hummer obligingly produced a midsized pocketknife from his pack and handed it to his older brother.

As they prepared and distributed snacks, Hummer kept his attention fixed upon the sluggish computer. He inserted the portable drive and began rooting through the copied files.

"What'd we get?" Hawk asked, almost dreading the response.

"A twenty-year-old memo from the then-head of the GCA to an undisclosed recipient or recipients," Hummer said. "Presumably the system deemed it old enough to downgrade its classification status. Listen to this: 'The organization known as "Altair" must be seen as hostile to our goals and treated accordingly. It is to be classified among the subset of organizations described in Title III, Section 303(a) of the Federal Domestic Security Act of 2026, and treated according to (b) of that same section.'"

"Gibberish," said Hawk.

"Luckily," said Hummer, "another of the files we got was a copy

XII

of the Federal Domestic Security Act of 2026. Someone must have gone back and tagged it as pertaining to Altair. Let's see . . . Title III, Title III . . . Here we are: 'Title III: Intellectual, Philosophical, and Ideological Insurgents.' That doesn't sound good."

"Oh!" cried Hawk with sudden realization. "That's the information-control act. It's the one that makes you a terrorist if you think differently than the government does."

Hummer's eyebrows shot up, and he immediately returned his attention to the screen. "Section 303 is titled 'Ideologically Insurgent Persons and Organizations.' Well, doesn't that look promising? '(a) Any person or organization that espouses or encourages others to espouse an ideology that runs counter to the established laws of the nation may be deemed ideologically insurgent and shall be viewed as a threat to national security.' Blah, blah, blah, legalese. Basically all this says is that if you preach anything contrary to what they want you to, you're a traitor."

"So much for free speech," Honey muttered.

"Incendiary rhetoric can lead a lot of people to do stupid things," said Hawk. "At least, that's how they justified it. The anti-political fervor of the time was so high that they equated speaking out against the government with yelling 'Fire!' in a crowded theater."

"In other words," said Hummer grimly, "speech is only free if the government agrees with what you're saying. Otherwise, you're calling for insurrection. The (b) section here just references some other law on how to prosecute and punish any person or organization that falls under the (a) section. Public Law No. 118-217, it says here, but it doesn't give any other title or reference."

"I don't think we're really interested in the punishment," said Hawk. "It's enough to know that 'Altair' refers to an organization that the government deems 'ideologically insurgent.' Did we get anything else?"

Hummer typed a couple of commands into the computer. "Another memo a couple years later: 'Any GCA personnel affiliated with an insurgent organization (such as Altair) must be terminated immediately'—I hope that means terminated as in fired and not terminated as in killed—'and all work and personal effects must be confiscated and classified until they have been determined harmless.' So there were members of Altair working for the GCA at one point, apparently. It must have been a fairly persistent problem—there are two more memos here where they're discussing what to do. 'Altair must be wiped out of existence,' this one says."

"Someone struck a nerve," said Hawk wryly.

"Listen to this last one: 'The current administration has determined that insurgent organizations such as Altair must be isolated and marginalized, so as to discourage any recruiting efforts. From this time forward, any mention of the name on GCA premises will be considered a violation of this decision, and the offending party shall be dismissed from service within the agency and subject to interrogation regarding their knowledge of the organization.'"

"What exactly does that mean?" asked Honey with a confused frown.

"Pretend it doesn't exist, and eliminate anyone who says it does," said Hawk. "It's kind of the same tactic Prom-F took last year when a couple of students made a compost pile by the back field explode. The grounds crew cleaned up any evidence that it had ever happened, and anyone who asked questions about it was sent to the principal's office."

"Did they catch the students?" Honey asked.

XII

Hawk and Hummer exchanged a telling glance. "No," Hawk said slowly, "not on that particular occasion."

"So it was you two?"

"No," said Hawk. "I had nothing to do with it."

"It wasn't meant to explode like that," said Hummer. "Pierce and I miscalculated the chemical components of the pile and how much heat it was actually producing."

Honey closed her eyes as though a sudden headache had descended on her. "And why exactly did you want to blow up a compost pile to begin with?"

Hummer looked like she had asked him why he wanted to breathe. "Because it was there. We were learning about organic decay in one class, and combustible elements in another, and that was the perfect way to field-test what we were being taught in both classes together. It didn't make *that* much of a mess."

"It left burn marks in the grass as far as fifty feet away," Hawk said. "That wasn't really the point of bringing up the story, though. The point was that the administrators didn't give the incident any sort of publicity. They hushed it up to keep anyone else from trying the same thing. That sounds a lot like what this memo is saying to do about Altair. Are there any other files?"

"Just one more," said Hummer. He brought up the final document. "This one doesn't make any sense at all, though. It's just a huge list of words and phrases. I don't know what it has to do with Altair, or with anything at all."

"What phrases?" asked Honey.

"Ones that don't even make sense: aerial theirs, earthrise ail, hairier tales, a saltier hire, a trashier lie, I the rare sail, her a teal iris, the air is real . . . There are . . . hundreds . . . *thousands* . . . Holy cow, this list goes on *forever*."

"And what's any of it got to do with Altair?" Hawk asked.

A Rumor of Real Irish Tea

"What's any of it got to do with anything?" Honey corrected.

Suddenly a smile broke across Hummer's face. "Well, I can answer Honey's question at least. They're all anagrams of the file's name: Real Irish Tea."

"Real Irish Tea?" she echoed in skepticism.

"Yeah, they all use the same letters," said Hummer. Then, "Hang on." He snatched a notebook and a pencil from his bag and jotted a couple of phrases on the first blank page. Quietly he tapped the tip of his pencil against the letters in different orders. An ironic chuckle escaped his lips.

"What?" Hawk and Honey asked together.

Hummer looked up with a faint, rueful smile. "Altair is here," he said, and he pointed to the screen. "Every phrase listed in this file can be rearranged to spell 'Altair is here.' Coincidence?"

"Doubtful," said Hawk. "So what, we just came across an old code or something?"

"Looks like it," Hummer said.

"That and a handful of old memos was hardly worth risking capture over," said Honey glumly.

The two older boys exchanged an uncertain glance. "You never know," said Hummer. "It may come in handy someday." Even he didn't sound too sure of himself, though.

XIII
On the Road Again

JULY 31, 11:53AM MDT, IN TRANSIT TO GREAT FALLS, MT

EMILY STARED OUT the window, sincerely hoping that it would be the last time she saw the endless crop fields that lined the highway into Great Falls. She had only faint cause for that hope—arriving to discover all of her belongings had been shipped from New York had pretty much solidified that she was at Prom-F to stay—but Principal Jones's pointed warning had been aimed as much at her as Oliver. Perhaps, if everything went well this time, she too could be reinstated at Prom-A. If they could track down the Wests quickly and efficiently, it might offset all the misery of the past month.

But who was she kidding? These kids had already outsmarted the GCA several times over. There was no point in getting her hopes up.

Her gaze shifted from the window to the other passengers: Oliver, Quincy, Quincy's new handler Alyson (who was enthused to be leaving Prom-F for the first time in fourteen months), and Ben Birchard. Emily was surprised that he hadn't opted to ride with General Stone in the other car. He sat up front with Maggie, who was driving, but even from behind it was obvious that he was brooding. The so-called promotion had blindsided him.

From Emily's limited perspective, there wouldn't be much difference between working for Principal Jones and General Stone. Both were stringent, austere people who probably demanded job performance beyond what most of their underlings could accomplish. Ben had excelled under Principal Jones, so there was no reason he wouldn't do the same under General Stone.

But then, being yanked from administering at the Prometheus Institute into serving under a military leader had probably never figured into Ben Birchard's career ambitions. He might not view it as a promotion at all. In that case, why had he not utterly refused?

Emily determined not to feel sorry for him. He was slippery as an eel, so he would squirm his way out if the situation truly disagreed with him.

The other occupants of the vehicle were quiet. Oliver pretended to read a textbook, but he hadn't turned a page in a full five minutes. Quincy, subdued, clasped her hands in her lap and only hazarded fleeting glances at the window. She looked like a prisoner being sent on work release, with plans to escape dancing through her enterprising mind while she did everything she could not to let it show on her face. Or so Emily guessed. The girl had worn a shell-shocked expression when she came down from her dorm to the waiting van. It didn't completely fade until an hour into the drive.

Her new handler, Alyson, was just over a year into her Prometheus internship and had served the whole of it at Prom-F. She was a jittery person, small in stature and wary of her surroundings. Emily wondered if she'd suffered one prank too many from her precious little charges, or if that disposition was natural. Her excitement manifested in her hands, which seemed unable to

XIII

keep still for more than a few seconds at a time. The occasional flash of anxiety crossed her face, as though she feared that the treat now dangled before her might suddenly be snatched away.

Or maybe she was trying to remember whether she'd left the iron on in her dorm room. Either way, Emily only caught the fleeting emotion by studying the woman's face in the rearview mirror.

Three weeks of blank walls in a confinement cell had taught her to appreciate her surroundings more.

When they finally pulled onto the airport tarmac, a small private jet waited, complete with the Prometheus Institute's crest emblazoned on its tail. General Stone's sedan pulled in ahead of them, and he exited the vehicle. The airplane staff member who met him saluted. The younger man was not wearing a military uniform. Emily frowned at the show of respect.

"Here we are," Maggie said as she put the van into park. "Mind you behave yourselves while you're gone, children."

"Oh, we will, I'm sure," said Ben, much to her amusement. He exited first and crossed around to the back to retrieve his bag. Alyson and Quincy went next, followed by Emily and Oliver. Airport attendants rolled a cart over to assist with the luggage.

"I need to use the bathroom," Oliver said loudly.

"Hold it until we're in the air," Ben advised him. "General Stone's not the sort of man you ask to wait for you." He strolled away to follow the general up the stairs into the aircraft.

"Can you hold it?" Emily asked Oliver, determined to speak up for him if he couldn't.

He shot her a disgusted glance. "Of course I can. I'm not some diaper-clad two-year-old."

"Well excuse me for asking," she said.

Alyson glanced sympathetically her way as she followed Quincy toward the stairs. Handlers were routinely treated like dirt, that look said, so get used to it. Emily, who knew that much at least, lifted her chin in defiance.

"What are you getting all uppity about?" Oliver scornfully asked. "Come on, or you're going to make the rest of us late. And General Stone's not the sort of man you ask to wait for you." He favored her with a snotty little smirk.

Emily ruffled his hair as she strolled past him. "Come on yourself."

"Hey!" he cried in outrage.

They had a jostling race up the stairs, with Oliver trying to wedge past her and failing. When they stumbled into the cabin, half-laughing and half-annoyed with each another, they realized that General Stone had seated himself in the very first row and was staring directly at them.

"Sorry," Emily murmured, straightening.

"You should be," said Oliver, and he slipped past her up the aisle.

It took every ounce of her self-discipline not to chase after him and thump him on the head. With the general's steady gaze upon her, though, she maintained her composure and walked between the rows to join Oliver. The interior was identical to the first Prometheus jet she had ridden. Were they one and the same, or did the Institute have a whole fleet?

Oliver settled at one of the tables on the right, halfway back in the main cabin. Quincy and her handler were on the left, two tables closer to the exit. Ben slouched in the back corner, presumably to sulk.

They were airborne in no time at all. No sooner did the seatbelt light click off than Oliver unlatched his restraint and bolted for the lavatory at the back of the plane.

Alyson hissed from two seats up. "Aren't you going with him?"

XIII

Emily wanted to ask what sort of damage a ten-year-old could perpetrate between an airplane lavatory and his seat, but then she decided that she didn't want an answer to that question. Alyson and all her experience at Prom-F could probably provide any number of possibilities.

Accordingly, Emily unlatched her own safety belt and trudged to the back of the plane. She sat in the aisle seat directly across from Ben, who looked up inquisitively.

"Apparently I need to follow Oliver to a lavatory twenty feet down the aisle," Emily said dryly. "I'd hate to be a negligent handler."

"There are worse things to be," Ben said with well-controlled bitterness.

She suppressed a laugh. "You don't seem excited about this trip. Are you worried that work will pile up too much while you're away from Prom-A?"

"If I ever return to Prom-A," he said darkly. "I can't figure out whether General Stone was serious about this being a promotion or not."

"Oh, were you promoted?" Emily asked, trying to feign surprise.

His answer was a slant-eyed glare. "Cute," he said flatly. "For future reference, tell Oliver that if he wants to listen to a computer located in a quiet hallway, he needs to turn the speakers down almost to nothing."

Emily had the grace to blush. "I kind of suspected you knew."

"Luckily, Principal Jones didn't notice anything. I'm surprised you would let him tamper with someone else's computer while they were out of the room."

"I told him not to, but he never listens to me. And somehow, I don't think you're really that surprised." Ben Birchard was

127

anything but stupid. He must have known that walking away from a computer rendered the contents of that computer vulnerable, especially when there were other people in the room he vacated.

He tipped his head in vague acknowledgement, a faint smile pulling at one corner of his mouth. So he'd known that Oliver would jump at the chance to eavesdrop on a secret meeting of Prometheus principals, and he'd allowed that situation to come to pass. But to what purpose? The question nagged at her. Were she and Oliver still being assessed for loyalty?

"You know," said Ben abruptly, "I was doing really well at Prom-A. This so-called 'promotion' is just about the worst thing that could've happened to me right now."

"Is it even legal for the military to conscript someone who works for the GCA like that?" Emily asked.

"When it's General Bradford Stone doing the conscription, you don't ask those sorts of questions," Ben said. "Besides, it's not like I can protest. He's the GCA's military liaison, for one thing, and it's not like I'm being transferred out of the Prometheus network, for another. But the last thing in the world I ever wanted was to end up at Prom-E."

"Prom-E?" Emily repeated sharply. "There is no Prom-E."

Ben frowned. "How idiotic would that be for them to skip a letter of the alphabet? The school for geniuses can't even get its ABC's right? Of course there's a Prom-E."

"But—"

"It's not in the system like the others, I'll give you that," Ben continued. "That's because it's the military branch of the school, the one for the true delinquents and troublemakers. There are minimum age limits for enrollment, and it extends past high school into adulthood. Our lovely General Stone up there is the principal,

XIII

and I'm his new administrative assistant, it seems. I suppose he's just itching to get his hands on Hawk and Hummer West."

"They're not going back to Prom-F?" Emily asked in surprise. Hadn't Quincy once said something along those lines?

"They've already escaped from Prom-F once," said Ben. "They won't get a second chance. Prom-E is the only other place to send them." He looked like he was about to say more, but their conversation was interrupted by a muffled flush and the lavatory door opening.

"What took you so long?" Emily asked Oliver.

He recoiled, not having expected her there. "I was enjoying the solitude. Two blissful minutes where I didn't have to look at your ugly face."

"And here I thought we were going to have to introduce prunes into your diet," Emily wryly said, much to his horror.

"Gross!"

"Back to your seat." She tipped her head up the aisle and followed with only a goodbye glance toward Ben.

As Oliver buckled himself into his chair, she leaned eagerly over the table and asked in a whisper, "Hey, did you know that there's a Prom-E?"

His face contorted. "Not you too."

"Huh? What's that supposed to mean?"

"My idiot roommate Tyler went off about that last night: the *shadow campus*"—he wiggled his fingers aloft in a farcical pantomime—"where all the Prom-F graduates get erased from the world. He's got this whole conspiracy theory. I knew you were dumb, but I didn't realize you were so far gone that you'd believe in something as preposterous as that."

"I didn't," Emily said. "Ben just told me about it. It's the military branch of the school, and General Stone's the principal."

A Rumor of Real Irish Tea

Oliver tipped his head in a critical glance. "He's pulling your leg. You should know better than to believe anything Birchard tells you."

"I should know better than to believe anything he tells *you*, you mean," Emily corrected, but the doubts he expressed seemed legitimate the more she considered them. Ben could easily be making fun of her, taking advantage of her gullibility to see how many ridiculous stories he could pass as genuine.

Still, "He seemed serious," she said, tapping her lower lip.

"Gullible," Oliver said with a derisive sneer.

They landed in Phoenix and deplaned beneath a scorching afternoon sun. Emily could have sworn it was a hundred fifty degrees outside as she stripped her tailored jacket from her shoulders. Never would she understand why people chose to live in such an uninhabitable climate.

Two cars waited to take them to their final destination. General Stone climbed in one and commanded Ben to join him. Quincy, Alyson, Emily, and Oliver piled into the other, the two children and Emily squishing into a crowded back seat while Alyson sat up front with their stoic driver. The airport was located centrally within the sprawling city, and it was only a ten-minute drive to the GCA office where they would stay. It was the same office that the Wests had ambushed just that morning.

From the outside, it looked like any other office building. They filed through the front door and the metal detectors under the watchful eyes of two security guards. General Stone commanded for the luggage to be taken to rooms on the fifth floor—probably where the holding cells were, Emily thought sourly—and then he led the small troupe to an elevator. They got out on the third floor, where several guards stood along the hallway with their weapons at the ready.

XIII

"And here is our crime scene," he said grimly. "Who's the man in charge here?"

A harried, middle-aged agent appeared from a room at one end of the hall. "General," he said as he hurried forward, "I'm Agent Knox. I'm the one in charge."

"Were you here this morning when the incident occurred?" General Stone asked.

Knox shook his head. "I was en route to pursue a lead we received from the national hotline."

"The waffle house," said the general flatly.

"Eight different calls over a ten-minute period from eight different citizens who had no discernible ties to one another," said Agent Knox grudgingly. "Not until we went back and traced the location of their phone calls, that is. They were all made along a bus route that led to this city block. Not a single person from the bunch was anywhere near that waffle house."

"And that, Agent Knox, is the danger of dealing with a savvy human-projector," said General Stone.

"The hotline people didn't bother to triangulate any specific locations for their callers," Knox said. "They're on alert to do so from now on. This won't happen again."

"I highly doubt it would happen again regardless. Those kids got what they came for, didn't they?"

Knox shifted uncomfortably. "They got something, but whether it would be of any use to them, I don't know. If you'll come this way . . ." He motioned down the hall, and his inquiring eyes traveled back to the others who accompanied the general, especially to the two children.

General Stone followed his gaze. "Birchard, you'll come with me. These other two can be escorted up to their rooms for the time being."

A Rumor of Real Irish Tea

No mention of the handlers even being present. Once again, Emily felt like she didn't exist.

At least she had a companion in her misery this time, though. She looked to Alyson expectantly, only to discover that the other handler had already turned back to the elevator, careless of the general's slight.

Emily glanced unhappily down at Oliver, and he scowled back up at her.

Yes, things were entirely back to normal.

XIV
Insufferable Know-It-All

AUGUST 1, 9:15AM MST, GCA REGIONAL OFFICE, CENTRAL PHOENIX

If Emily never saw another vending machine pastry so long as she lived, it would be too soon. "How can you eat that?" she asked Oliver as he took a giant bite from a leathery donut.

"They didn't have any spaghetti," he replied through the mouthful. He chewed laboriously and swallowed. "What, am I supposed to starve?"

She shook her head. "You'd expect a government agency to have something healthier than prepackaged sweetbreads to eat."

"Sweetbread isn't bread that's sweet," said Oliver. "It's animal pancreas. I don't think they prepackage that sort of thing, and if they did, it would be a pretty smelly vending machine."

"Sweet rolls," Emily corrected herself. "Sweet pastries. Sugar-covered over-processed bread-like foods. Government agencies should be selling healthy things like carrots and apple slices."

"Carrots and apple slices are perishable. Sugar-covered over-processed bread-like foods have six months of shelf-life. They're more cost-effective."

"So the one place we save money is the one place we shouldn't," said Emily like the health-food fanatic that she was.

A Rumor of Real Irish Tea

Oliver shrugged. "There's a cold-food vending machine in the first floor break room. It has yogurt and apples and sandwiches. If you're so concerned about what to eat, go get something from there."

They were sitting in a small communal kitchenette on the fifth floor, just down the hall from their allotted rooms. "You'd have to come with me," Emily said. The last time she'd left his side on a field mission like this, she'd ended up hypnotized by Honey West.

Oliver cocked an incredulous look upon her. "It's a few floors down, not halfway across the city."

"It's more than twenty yards, and I'm not taking any chances this time around."

"Yeah? Well, I'm busy right now."

"Doing what, procrastinating your homework?"

He lifted his nose in the air and took another bite of donut. She'd hit the nail right on the head, in other words. This time around, no one was pretending that Oliver had any other purpose beyond his null-projection. No one informed him of any updates on the Wests' whereabouts, no one consulted him for his opinion on their movements, and—above all—no one gave him meaningless busywork to make him feel like he was useful. He and Quincy both had their school assignments, and they were expected to sit quietly and wait until they were needed.

It was a waste of resources, Emily thought. Oliver and Quincy would probably have insights to the Wests that had escaped the notice of General Stone and the collection of GCA agents that were working this case.

"Whatever. I don't care," she said aloud. "It's not like I was hungry anyway."

In direct contradiction of those words, her stomach let out

XIV

a loud gurgle. Oliver choked on his donut in an attempt not to laugh, but he recovered almost immediately.

"Good," he replied, pretending that his face was not bright red from the indignity of nearly suffocating in front of his handler, "because I don't feel like going down to the first floor. I'm perfectly comfortable here."

Emily looked at the ceiling and lamented that such a selfish little brat got to dictate her movements. Oliver simply polished off the last of his donut.

A light tap on the open door interrupted their unfriendly solitude. "Hello," said Ben with a fake smile, and he held up a large brown paper bag. "I brought up some breakfast. Are Quincy and Alyson not up yet?"

"Haven't seen them," said Emily as she suspiciously eyed the bag. It was probably an assortment of crullers and pastries, if it was even breakfast food at all. Every guy she knew in college seemed to think that pizza and burgers could be eaten at any time of the day or night. Men in general didn't know what constituted a proper morning meal.

Ben's attention moved to the table where Oliver sat. "Looks like you've already had a little something," he said, nodding toward the empty donut wrapper. "I'm surprised your handler would let you eat that."

"What's she got to do with it?" Oliver asked. "I don't need her permission to eat whatever I feel like eating."

"Sure," said Ben with a slight smile, and he set the brown bag on the table. "I took the liberty of guessing what to get everyone. You two can start while I go round up our missing pair." Without further ado, he strolled from the room as abruptly as he had come.

Emily waited until he was gone before pouncing on the bag. It did not, as she had originally suspected, hold an assortment of pastries or a mess of burgers. Instead, there were individual boxes stacked one on top of another, the logo of a Phoenix bistro prominent on their packaging.

She pulled out the top box and noticed the initials OHD scribbled in one corner. The box itself was warm on the bottom. "This one's yours," she said to Oliver, bewildered as she handed it over. "What did he get you?"

Oliver eyed the package suspiciously, as though he didn't want to open it to find out.

"Go on," said Emily with growing amusement.

He leveled a sour glare at her but gingerly flipped the box open. Just to be a snot, he tipped it toward himself so the contents were out of Emily's sight. She resisted the temptation to crane her neck or cross over behind him.

"Well?"

"Pancakes," he said flatly, "with extra syrup, two sausage links, and some scrambled eggs. How am I supposed to eat all of this?"

"You don't like it?" Emily asked curiously.

He made a disgruntled noise and slouched down in his chair, sulking.

She pulled out the second box and read the initials from the top. "QI. What's Quincy's last name?"

"Ivers," said Oliver. "She'll get mad if you go snooping in her food, though."

"I wasn't going to." Emily pettishly set the box aside. The next one read AEM, which she took to indicate Alyson. The final box had Emily's initials on it—EJB, she noticed with annoyance. Where exactly had he learned her middle name? She hadn't used it on her internship applications.

She decided to forgive him when she saw the contents, though. Nestled within were half a grapefruit, two triangles

XIV

of whole-wheat toast with a side of marmalade, two eggs sunny-side-up, and four—yes, *four*, she realized with growing excitement—slices of real, honest-to-goodness bacon. A set of plastic utensils was included, along with a folded paper napkin. It was like the dream breakfast she had never dared hope for.

"Isn't there anything to drink?" Oliver asked.

Emily pulled out a smaller bag nestled within the larger one and removed the contents: two bottles of orange juice, one regular soymilk, and one chocolate soymilk. This last item was labeled with Alyson's initials, but none of the others were marked.

Oliver immediately grabbed an orange juice and cracked it open to take a swig. Emily thought she ought to take the other orange juice, but she wanted the soymilk. As a couple of voices sounded in the hallway outside, she hastily set the soymilk in front of her own box and sat down. She didn't go so far as to open it, but she sincerely hoped that Quincy would not demand it from her.

Quincy was the first to appear in the doorway. She spared a suspicious glance at Emily as she joined them at the small round table. Her hand immediately shot out to snag the second orange juice from the center where it sat next to Alyson's chocolate soymilk.

"Did you want a regular soymilk?" Emily asked, eaten with guilt for her own stinginess.

"You're not supposed to talk to her," said Oliver mechanically.

"I *hate* soymilk," said Quincy with venom, and Emily wasn't sure whether it was directed at her or the drink. Either way, she got to keep her beverage of choice.

Ben and Alyson were not far behind. A nervous, twittering laugh from Alyson announced their presence as they arrived, strongly reminiscent of how Principal Lee's assistant Michelle had acted only a couple nights ago. Emily looked at Ben dubiously. How did he have that effect on women? It wasn't as though he was devilishly handsome or excessively witty.

"I see we've got everything distributed properly," he said when he saw the table. "Sorry if I got any of the orders wrong, but I did have only limited resources to work with. I heard you only drink chocolate soymilk, Alyson, so I got one of those for you."

Alyson turned a delicate shade of red, flattered by his pointed attention. "The regular kind tastes so foul," she said as she slid into the last open chair.

Emily wryly took a gulp of her "foul" drink and watched with tempered interest as both Quincy and Alyson opened their boxes. Alyson was by far more vocal in expressing her thanks.

"Oatmeal and fresh fruit salad! It's been so long since I've had a decent bowl of oatmeal!" She might have stopped there, but a tentative glance toward Ben showed him smiling pleasantly back at her. Emboldened, she continued, "The stuff they sometimes serve at Prom-F is all over-cooked and has the consistency of glue. This bowl looks wonderful! With brown sugar and butter and everything, even! And the cantaloupe and honeydew look so good! How did you know to get this for me?"

Couldn't she see that smile on his face was fake? Or was she so desperate for male attention that she overlooked that detail?

"I just took a wild guess," he said, and he neatly averted his eyes toward the window.

It wasn't any wild guess. Even if Quincy didn't make loud exclamations like her handler, the sudden glow to her eyes when she opened her breakfast box testified that she had received an appealing meal as well. In fact, the only one who had expressed discontent was Oliver. Emily turned to discover him

XIV

in the midst of dipping one sausage link in the extra syrup from his pancakes.

Surprise jolted through her. He wasn't upset at all. He just didn't want to express thanks to the likes of Ben Birchard.

Her attention shifted to her own meal. The grapefruit, toast, and eggs made a familiar trio—she had ordered that particular combination any number of times over the past four or five years before she came to Prometheus. The bacon was a new addition, but if bacon weren't beyond her price range, she might have eaten it every day of the week.

How had Ben known that? She raised suspicious eyes to his face, but he was still patently avoiding anyone's gaze.

"Thanks, Birchard." This quiet expression of gratitude came from Quincy, who had picked up a large, sugary scone from her box.

"I know you don't really like eggs," Ben said, "but you need to eat a couple bites at least—you don't have any other protein in there."

"That's right, Quincy," said Alyson encouragingly. "Make sure you eat everything that Mr. Birchard was nice enough to bring you."

Quincy made a face at her handler and defiantly bit into the scone. Oliver, meanwhile, was fixated on sopping up syrup with pieces of his pancakes. Ben took the momentary lull in conversation as a cue to leave.

"Now that everyone has what they need, I'll be on my way. If you have any particular wishes for lunch, let me know. The GCA is footing the bill, after all."

He was out the door with a cavalier wave. On impulse, Emily bolted after him. "Wait," she called as he moved to the elevator. If there was a car there waiting for him, she was going to throw a fit.

Ben turned curious eyes on her. "Let me guess," he said. "Turkey on rye, extra mustard, hold the mayo, with lettuce, tomatoes, alfalfa sprouts, and avocado if they have it."

"How do you do that?" Emily asked. He'd brought her a turkey sandwich the other night, but she hadn't realized then how specific the selection was to her tastes. "Have you been stalking us all for the last five years?"

"I don't know what you mean," Ben said in all innocence.

Emily pointed back toward the kitchenette and spoke in a fierce whisper. "Half a grapefruit, whole-grain toast, and two eggs sunny-side up. I've ordered that a hundred times. Not the bacon—that was too expensive."

He shrugged, his hands in his pockets. "It's fascinating how extensive the GCA is in their background checks. It's even more fascinating the amount of information the government stores on any one individual. Try buying things with cash in the future instead of using your bank card. Although, they do have plans in the works to track individual bills, so even that won't be safe for much longer."

"So you just . . . went and looked up our preferences?" asked Emily, feeling somehow violated.

"The information was there to look up," he said, with no regrets in sight.

"And what about the bacon?" she pressed. She'd never purchased such a luxury item before.

"Ah," said Ben knowingly. "That was a tip from the Prom-F lunch lady. She said you were almost in tears one morning because she offered you bacon. She remembers your face quite well, actually."

Behind him, the elevator chimed and the doors slid open. Emily gaped as he waved a cheery farewell and got into the car. The doors slid shut again.

XIV

"He really is a terrible gossip," she muttered when she had gathered her wits again.

Back in the kitchenette, Alyson raised jealous eyes to glare as Emily returned to her seat. Emily felt like telling her to put a sock in it, that she wasn't trying to flirt with the ever-so-charming Mr. Birchard. Instead, she focused on her breakfast.

"I'm missing a slice of bacon." She turned accusing eyes on Oliver.

He grinned and crunched down on the last half of the missing slice.

"Pest," said Emily. "You don't have anything worth stealing in your box."

"I have syrup," Oliver replied, and he waved the extra little vat enticingly. "It's re-e-e-eally good with bacon. It's really good with everything," he added with a studious little frown.

So Ben had known about Oliver's love of syrup. Had Prom-F ever served it in the times they were there? She couldn't recall. Perhaps it had been a staple of Prom-A breakfasts, though.

She obligingly dipped a slice of bacon in the syrup, much to Oliver's shock. "That is really good," she agreed. "Oh, don't get your panties in a twist. I'm not going to take any more of your precious syrup."

"I don't wear panties!" Oliver cried in outrage.

She couldn't help the laugh that bubbled up, and only the sudden recollection that they had an audience stopped her from remarking on his unfortunate choice of words. He remembered Quincy and her handler at that very same moment, because a deep blush descended upon him as he turned his eyes on them.

"What?" he asked belligerently.

Quincy said nothing. Alyson nervously looked around the room and homed in on the television mounted in one corner.

A Rumor of Real Irish Tea

"Shall we have a look at the news?" She hurried to switch the screen on to NPNN.

Emily inwardly groaned.

"It's Veronica Porcher," said Alyson eagerly. "I just *love* her."

The beautiful newscaster's face did indeed fill the screen. Quincy and Oliver looked away with indifference, but their attention snapped back as Alyson turned up the volume.

"There's been a bizarre new twist in the kidnappings of Maddie and Alex North," Veronica reported with a solemn expression. "Residents here in Phoenix, Arizona have reported multiple sightings of the pair, but in a strange development it seems the two are always in the company of another pair of boys. Surveillance videos show the foursome at a local shopping center"—the video cut to a grainy camera shot and what appeared to be four children, though their faces were not at all discernible—"and police worry that what they originally thought to be two kidnappings in fact involves four or more children, and that they are now looking at a kidnapping ring. The identity of the two older boys remains a mystery, though police sketch artists have released these pictures based on eyewitness accounts."

Two rough sketches of Hawk and Hummer West flashed up on screen. The nose was too big on Hummer, and the forehead too narrow on Hawk, almost as though the pictures were intentionally inaccurate.

Veronica's report continued. "Anyone who sees these children out on the streets is encouraged to call the national hotline, but police have asked concerned citizens not to approach. It still remains uncertain who is behind these kidnappings, but the children have behaved as though they were under constant surveillance, and any interference may cause them harm."

XIV

"Then why broadcast their information all over the national news?" Emily asked sarcastically.

Oliver and Quincy both turned inquiring eyes on her.

"No, I'm serious," she said. "If there really were some nefarious kidnapper lurking in the shadows and he was going to hurt these children if people try to approach them, wouldn't having their faces on the national news make him even more likely to do something? I mean, what kidnapper sends his victims out into public, anyway? Who actually believes any of this?"

"Are you questioning the journalistic integrity of Veronica Porcher?" asked Alyson with a tremulous voice.

Emily flung an angry hand toward the screen. "You *know* that story's false. Hawk and Hummer escaped from Prom-F, and they broke Honey and Happy out of Prom-B. Oliver and Quincy were sent here to recover them. There were never any kidnappers. I know the public has to be told something," she added self-consciously under Alyson's reproachful glare, "but couldn't they have come up with a better story than that?"

"They didn't have that many options," Oliver said. "They'd already reported Honey and Happy as kidnapping victims. They couldn't exactly report Hawk and Hummer as the kidnappers, because that would draw all sorts of questions: where did these pint-sized miscreants come from? Why wasn't it readily apparent who they were to begin with? Wouldn't their parents or teachers have reported them missing as well? And then there's the problem of facial similarities—when you see them all together it's obvious they're related. Those sketches were terrible, though. No one's going to see those on the news and think it was one big family outing like they would if they used pictures instead."

"It's easier to create a villain," said Quincy. "This way, if anyone does try to help Hawk and Hummer, they'll be pegged as the kidnapper. It identifies them to the public and cuts them off from receiving any help."

"Except that they have Honey with them," Oliver said.

"But even Honey's projections wear off," Quincy countered. "They'll have to be a whole lot more careful about where they go and who they talk to, because the public now knows to look for four kids instead of two."

Oliver tacitly conceded that point.

Emily, though, still fixated on the terrible story. "But the report itself makes no sense. No kidnapper in his right mind would march his victims out where everyone could see them."

"Unless he's just that twisted," said Quincy with a wry smile. "Look, it doesn't really matter *what* Veronica reports, just that she reports it. The more often she repeats a story, the firmer it gets rooted into her viewers' brains. They're not even going to think to question the details. Look at my idiot handler if you want proof of that."

They all simultaneously turned to Alyson, who stood next to the television with a horrified expression on her face. "I . . . I *like* Veronica," she said fiercely.

"But you have to admit there are holes in the story she's reporting," said Emily.

"Of course there are holes. She's reading what they tell her to. It's not her fault."

"Give me a couple weeks, and I'll have her nicely deprogrammed," Quincy said to Oliver. "It takes at least that long to reset the neural pathways when they've had so many repeated exposures."

"So you two knew that Veronica Porcher was a projector?" Emily asked.

"Everyone knows that she graduated from Prom-C," said

XIV

Oliver. "Principal Carter likes to brag about it, even though he wasn't even principal there when she attended."

"I never saw what the big fuss was about her," said Quincy. "Hit the mute button and she's just a pair of red lips and big hair."

"I *like* her," Alyson insisted, but she seemed less sure of herself. Emily supposed it was upsetting to discover that a long-time favorite personality was nothing but a sham made possible by a fluke of genetics. She'd be upset herself if not for her three weeks in confinement with Oliver in the next cell over. In that time, she'd come to thoroughly despise Veronica Porcher and every other NPNN reporter.

How many more of them were projectors? Or was Veronica the only one?

The government so rarely did things in small degrees, but projectors were not all that common. It seemed unlikely that too many of them aspired to be news reporters. Unless the Prometheus Institute chose its students' career paths for them—which wouldn't have surprised her in the least at this point—the likelihood of another projector on the national news did seem slim. Besides that, Veronica had done most if not all of the reporting on the kidnapping of Maddie and Alex North. If there had been another projector available, surely they would have split the duties.

Or not. At this point, Emily had absolutely no clue how her government ran things.

XV
Misguided Projection

AUGUST 1, 12:07PM MST, GCA REGIONAL OFFICE, CENTRAL PHOENIX

THE FOUR WERE left on their own for the morning. Quincy and Oliver had homework, and Alyson stubbornly insisted on watching the news. Emily retired to the small sofa in the corner with a presidential memoir she had found on a sparsely populated bookshelf. She soon abandoned it in favor of staring out the window.

The scorching Phoenix sun seemed like it could melt the cars on the street below. Pedestrians were few and far between, though a few bicyclists did brave the heat. When Ben Birchard's head poked out of a cab, Emily perked with interest. He had a brown paper bag with him—lunch, she sincerely hoped.

He jogged across the hot pavement toward the building and out of sight. Emily turned from the window and pretended to read the memoir on her lap. The elevator down the hall chimed and Ben appeared, sack in one hand and a thick manila file in the other.

"I've brought lunch," he announced as he set both items on the table.

Alyson flipped off the television and scampered to his side

XV

with a nervous laugh. "You shouldn't have." Ben smiled at her, which triggered more fluttering eyelashes.

Emily scowled.

"I hope you didn't get me anything with pickles," said Oliver. "I hate pickles."

"I got you pickle loaf smothered with extra pickles and pickle relish on the side," Ben said as he fished around in the bag. "Enjoy." He handed a wrapped sandwich to Oliver, who opened it to reveal a cheeseburger. The boy thoroughly examined every layer.

Ben, meanwhile, continued to hand out the contents of his sack like Santa Claus on Christmas Eve. "For Quincy, another burger. I hope you like sauerkraut, Miss Alyson, because I went out on a limb and bought you a Reuben."

"My favorite!" Alyson received the sandwich with worshipful eyes. Emily and Oliver each suppressed a gag, but for entirely different reasons.

"And for Ms. Brent." Ben handed her the final packet with a murmured, "I hope it's to your liking."

She made a mental note to order something new the next time she went to a deli. Much as she loved turkey on rye, she did not like someone else anticipating her order.

To her astonishment, however, the proffered sandwich was not turkey on rye. She unwrapped, instead, a ham-and-cheese on toasted sourdough. Lettuce, tomato, and extra mustard completed the creation. She lifted curious, confused eyes to her benefactor.

Ben was in the midst of receiving Alyson's extended gratitude "Reubens are so expensive that I only get to treat myself once a year, but I haven't had one since my internship started because they don't ever get corned beef up at Prom-F! Thank you so much!". In the midst of this exuberant speech, he ventured a wry glance toward Emily in the corner.

He was making fun of her. He *knew* she always ordered turkey on rye, and he had intentionally bought her something different. Well, she'd show him. She didn't care what kind of sandwich he brought, as long as it didn't come from a vending machine.

On that thought, she took a hearty bite of the ham on sourdough.

It was all right, but she liked turkey on rye more.

"What's in the file folder, Birchard?" Oliver asked between bites of his burger.

"It's a printout of commercial and residential rentals for the last three weeks. The government has a database to keep track of housing contracts, and General Stone gave it to me to review. Care to have a look?"

"Why? You want me to do your job for you?"

Ben smiled and shrugged. "I just thought you might be bored of homework. But actually, you can't look at it. General Stone gave it to me to take care of, and it wouldn't be responsible of me to hand it over to a ten-year-old without his say-so."

Oliver glowered as he chewed.

"Is there anything to drink?" Quincy asked quietly.

"Oh, almost forgot." Ben dug four water bottles from the bag. "The agents downstairs warned me that the tap water here is horrendous. Make sure to toss your bottles in the recycle bin when you're finished with them."

Alyson beamed her thanks as he handed around the water. Emily warily took hers, careful to keep her expression neutral. Ben waited until she had lifted the rim to her lips before he announced, "General Stone said he wants to meet with you after

XV

lunch, Quincy, Oliver. I'll escort you down to the conference room he's commandeered once you're done eating."

"What's he want?" Oliver asked sourly.

"I imagine he wants to pick your little brains. He's good at using whatever resources he comes across, and it would be foolish to let a couple of those resources rot away doing homework. I told him you had a personal interest in seeing the Wests brought home, Oliver," he said.

Oliver eyed him suspiciously.

"What did you tell him about me, Birchard?" asked Quincy.

Ben only smiled and arched his eyebrows.

"Great," she muttered.

Emily ate only half her sandwich and wrapped the other half up again, intending to save it for a late-afternoon snack. The refrigerator stood empty except for a couple of ice trays in the freezer, so she didn't feel the need to label the wrapper.

"Ham-and-cheese isn't your favorite?" Ben asked her in a low voice as she stooped to put the sandwich away. Alyson and Quincy had gone to use the restrooms, and Oliver was polishing off the last of his burger, heedless of anyone else in the room.

"It was very good, thank you," said Emily diplomatically.

"I thought with the bacon obsession that ham was a decent bet to make. I guess I got it wrong."

"I said it was good," Emily repeated, annoyance thick on her voice.

He shrugged, and she could tell he didn't believe a word she had said. That only annoyed her further.

"How did you know that Alyson likes Reubens?" she asked accusingly. "She said she only buys them once a year."

Ben tipped his head. "On her birthday. It's not only a matter of reviewing data, but of interpreting it. I'm rather proud of my abilities. I think I'll get you a club sandwich next time. Maybe a turkey club. I'll have to mull it over."

"Turkey on rye is what I always get," Emily said.

"But you also hate to be predictable," Ben replied. "It shows on your face plain as day. But if you'd like to *request* turkey on rye for tomorrow's lunch, I'll abide by your demands."

"What if I want a strip steak with a baked potato and extra gravy?"

He winked. "The GCA's paying."

Her breath caught in her throat. "I don't really want one. I was just trying to think of something expensive. I don't even *like* steak, not that I've ever had more than a taste of it . . ." She was babbling, she suddenly realized, and he was laughing at her. "Ooh!" she cried in frustration, and she stalked away from him.

And not a moment too soon. Alyson and Quincy returned from the lavatory. The other handler had shown a marked desire to monopolize Ben, and as far as Emily was concerned, she was welcome to him.

"Shall we head downstairs?" he asked. "I'm sure General Stone is ready and waiting for you."

He ushered them to the doorway. As they moved toward the elevator, Oliver suddenly snagged Emily's sleeve. "We'll take the stairs, Birchard," he said. "It's the second floor? We'll meet you there."

Ben was nonchalant. "Yes, second floor. Are you sure you want to take the stairs, though? The elevator's quicker."

"I need the exercise to work off that fatty burger you fed me," Oliver retorted.

"Oh, it was mostly soy and you know it," said Ben. "But if you want to take the stairs and your handler has no objections, I certainly don't care. We'll see you downstairs."

XV

The elevator doors slid open and the three got on. Quincy favored Oliver with a suspicious glance as he led Emily to the stairwell.

"What gives?" Emily asked.

Oliver waited until the landing door shut behind him before he answered. "Would you kindly stop flirting with Birchard? It's gross."

She bristled. "I am *not* flirting. I don't even like him. He's an infuriating *know-it-all*."

"Yes, infuriating," said Oliver. "He knows everything about everyone, and right now he's showing off like a bowerbird dancing to attract a mate."

"Ugh!" Emily recoiled at the analogy, but her reaction had no effect on her pint-sized scold.

"Quit giving him the time of day. It only encourages him."

"*I'm* encouraging him?" she said incredulously. "Quincy's handler is ready to lick his shoes clean, and *I'm* encouraging him?"

"I'd tell her to cut it out too, but I'm not allowed to talk to her," said Oliver with a dark scowl. "I'm pretty sure she's a lost cause anyway. Women are so stupid."

"Hey." She grabbed his shoulder so that he would look at her, her expression deadly serious. "That's not appropriate. I know I let you get away with a lot of things—you can tell me I'm an idiot, you can say that Alyson's an idiot, but don't just categorize all women as stupid because a few of them have bad judgment. And I am certainly *not* flirting with Ben Birchard."

Oliver's face flushed a mottled red. He shrugged out of her grip. "Fine. But don't encourage his antics, either. Just take whatever he gets for you and keep quiet about it."

"I *did* keep quiet about it," Emily cried, feeling unjustly accused. "He gave me a ham sandwich, and I didn't say a word!

A Rumor of Real Irish Tea

I can't help it if he starts up a conversation with me. I mean, I guess I could be all surly and glare at him like you do, but most people don't think that's polite. And he finds it amusing enough coming from you. He'd probably laugh himself silly if I tried to stonewall him like that."

The scowl on his face grew deeper. He harrumphed. "There's never a right answer with Birchard. You'd better hurry, or he'll come looking for us." He swept past her down the stairs.

That little punk, Emily thought. He'd been the one who wanted to discuss something privately—not that she expected any privacy within a GCA office. The security cameras that overlooked each landing reminded her of that quite nicely. She supposed that Ben would hear the entirety of their conversation before nightfall.

As they exited the second floor stairwell, the man himself stood waiting. Quincy and Alyson were nowhere in sight, but voices traveled from a conference room down the corridor.

He smiled. "This way," he said, and he led them forward.

"Snake," Oliver muttered, aptly voicing Emily's misgivings aloud.

If Ben heard the quiet insult, he made no such acknowledgement. Instead, he motioned them through the doorway of the conference room. Within, General Stone stood at a table of GCA agents. Quincy sat in a chair near the far end, with an empty seat next to her that was undoubtedly meant for Oliver. Alyson had been relegated to a chair in the corner, and Emily rightly surmised that its adjacent companion was meant for her. Wordlessly she took her spot.

"And now that we're all here," General Stone said with just enough control to indicate how annoyed he was, "let's begin. We've established that the Wests targeted this office in particular,

XV

that they must have gleaned information from both public archives and the low-level agents that you sent to track them. We know what they seized and how they escaped. We're only missing where they ended up. Agent Knox and his team have established from sighting reports that they're moving from one place to the next every day or two. Is that correct?"

Agent Knox sat up straighter in his chair. "Yes, sir. We've been able to pinpoint a hotel room in Glendale, an apartment in Peoria, and a small business office downtown as places that they definitely stayed at some point. The hotel room was only rented for one night, but there was a signed lease on both the apartment and the office. We've kept the areas under surveillance since their discovery, but they haven't returned there yet."

"Three places in what's likely a very long string," said General Stone, "with three different names on the rentals and payment by money order. They have an extraordinary number of resources at their disposal, but they are limited in what they can do. They're not buying any property because the process takes too long. We've narrowed our search to business and private rentals that have payment by money order rather than by check or bank transfer. Anything else?"

To Emily's great surprise, Oliver raised his hand. "General Stone," he said. All eyes turned upon him. The general looked more irritated than interested in what he had to say, but Oliver didn't care. "You'll want to look for something that was rented at a significantly lower price than the landlord originally asked. Honey West likes a bargain. At least, she did in Las Vegas and Flagstaff."

Grudgingly, Stone shifted his attention to Agent Knox. "Do we have access to that information?"

Knox shifted through a stack of papers. "The hotel room was

rented at half its usual price. The office space . . ." He paused to glance over a few different pages. "Its rent was significantly lower than the comparables in the area. The apartment seems on the low side as well."

"You'll want to look for contracts where the utilities are included in the asking price too," said Oliver. "I doubt they'd want to take the time to set up those services or pay those bills."

"No one includes utilities in the rent these days," said a balding agent halfway down the table.

"They do when a projector like Honey West asks them to," said General Stone grimly. "From everything I've heard, she could sell a crate of light bulbs to the Amish and have them thanking her for the honor."

A few of the older agents exchanged knowing glances. Everyone else looked around in confusion. Ben was the one to voice their collective uncertainty.

"The *Amish*, sir?"

General Stone grunted. He deigned to explain himself, though with a hint of contempt on his face. "I guess I'm showing my age with that remark. The Amish were a community of people in Pennsylvania that shunned modern technology. They were assimilated into the general population back in the twenties, but before that they drove around in horse-and-buggy rigs and led a primitive lifestyle."

"Ah," said Ben.

The general redirected the conversation back to more pertinent matters. "So we're looking for units that were rented at a lower asking price with all utilities inclusive. Agent Knox, would you be so kind as to divide the contracts among the proper parties?"

"Wait," said Oliver. "Aren't these in a database? Can't you just whittle down the possibilities with search terms?"

XV

A muscle clenched along Agent Knox's jawline, and a controlled breath left his throat. "The properties are in a database, but most of the contracts are submitted as images. The Housing Department is roughly three years behind in verifying that those contracts match the information tied to them." On this monumental tribute to government efficiency, he shuffled around the table to distribute the papers he held. "These are all the rental contracts from the past three weeks for the entire valley. Star any likely candidates, and when you finish with your pile, pass it to the right. We're double-checking to make certain that we don't miss anything."

Emily was supremely relieved when he bypassed the two handlers. She'd had a boring enough morning and didn't want to spend the afternoon looking over rental agreements. Her relief was short-lived, though.

"Oliver, you should trade places with Alyson," said Ben. "You and Quincy can have your handlers help you go over your contracts."

"You don't trust a couple of kids to do the work of adults, Birchard?" Oliver asked snidely, but he pushed away from the table as instructed. Alyson, eager to impress one person in the room at least, moved out of her chair to replace him.

Quincy simply glared at Birchard with disgust.

Oliver split his pile and handed half to Emily the moment he sat down. "You aren't too keen about combing through rental agreements either," she surmised as she took it from him.

He wrinkled his nose, but he turned his attention to the set of pages he had kept.

It was slow-going. Most of the rentals didn't have an original list-price included in the government registry—nor were they required to—and only by looking at comparables in the same neighborhood could they figure out whether the price was appropriate or not. This meant frequent consultation of a computer database, and while the GCA agents were nice enough to provide laptops for everyone, the work still took forever. As the hours passed, they slogged their way through contract after contract. In a city this large, there were literally thousands of rentals to review. Emily couldn't blame General Stone for enlisting all the help he could get, child labor laws notwithstanding.

The task had long since become mind-numbing when agents began to stand up, stretch, and take extended breaks away from the conference room. When Emily chanced a peek at General Stone, she discovered him thumbing his cell phone, much to her disbelief. The only ones who seemed to take the task at all seriously were Oliver, Quincy, and Ben.

Of course Ben would take it seriously. He was probably creating a personal catalogue of Phoenix residents and their preferred breakfast foods. Why anyone let him anywhere near a database of any kind she would never understand.

Just after four o'clock, when she thought her brain might combust from sheer boredom, a chime sounded from the elevator. A couple of agents who had been loitering in the hallway scampered back into the room and took their seats at the table. They leaned over to their colleagues and whispered something, their excitement simmering.

Emily's attention shifted to the door as a pair of voices approached.

"It's just a formality, I assure you. I see no reason why the general wouldn't agree to such a tiny request." The man sounded vaguely familiar, but Emily couldn't put her finger on where she had heard him before.

XV

"I do hope so," a woman replied, and Emily sat bolt upright at the sound of that lush voice. The whole conference room turned to watch as none other than Veronica Porcher sashayed in, with Principal Rupert Carter of Prom-C on her heels. It was the first time that Emily had seen him from a normal vantage point instead of from above. From here his comb-over didn't look nearly as atrocious.

General Stone stood. "Principal Carter," he said in greeting, and he extended his hand, which Principal Carter promptly shook.

"General," he said with a deferential nod. "Of course you know Ms. Veronica Porcher of the National Public News Network. Veronica, this is General Stone."

"Charmed," said Veronica as she also shook his hand. Her lovely mouth curved into a beautiful smile, and Emily instantly hated her for it.

"Unfortunately for you, I'm not," said General Stone. "Principal Carter sent me a message that you want to be put up in a hotel for the duration of your stay here."

"It's customary," Veronica said, trying not to look perturbed at his brusqueness. "I've been on several assignments like this, and the NPNN executives always provide me with a hotel room."

General Stone remained unmoved. "We're not the NPNN executives. This is a GCA operation, and you're here as a resource. You'll be treated like any other resource."

Emily's heart froze as the meaning of that sentence sank in. Oliver and Quincy were resources, and they were staying on the fifth floor of this very office. Did that mean that Veronica . . . ?

She didn't have to wait long for her answer. "Surely you can see that I'm more than a mere resource, General," Veronica said in her most persuasive voice.

A Rumor of Real Irish Tea

"Have Ms. Porcher's things taken to the fifth floor," the general said to Principal Carter. "We're on a budget here, and there's no reason for an extra expenditure like a hotel room when there are perfectly serviceable quarters within the office. And before you waste your breath on any more arguments, Ms. Porcher, I should point out a couple more of our resources at the end of the room: Oliver and Quincy, from the Prometheus Institute. They're both null-projectors, so there's no point in you trying to change my mind."

A momentary pout crossed her face, but she quickly schooled it away. "How nice to see students of my alma mater using their talents for good in the world," she said with a contrived smile. "And is that—" Suddenly her face lit up. "Do my eyes deceive me? Is that you, Ben Birchard?"

He stood from his place at the table. "Hello, Veronica," he said warmly, and he embraced her in a very familiar greeting. Emily could have sworn she heard Alyson growl when Veronica kissed him on the cheek.

"Darling Ben! I had no idea you were here. It's been ages since we saw each other! How have you been?"

"Well enough," said Ben. "And you? You look wonderful as always."

She laughed, a low, indulgent sound.

General Stone loudly cleared his throat. "Birchard, since you seem to know Ms. Porcher so well, why don't you escort her upstairs. Take one of the null-projectors with you," he added with a suspicious glance at the news reporter. Veronica pretended not to hear him.

Ben, ever obedient to his master, turned first to Oliver and Emily, but he must have thought better of that decision, because he suddenly shifted his attention away. "Quincy, Alyson,

XV

how would you two like to take a short break with me up to the fifth floor?"

Quincy wordlessly stood and straightened the stack of papers she had been looking through. Alyson was equally ready to comply, though a nervous hint of jealousy gleamed in her eyes as she smoothed her rumpled suit. Emily didn't know why she bothered. Not a hair was out of place on Veronica, who looked as though she had just come from an extended session with makeup and wardrobe professionals. No one in the room could compete with her as far as looks went. An anxious dab of a thing like Alyson had no chance.

And why she would want a chance with the likes of Ben Birchard, Emily would never understand.

The foursome exited the conference room, leaving behind a number of star-struck GCA agents in their wake. General Stone turned to Principal Carter. "You really thought it was appropriate to put your little prima donna up in a hotel for an unknown period of time?"

Carter shifted uncertainly from one foot to another. "It seemed reasonable enough when she asked."

General Stone smiled sarcastically. "I'm sure it did. Has she been briefed on her role in this charade?"

"Yes. She has a set of broadcasts to run this evening from seven to eleven, so she'll need to go back to the studio in a couple of hours. She wanted to get settled where she was staying before then, which is why we've come."

"She came now because she wanted me to approve a five-star hotel room for her," General Stone said.

"Not five-star," Principal Carter protested faintly.

"Have you seen where she usually stays? NPNN should know better than anyone to keep an eye on human-projectors in their midst. This one in particular has been using her talents to upgrade her lifestyle, and the government gets to foot the bill. I will not tolerate that sort of insurrection, Carter. She is a tool, and she will behave accordingly."

"I'm sure she understands, General," Carter said quickly, and he glanced around the room in growing embarrassment.

General Stone continued. "I have very little patience for projectors. If we didn't need her . . ." He left that sentence hanging so that everyone within hearing distance could imagine a suitably disagreeable ending.

"I—I understand," the Prom-C principal said, appropriately cowed by the general's menacing aura. "I'm one hundred percent certain that Veronica knows her place and won't cause you any trouble. She's always done excellent work in the past."

General Stone grunted and turned away. "And now that she's here safe and sound, I'm sure the Prometheus-C campus is awaiting your return."

"Yes, sir." Principal Carter made a short bow, looked around again in confusion, and then retreated from the room. The GCA agents exchanged uncomfortable glances.

"Everyone stop what you're doing and hand your papers back to Agent Knox," General Stone abruptly announced. "We've done enough for today. Knox, have the likely locations compiled into a separate list by tomorrow morning."

"Yes, sir," said Agent Knox, but his expression looked like he'd been commanded to dive into a vat full of mealworms.

Emily didn't begrudge him his task. It was sure to be long and boring, and she was glad it hadn't been allocated to her. She quickly handed the remainder of her pages to Oliver, who shuffled them in with his own and added the whole to Knox's growing pile.

XV

"Can I go back to my room?" Oliver boldly asked.

General Stone was busy checking his phone again, but he took the time to wave one hand dismissively, as though shooing away a fly. Oliver caught Emily's eye and tipped his head toward the doorway.

She was more than grateful to make a retreat. "You want to take the stairs again?" she asked once they were out in the hall.

"Why would I choose to climb three flights if I didn't have to? It's not like Birchard's going to be in the elevator poisoning the air with his smugness."

"True," said Emily.

As he pushed the button to go up, though, the elevator chimed and the doors slid open to reveal the object of their conversation.

"Oh!" said Ben, halfway out before he registered that they were standing right in front of him.

"We've been excused for the evening," Oliver said shortly. "You'd probably better report back to General Stone so he can give you your marching orders."

Ben smiled wryly. "Yes, I probably should. I'll see you two later." He slipped past them, not one bit upset by Oliver's peremptory dismissal.

"That was easy enough," said Emily as the elevator doors shut behind them.

Oliver grunted, Ben's nonchalant attitude having rubbed him the wrong way as usual.

Their adventures were not quite over, though. Emily saw Oliver to his room, and when he was safely inside, she turned to her own. She was surprised to discover Veronica coming down the hall, an eager attendant in tow with her baggage.

"Is this your room?" she asked Emily, pointing to the nearest door.

A Rumor of Real Irish Tea

"Yes," said Emily tightly.

"I was hoping you might do me a little favor," Veronica said with a disarming smile. "Since I have to leave early in the mornings and come back late at night, I was hoping for something a little closer to the elevator. Would you mind switching rooms with me?"

Yes, Emily thought with growing irritation. "My room is next door to Oliver's," she said aloud. "I'm supposed to stay next to him—you know, Prometheus handler and all."

The disarming smile looked a little strained. "You'll still be on the same floor. I'm sure no one will mind. General Stone probably won't even know. I mean, there's no reason for him to come up and check where we're all staying, is there? Pretty please? I'd be so grateful to you."

Emily didn't care to have gratitude from someone like Veronica. She was more annoyed that, even in government-regulated quarters, she was being asked to move aside for someone more important than her, someone who regularly stayed in five-star hotel rooms, someone who was a human-projector who always got her own way. *Like Honey West.*

Before she could voice her anger, Oliver's door opened behind her. "She said no, ya harpy," he told Veronica in his brattiest voice. "Go back to your own room and quit trying to project your wants on everyone else. It's not going to work as long as I'm around."

Then, he slammed the door.

Gratified as she was for the interruption, Emily was still embarrassed. "Sorry," she said to the astonished television reporter. Mortified, she skirted past her into her own room. Veronica remained speechless, clearly unaccustomed to such treatment.

XV

Emily leaned against the closed door with a sigh of relief. If not for Oliver's presence she would have caved to the beautiful woman's demands. She would have had no choice, just like she'd had no choice with Honey West.

How grateful she was to Oliver just for being there. Maybe she should buy him his own bottle of pancake syrup in thanks.

XVI
Real Irish Tea (Reprise)

AUGUST 1, 6:45PM MST, GCA REGIONAL OFFICE, CENTRAL PHOENIX

"Wow," said Oliver to Emily. "Birchard must hate you. He brought you fish for dinner."

"I happen to like fish." Emily stabbed the mahi-mahi filet with her fork perhaps a little too vigorously. She did like fish. She just didn't like that Ben obviously knew as much.

But then, it wasn't a strip steak and baked potato, so she should have been grateful rather than annoyed.

She glanced over at Oliver's entrée. "How's the chicken?"

Oliver's attention darted to the corner, where Ben sat talking with Alyson. He made an unhappy noise in the back of his throat, which Emily took to mean that it was delicious.

"What did Quincy get?"

He made a face. "Some gross vegetarian thing. I think it has eggplant in it."

"Did she want some gross vegetarian thing?" Emily enjoyed a lot of vegetarian meals, but she could understand why such cuisine wouldn't appeal to a couple of grade-school kids.

"Probably. She doesn't eat meat," said Oliver.

Emily stared. "She had a burger for lunch."

XVI

"Veggie-burger. And her breakfast was scones and fruit salad with a side of eggs that she didn't eat. She says eggs are proto-meat. She'll eat them if they're mixed into something, but she doesn't like them plain."

"Maybe she could try adding ketchup," said Emily dryly. Oliver leveled his standard "you're such an idiot" look directly at her.

There was no need to ask what Alyson's dinner was. In her ecstasy over the fettuccini alfredo, she'd taken five minutes to express her nervous, excited thanks. Emily imagined that she didn't have much experience with men, because she seemed to think Ben's attentions were personal instead of realizing that he catered to everyone he met.

It was sad to watch.

The conversation in the corner took an interesting twist. Alyson asked, "So, how long have you known Veronica Porcher?"

Emily, careful not to make any jarring movements, lifted her gaze from her food to study the pair.

Ben smiled. "Oh, it's been a few years or more now," he mused as though recalling blissful days. "We dated for a short while."

"O-oh," said Alyson, who looked supremely disappointed. "She . . . she's always been one of my favorite reporters. She's so beautiful and well-spoken."

He nodded, much to her dismay.

"Hey." Quincy abruptly stood from the nearby table, where she'd been sitting alone. "I need to go to the bathroom."

Alyson extracted herself from the conversation with apparent relief and hurriedly followed her charge out the door.

"When do you go to the bathroom?" Oliver asked Emily impertinently.

She plastered a bland smile on her face. "I wear an adult diaper during the day so that I never have to leave your side."

He recoiled. "Ew! Gross!"

She lightly swatted his head. "I go when you go. Or what, did you think I just always stand outside the boys' room like a faithful dog?"

"You're always there when I get out."

"You always take too long looking at yourself in the mirror," Emily said. That was only a guess, but by his outraged expression she'd hit the nail right on the head.

"You two look like you're having fun," said Ben as he sauntered from the opposite corner. "How's your dinner?"

Oliver grunted.

"It's excellent, thank you," said Emily with a fake smile.

He suppressed a laugh. "No love lost for me on this side of the room, I see. Have I done something to offend you?" This question was directed at Emily, as he apparently knew Oliver was a lost cause.

"No," she said lightly.

"Your girlfriend tried to kick her out of her room earlier," said Oliver. Emily shot him a warning glance, but that only made him defensive. "What? She did. And if not for me, you would've let her."

Ben watched the interchange with interest. "If by 'girlfriend' you mean Veronica," he said apologetically, "then I'd appreciate it if you didn't refer to her by that particular title."

"Rough breakup?" Oliver snidely asked.

"Nothing's ever rough for her," said Ben, but then he added, "except when she's around the likes of you. No, Veronica can have any man she wants, and for a few short days, she wanted me. Just between us, though,"—he leaned in closer, as though

XVI

telling Oliver a secret—"it was all part of my interview process with the GCA. She and I are on good terms because we have no reason to be otherwise."

"Part of your interview process involved you dating Veronica Porcher?" Emily asked skeptically.

"They didn't say so at the time, of course," said Ben, straightening, "but the GCA always exposes potential staff members to a low-level projector to assess their susceptibility. I conveniently met Veronica on my way out from my third interview at Prom-A, she conveniently was interested in spending time with me, and we conveniently broke up all within two weeks. I got my job three days later."

"I guess handlers don't merit that sort of scrutiny," said Emily. She certainly hadn't dated any extra-charming individuals during her interview process.

Ben shook his head, but his answer surprised her. "Not to such an extent as full-time staff members, no. You did meet with a projector at some point in the process. I told you that you scored high for obedience on your personality assessment, didn't I?"

She opened her mouth but then shut it again without speaking. She had naturally assumed that the "personality assessment" had been one of the myriad questionnaires she'd filled out with her applications. She racked her brains to recall all the people she'd met with, but it had been so long ago, back when she'd just been starting her graduate program.

"Girls always take so long in the bathroom," Ben said absently. He glanced toward the doorway and then shifted a wry look upon the surly ten-year-old next to him. "Almost as long as you do, Oliver. I wonder how much longer they're going to be."

"Did you need something from them?" Emily tightly asked.

A Rumor of Real Irish Tea

Why didn't he just follow the pair into the girls' room, since he didn't have any scruples about snooping elsewhere?

"Actually, I had a matter to discuss with all of you." Ben pulled a set of keys from his suit pocket. "It took me a while to get General Stone to agree with me even bringing it up, because it's something of a sensitive subject. We'll have to wait until they get back to discuss it any further."

He was just trying to drum up their curiosity, probably for his own amusement. Well, it wouldn't work on her. She kept her expression neutral, as if she didn't care what sensitive subject General Stone had agreed to let Ben broach.

Except she did care. It had to do with the Wests, because everything right now tied back to the Wests, and Emily wanted nothing more than for those four kids to get caught and dragged back to Prometheus. She was willing to do whatever she could to help in that endeavor.

But no one wanted her help. It was Oliver and Quincy they needed. She and Alyson were a couple of warm bodies there to make sure those two didn't disappear into the sunset as well.

"Here you are," Ben said as Quincy and Alyson returned from their bathroom break. "Let's all adjourn to the computer lab down the hall, shall we?"

"There's a computer lab down the hall?" Oliver asked with interest.

"Restricted access," Ben replied, and he swung his keys on one finger for emphasis. He led them around the corner to a plain-looking doorway, where both key and fingerprint were required to open the lock. He pressed his thumb onto the pad. "Fingerprint scanners are so easy to hack. All it takes is an authorized print and a copy machine, but it makes the higher-ups feel so much more secure when they have to use a body part

XVI

to gain access somewhere." He took the time to wipe his own print off the scanner before he held the door open for all of them.

"In you go," he said.

Within was a very small room, more like a closet than a lab, where two computers sat on standby. Everyone squashed in, with Oliver and Quincy taking the only two chairs while Emily and Alyson wedged themselves into the corners. Ben stepped between the two kids and tapped a password into a prompt on one computer.

"Now," he said, "what I'm about to tell you is completely confidential, and you're never to speak of it outside this room, do you understand? Quincy, Oliver, that means no discussing it with your little friends once you get back to Prometheus. Alyson, Emily, that goes double for you. Mere mention of the word can get you expelled from the premises and regarded as a threat to national security."

He was going to talk about Altair again. Emily's heart rate spiked. "What if we don't want to know about it?"

He tipped his head toward the door. "You're welcome to wait outside if that's how you feel. I wouldn't blame you in the least."

She might have taken him up on that offer, except that Oliver turned disparaging eyes upon her. "Stay where you are," that glare said, and it effectively killed any inner initiative that she had to flee.

When it became apparent that no one was making an escape, Ben proceeded. "I thought that so long as you both are here to help find the Wests, you should probably be aware of their movements and the GCA's efforts to get them back. I convinced General Stone to let you help with the property search this afternoon—"

"Oh, thanks loads," said Oliver sarcastically.

"—but it took me a little while longer for him to agree with me sharing what you're about to see," he continued seamlessly, as though Oliver had not spoken a word. "Do you want to look at surveillance footage first, or files?"

"We've been looking at files all afternoon," said Quincy in an exasperated voice.

Ben spared her a faint smile. "Surveillance footage it is, then. This is from yesterday morning's break-in. One of the GCA techs cobbled together all the pertinent footage into one loop."

He tapped a few keys, and a window opened up on the screen in front of Oliver. The camera angle showed the front security guards' desk and the door leading to the street. A time signature in the corner read 07:16. "It starts with the view from inside the entrance," Ben said. "Roughly ten minutes before, this branch of the GCA received notification from the national headquarters that Honey and Happy West had been spotted at a restaurant a few miles away. The agents on duty scrambled to put together a surveillance team, and most of them were away from the office when this occurred. Now, there—see the guard pick up the phone?" On screen, the security guard spoke into a handset. "If you squint you can make out the four kids through the glass of the front door. That's Honey on the other end of the phone. They called the accounting department first and had them transfer the call down to the security desk, presumably because they didn't have the extension for the direct line down there. The main phones were still switched over to the answering service, so they had to use a back-door line anyway."

"How did they get the accounting department's number?" Quincy asked.

He paused the video feed to explain. "The GCA had been sending low-level agents and techs to follow the Wests whenever

XVI

they got a report of their whereabouts, so that Honey wouldn't be able to extract any useful information from them when they were discovered. Even low-level agents and techs have the accounting department's phone number programmed into their phones, though. Number-crunchers aren't usually considered when the government looks to hide sensitive information. We assume that the Wests extracted the number from one of those cell phones, because they always confiscate the phones and wallets of anyone they find following them."

"Don't I know it," Emily muttered. She'd gotten her phone back in Flagstaff, but her wallet had disappeared completely. She'd had to beg the GCA to let her call her bank and put a freeze on her account before they tossed her into confinement.

"The items usually turn up in a trash can somewhere," said Ben sympathetically. "We've got a whole drawer full of them here."

"Shouldn't you give them back to their owners?" asked Emily. She had assumed that if they ever found her wallet it would be returned to her.

To her great dismay, though, he shook his head. "It's evidence in an open investigation. So here the guard, under Honey's influence, unlocks the door to let the Wests inside," he said, directing their attention back to the active computer screen. "And there you see Honey requesting his stun gun, which Hummer is going to confiscate from her."

"Rightly so," said Emily.

"You might not think so after you've seen the rest of this," said Ben with a wry glance. "There now: Hummer's crossed behind the security desk to get a look at the layout of the building."

"Photographic memory," said Oliver, annoyed. "Prometheus always underestimates the kid with the photographic memory."

"Yeah, as I understand it, once he's seen something it's stuck in his mind for good," said Ben. "This next bit we can fast-forward. They take the elevator to the third floor, Honey makes a juvenile face at the camera . . . Here we are: the accounting department, busy working on their end-of-the-month reports. You have to give the Wests some credit for ingenuity—it was the perfect day to attack."

"What are they doing?" Alyson asked in a mystified voice. On screen, the accountants had abandoned their work stations to line up in a circle with the youngest West.

"They're playing duck-duck-goose," said Ben. "We do have audio on these films, but every time they played it, whoever was watching ended up on the floor waiting for a tap on the head. I suppose with a pair of null-projectors here it would be safe enough to engage the sound, though."

He clicked a little icon at the bottom of the screen, and eager laughter met their ears. They watched in fascination as Honey commanded the supervisor to log into the main system on two separate terminals and then join the children's game in process on the floor. The two older boys, Hawk and Hummer, sat down and began typing. The game on the other side of the room grew in frenzy.

"I can't hear what they're saying," Oliver complained. "Those idiots are too loud."

"Hawk tapped into the branch's security system to watch for any signs that they'd been detected. Hummer stayed in the main system to enter a search term," said Ben. "Incidentally, it was the term he used that triggered an alert that something was wrong."

"What was the term?" asked Quincy.

Emily already knew the answer. Her stomach dropped when Ben said, "Altair."

"Like the star?" asked Alyson in confusion.

XVI

"Like the star," he said. "Just don't mention its name unless you're in the middle of an astronomy lecture. Now, there—they've copied their files and Honey starts a new game."

Her sweet voice rang out through the computer's speakers: "Okay, people! New game! It's time to trash the office! Whoever is able to get a computer through the window first gets ten extra bonus points! Go!"

"They actually did get a computer through the window," said Ben, "but it took several collaborated efforts."

"Are all those accountants being held in confinement now?" Emily asked.

He smiled but didn't favor her with an answer. "Here they are retreating down the stairwell. There goes one agent down via stun gun, courtesy of a fairly apathetic Hummer. And there goes number two . . . and three . . . and four. They get the car keys from number five, zap him, and escape through the parking garage out onto the street."

They watched the rest of the video play out in silence until Quincy suddenly asked, "Is that Revere?"

"Hmm?" said Ben.

"That raven—it must be Revere. Hawk just threw something to him."

"I didn't realize the bird had a name," said Ben. "Hawk threw him the drive they copied their stolen files onto, probably as insurance in case they got caught."

"If they'd been caught, it wouldn't have done them much good for a bird to have the drive," Oliver said scornfully.

"We think they split up after they ditched the car," Ben replied. "It would make sense, given all the other precautions they planned. So chances were in their favor for someone to get hold of the information they took so much risk to obtain."

A Rumor of Real Irish Tea

"Was the information worth the risk?" Quincy asked with muted interest.

A complicated expression flashed across his face, enigmatic in its brevity. "I guess that would depend on whether they knew what to do with it. Shall we have a look and see whether you can figure it out?"

In the wake of silence that ensued, he brought up a small list on the screen.

"And here it is," he said. "A trio of memos, a bloated thirty-year-old law, and a curious little file entitled 'Real Irish Tea.' Although, that file's not actually little either."

"Real Irish Tea?" Oliver repeated dubiously.

Ben smiled, but he didn't satisfy Oliver's interest by elaborating. "Shall we have a look at the memos first?"

Without waiting for an answer, he clicked open the first file.

"'The organization known as "Altair" must be seen as hostile to our goals and treated accordingly,'" Quincy read aloud. "'It is to be classified among the subset of organizations described in Title III, Section 303(a) of the Federal Domestic Security Act of 2026, and treated according to (b) of that same section.'"

"Is that Federal Domestic Security Act the same law that's been included in this list of files they stole?" Oliver asked intuitively.

"Oh, very good," said Ben with a nice smile. "We can probably skip that one. It's about two thousand pages long, for one thing, but it's also just a procedural definition they were using to classify Altair back in the day. Here's the second memo: it's fairly short."

On screen, a couple lines of text appeared. Goosebumps crawled along Emily's skin as she quietly read its contents: "Regarding the recent activity of subversive organizations, this office will no longer turn a blind eye. In particular, Altair must

XVI

be wiped out of existence before it becomes a further menace to our goals."

This was not the controlled language one expected from a responsible government entity. It outright called for annihilation of Altair. From everything Emily had heard of that shadow organization, it was the epitome of evil. She couldn't imagine what sort of crimes it had perpetrated to merit such a strong response.

"Oh, my," said Alyson faintly. "They must not be very nice people in Altair."

"The Wests are certainly playing with fire by seeking them out," Ben agreed. "Here's the final memo: 'The current administration has determined that insurgent organizations such as Altair must be isolated and marginalized, so as to discourage any recruiting efforts. From this time forward, any mention of the name on GCA premises will be considered a violation of this decision, and the offending party shall be dismissed from service within the agency and subject to interrogation regarding their knowledge of the organization.' And this would be the primary reason that you are never to discuss this subject in unauthorized situations."

Emily pressed one hand to her head, upset that she knew anything about Altair to begin with. She didn't need Ben's warning never to mention it again.

Alyson took that moment to revise her previous statement. "They must be *very bad* people," she said, her voice trembling with horror.

"I don't see what the big deal is," said Oliver peevishly. "So Altair is a subversive organization and the GCA banned any mention of them. So what? That doesn't tell us anything, and I don't see how it could be of any use to Hawk or Hummer."

A Rumor of Real Irish Tea

"What's the last file," Quincy asked, "the one about Real Irish Tea?"

Ben looked like a child about to unwrap his birthday presents as he brought up the final file in the list. "You tell me," he said.

They all turned their attention to the computer screen once more, where four columns of words stood. Emily couldn't find a page count noted anywhere on the document, but from the size of the scroll bar on the side, she surmised that it was extensive.

"Heal rarities?" said Quincy as she squinted at the list.

"Heartier sail?" said Oliver in disbelief.

"*Raise a Hitler?*" said Alyson with complete horror.

Ben fought back a laugh.

"What is this?" Emily asked.

"You tell me," he said again. "Actually, I'd be interested to know whether Oliver and Quincy can figure it out. They're roughly the same ages as the elder Wests, and I've given them the same information that Hawk and Hummer should have. So what do you two make of this?"

"Real Irish Tea," Quincy murmured as she contemplated the words on the screen.

"Yes, that's my favorite of the bunch," said Ben. "I mean, right behind 'raise a Hitler,' of course," he added with a wry glance toward the ashen-faced Alyson.

"They're all twelve letters long," said Oliver.

"They're all the same twelve letters," said Quincy almost immediately after.

Emily took a second look at the list to discover that they were right. "So it's a list of anagrams?" she asked, but Ben motioned for her to stay silent.

"Can I have a piece of paper?" Quincy asked, and she opened a drawer beneath the second computer to look for the wanted object.

XVI

Ben quickly pulled a folded sheet of paper and a pen from his pocket and set them both in front of her. "Have at it," he said.

"The file was tagged for dealing with Altair," Quincy said to Oliver as she jotted down that word. Then, she wrote above it "real Irish tea" and crossed out the letters r, a, l, i, t, and a. "So," she mused, "we're left with e, r, i, s, h, and e."

"*Altair is here*," said Oliver grimly. "It's a system of code."

"Not a very good system," said Emily. "Most of these are complete nonsense. They'd stick out like a sore thumb if someone tried to use them."

"Have you ever heard of steganography?" Ben asked.

She hadn't, of course. "What is that, like dinosaur writing?"

Oliver scoffed.

"What?" she said. "I have no clue what it is, so why don't you tell me."

"I don't know either," he retorted, "but obviously it has nothing to do with *dinosaurs*."

"I know that," Emily said through gritted teeth. "It was just the first thing that came to mind. Steganography, stegosaurus."

He shook his head in disgust. "You're so dumb."

"Well, not quite," said Ben thoughtfully. "They are both derived from Greek, and the root words are probably related, though they're not the same. Steganography is a form of cipher-writing, from the Greek *steganos*, meaning covered."

"Covered writing," said Quincy with growing impatience. "We get it, so get on with it, Birchard."

"Steganography is the process of hiding a code within another code. To be brief, this list comprises the dummy code. Someone who wanted to use this would select a few appropriate phrases and then mix their real coded message in with the dummy words. The recipient goes through line by line and marks out the dummy words in order to discover the intended meaning. Whichever lines have all of the words from one of these phrases are part of the code, and everything else can be discarded."

"That . . . sounds like a lot of work," said Alyson.

"Coding is always a lot of work, especially in the age of computers," Ben replied. "The GCA discovered this little trick a long time ago. I don't think Altair uses it anymore. It's a shame, too—Real Irish Tea is a brand name, you know."

"My mother drinks it," said Emily as an image of a green and orange label flashed into her mind.

Ben nodded. "A lot of people drink it. It's fairly popular on the coasts."

"Does it have anything to do with Altair?" Oliver asked.

"No. That's the beauty of it—or the irritation, depending on your point of view. They couldn't very well go around arresting and interrogating anyone who mentioned a specific brand of teas, could they?"

Oliver scowled. "So why didn't they just put the brand out of business?"

"It's international," said Ben. "Even in a global market we can't go to another country and put someone out of business. Besides, that would've required them to admit that Altair was a serious threat, and by the time they realized this code, they were past that point."

"It had already become taboo," said Quincy quietly. "So the code is defunct. There's not really anything Hawk or Hummer can do with it. Is there?" she added with growing uncertainty. Ben seemed to know more than the rest of them put together.

"What would you do with it?" he asked her curiously.

Quincy bit her lower lip and looked away. She didn't have an answer for him.

XVI

"I'd throw in the towel and look for something new," said Oliver. "This batch of files was a waste of their time. They risked being caught for a load of useless garbage."

"Maybe so," said Ben, but he didn't seem entirely convinced.

It was a suspicious response from a suspicious individual. "What do you know that we don't?" Oliver demanded.

Ben stood up straight, his expression like the cat that caught the canary. "Oh, quite a lot of things, I'd imagine," he said, and an amused smile played about his lips.

XVII
An Unanticipated Snag

AUGUST 2, 10:53AM MST, PHOENIX

THE DISAPPOINTMENT OF their nearly fruitless ambush threw the four Wests into the doldrums. They all agreed to lie low for a couple days, but there was only so much they could do in an empty house with nothing but the packs they carried to keep them occupied. Outdoor activities, even in their back yard, were impossible thanks to the scorching heat and late-summer humidity.

"I should've rented a house with a pool," Honey complained.

"Why, so the neighbors could hear children playing and wonder who moved in next door?" Hummer asked.

Wary of drawing too much attention, they determined to move locations when their meager supplies dwindled, so that they would not be seen leaving and returning to the same place. Thus, on this hot, sunny morning, they ventured out into the open to replenish their food stores and move to the next safe house.

"Does anything seem different to you guys?" Hummer asked as they walked down a residential street towards a nearby strip mall.

"You mean like how every car that passes us slows down to take a look?" Honey sarcastically replied. She had her hair in

XVII

pigtails and a pair of large sunglasses on her face so that she would bear as little resemblance as possible to the oft-broadcasted picture of Maddie North. Next to her, Happy had a baseball cap pulled low to shade his eyes from view. Four children walking down the side of the road on a Saturday shouldn't have been too much of a spectacle. Most kids were in school, certainly, but Saturdays were still technically a supplementary day rather than a mandatory one.

Only a handful of cars had passed them in the last five minutes, but each in turn meandered by before speeding up to the next stop sign.

"We should hurry," said Hawk. "Let's cut across that field and get indoors as quick as possible."

The field in question ran along the back fence of the strip mall. Overgrown, dried-out weeds choked its ground of any useful foliage, and spiked burrs caught at their socks and legs as they trekked across, but at least they were further from the road and the scrutiny of curious drivers.

Revere glided over them with a throaty caw. He perched on the building's roof and watched their progress with one beady eye. Together Hawk and Hummer hoisted Honey and Happy over the block fence, then pulled themselves up behind. On the other side ran a quiet driveway along a row of deserted loading docks. They kept close to the wall as they crossed through the nearest corridor to the main parking lot.

Saturdays were a busy day for areas like this, and the Wests had every hope of blending into the crowds. As they walked down the main promenade toward the grocery store at the end, though, something upsetting caught Hummer's eyes.

He snagged Hawk's sleeve, and the strangled noise in his throat caused Honey and Happy to halt. Their gazes followed his to the display window of an electronics store and the row of televisions that broadcasted NPNN for all passersby. Side-by-side rough sketches of Hawk and Hummer graced the screen.

Hummer yanked his older brother to the store's door; the moment it swung open, they could hear the content of the report.

"Authorities are still unsure how many young victims may actually be involved in this kidnapping ring," a well-manicured reporter said as the four children gathered in front of the largest television on display. "Federal and local police believe the perpetrators belong to one of a handful of domestic terrorist groups, and that they are attempting to indoctrinate these children to their extremist views in order to build up their membership. Phoenix residents are cautioned not to approach any suspected victims, but they're encouraged to keep an eye on their neighborhoods for any signs of suspicious behavior, especially around vacant or recently rented properties. And, as always, if you have any information regarding any of these four children"—here the pictures of Maddie and Alex North joined a split screen of the other two sketches—"you are encouraged to call our national hotline at—"

"Maybe we should call ourselves in," said Hummer vaguely.

Honey shoved her elbow into his ribs. "Idiot!" she hissed, and she jerked him and Hawk away from the television display, toward a more sheltered corner of the store. Happy followed faithfully behind. Once they were safe from the prying eyes of customers, Honey stomped on her older brother's toes for good measure. "Pull yourself together, Hummer. That reporter's obviously a projector."

He blinked away the short-lived haze of influence. "Not *fair!*" he cried with dawning realization. "They're . . . they're *programming* people to look for us!"

XVII

"What's not fair is that there are probably a dozen or more calls into the national hotline by now," said Hawk grimly, "and within such a short distance of one of our safe houses, too. We need an emergency exit strategy."

"I can drive a getaway car," said Hummer.

Hawk turned to Honey. "Can you get us some car keys?"

"Piece of cake," she said, and she bolted away.

"We'll have to abandon the car at a neutral point and use different transportation to get to our next place," Hawk told Hummer. "Any ideas?"

"We can split up again," said Hummer uncertainly. "Beyond that, I don't know. Before now, the public has only been looking for two kids, not four. We're going to stick out like a sore thumb wherever we go."

"Happy, do you have any ideas?" Hawk asked.

The six-year-old shook his head, all of his energy focused on containing his growing panic. The emotion emanated from him in waves.

"Where's Honey?" asked Hummer with a nervous glance around the store.

She reappeared a moment later, keys hooked on her thumb. A quick assessment of her three brothers had her running. She practically collided with the youngest, enveloping him in a protective hug. "It's okay, Happy. We're going to be okay. It's okay."

He nodded into her shoulder, his body still taut with anxiety.

Honey extended the keys to Hummer. "It's a blue car parked just outside," she said. "You go first, and we'll follow."

Hummer darted from the store and out into the parking lot.

"The lady who owns the car was really proud of her parking space," Honey said to Hawk. "I told her to take her time shopping. She seemed nice."

A Rumor of Real Irish Tea

"We'll leave the car somewhere easy to find," said Hawk reassuringly. "It's not like we can drive it to another safe house anyway. Are you ready to go, Happy?"

The six-year-old nodded, and together the three linked hands and bolted for the exit. Honey suddenly dug in her heels as they came to the door. "Listen up, everyone!" she called, much to Hawk's horror.

Every person in the small store turned their attention upon her. The televisions hummed with NPNN reports in the background, but she raised her voice to drown them out.

"The government is going to come and put you all in prison. You need to hide! If they find you, don't answer any of their questions, or you'll never see your families again. Quick! Go hide, now!"

Utter panic descended. Hawk yanked Honey out the door. "What was that?" he asked as they all scrambled into the waiting blue car. "Your projection's going to wear off, and they'll tell the GCA exactly how we escaped!"

"What'd she do now?" Hummer asked at the wheel. He put the car into gear and tore out of the parking space the moment the door shut behind them.

"She just told them that the government was coming to arrest them all," Hawk said angrily. "The last thing we needed was a big scene back there!"

In the back seat, Honey made a face. "The projection will wear off, but the emotions linger. People are paranoid, and if you send them into panic, they'll stay there for longer than they would with a regular projection. And since Happy was already on the verge of panic, I played it up a bit." She looped a protective arm around her little brother and hugged him close.

"I hate to say this," said Hummer to Hawk, "but she probably

XVII

did the right thing. Fear is a funny motivator—you don't have to be a projector to use it properly."

Despite the logic behind this reasoning, Hawk still didn't like it. "Where are we going?" he asked.

"Nowhere residential," Hummer said. "They've got every neighborhood in the city on the lookout for some bogus kidnapping ring. Is Revere following us?"

"Yes," said Hawk, and he glanced up to see the raven gliding through the blue sky above. The visual check wasn't necessary, but it reassured him.

"GCA sedan on the left," said Hummer, and the four children instinctively ducked as a black car whizzed by them on the opposite side of the road, presumably headed straight for the strip mall they had left behind.

"I know why we duck, Hummer, but could you please keep your eyes on the road?" Honey said as she straightened again.

"I've got it under control," he muttered. Traffic on a Saturday morning was nothing to get concerned about. He obeyed the speed-limit laws so as not to draw attention to them, and everything else went smoothly.

They abandoned the car in a public lot and boarded the mass transit system in pairs. Honey and Hummer moved to the back of the bus to sit alone, while Hawk and Happy lingered by a group of teenagers near the front. The bus was sparsely populated, and no one paid them any heed. They exited several stops down the line, tagging behind the oblivious teens, but then peeled away into a shadowed alley.

Ever vigilant in following them, Revere perched himself on a security camera that overlooked the spot. He intuitively lowered one wing to block the lens.

"These are our three options," said Hummer, and he revealed

a short list of their leased properties. "There are two commercial spaces and one industrial. They all have more than one exit and they're all situated pretty well if we need to get away. If we're going to stay in Phoenix, our only other choice is to rent a hotel room for the night."

"There's no reason we have to stay here," said Hawk. "It might be better just to cut and run."

"Weekend train schedules are spotty," Hummer said. "If we can hunker down until Monday, we may have a better chance of getting out undetected."

The four children exchanged uncertain glances. "My vote is for this place," said Honey, and she stabbed her finger at the second address on the list. "And I'm not trying to project that onto any of you."

"You don't need to," said Hummer. "That one is my choice as well."

"Did you two plan this in the back of the bus?" Hawk asked suspiciously.

Hummer made a face. "When have Honey and I ever been able to plan anything together?"

"If that's the obvious choice to us," said Hawk, "will it be obvious to the people looking for us?"

"We have to get off the streets," Hummer answered grimly. "We're taking a bigger chance out here than we would be in any one of these spots. I'm not sure how much longer Revere can block that camera feed without raising suspicions, either," he added.

Hawk glanced up at the raven, who cawed encouragingly at him. "All right," he said reluctantly. "Let's go."

XVIII
Ten Minutes Too Late

AUGUST 2, 11:07AM MST, IN TRANSIT, PHOENIX

EMILY HAD A massive headache pressing down on her, one which no amount of rubbing at her temples would relieve. The lumpy, GCA-issued pillow she'd been sleeping on was the most likely culprit, but she preferred to blame the massive levels of stress she currently battled. Capturing the Wests was of utmost importance, but right at this moment she wished the driver of the van she was riding in would take the corners just a little slower.

"We'll be there in a couple of minutes," said a GCA agent from the front seat.

She shifted her gaze first to Oliver, who looked grim and determined, and then to Quincy, who kept her eyes fixed on her hands. The back of the van was configured with seats along both sides facing one another. They had come in through the doors at the rear, and Emily felt like a SWAT team member from an old action movie as they raced through the city to their destination.

Whatever complaints she had against Veronica Porcher, she had to admit that the beautiful reporter's news alerts were working. Less than ten minutes ago, Ben had burst into the fifth-floor kitchenette and ordered Quincy and Oliver down to the parking garage. The Wests had been spotted along a residential street.

"You sure they're not trying to hit up another GCA office by calling in phony reports?" Oliver had asked acerbically.

"The calls are all coming from the same area as the report," said Ben. "Two days ago, that wasn't the case."

"So we're going to go nab them in broad daylight?" Quincy asked with thinly veiled concern.

He smiled ruefully. "I'm just following the general's orders. Hurry now. You'll be riding in the van with a few members of the elite retrieval squad."

The "elite retrieval squad," as it turned out, was comprised of military-type men suited in black uniforms and armed with tranquilizer guns. Emily recognized among them a few GCA agents from the previous afternoon. The squad was probably a small division of the enormous government agency.

Up until a month ago she had assumed that the GCA only dealt with government-sanctioned volunteer work and defending civil liberties. How many more times over the course of her internship would she have to recalibrate her understanding?

Blissfully, Ben was riding in another car with General Stone. Emily's head couldn't stand his extended presence this morning without splitting wide open. No one had bothered to tell them how long the car ride would be, and there were no windows in the back for her to direct her attention, so she was left to stare at the floor and pray for a speedy arrival.

"Are you all right?" asked Alyson from the seat across from her. "You look a little pale."

"It's just a headache," said Emily dismissively. "I took some painkillers back at the office. I'm waiting for them to kick in." It was a lie, but she didn't want Alyson's help or sympathy. Oliver,

XVIII

who knew perfectly well that she hadn't popped any pills within the last hour, shot her a skeptical glance, which she studiously ignored.

They really needed to catch the Wests. Then she could get shipped back to Prometheus—A or F, she didn't care—and not have to be subjected to the likes of Ben Birchard and Veronica Porcher. Her dislike of both was petty, but she couldn't help it. Ben seemed to be the guardian of all important information, and Veronica was the embodiment of the privileged elite. To a nothing-nobody handler like Emily, their very existence was a reminder of her insignificance.

Maybe she wasn't cut out for government work after all.

The van swerved around one final corner before coming to rest in the parking lot of a strip mall. "Everybody out," said the squad member in the front passenger seat, and one of his fellows in the back opened the door to the bright Arizona sun. Emily followed Oliver, who had already hopped down to the asphalt. She blinked against the brightness and looked around herself.

Law-enforcement vehicles and black government sedans infested the whole place. Ordinary citizens lined the walls, talking with policemen or GCA agents. Emily spotted General Stone striding purposefully toward the van, with Ben close on his heels.

"Get those two nulls over here," he bellowed.

"There's no way they're still here," Oliver muttered as an agent led him forward. Emily, following behind him, was inclined to agree. Unless the Wests had holed up in one of these storefronts, there was no chance that they would hang around a place so crawling with cops. A quick survey of the trees in the parking lot showed no unusual bird presence. From past experience, she was fairly certain that Hawk West would be summoning them in droves if he was in any danger.

"They're long gone," said Ben. She jumped, unaware that he had fallen in step beside her. "This place is an absolute mess."

"What does General Stone want with Oliver and Quincy, then?" Emily asked. Ahead, the two null-projectors were being escorted inside an electronics store.

"He probably thinks they can help calm some of the panic in there. It's doubtful. I was talking to one of the agents from the South Phoenix office. They were the first on the scene here. According to his timetable the Wests have been gone for a quarter of an hour at least. No single projection lasts that long unless the recipient is prone to that sort of behavior already."

Emily stared at him. "How much sooner than us did you arrive?" He had been the one to usher them to the parking garage at the downtown branch. He and the general shouldn't have been too far ahead of the van. So what, he'd barely stepped foot on the scene and was already gleaning information from the other offices?

He read her confusion perfectly. "I spoke to him on the phone, in the car on the way here," he said, and he waved his cell phone for emphasis.

Of course he had. "So you know agents from the other Phoenix offices? Why am I not surprised?"

"I've never met the man in my life," Ben said, "though I suppose he's around here somewhere." He scanned the parking lot with vague disinterest. Beneath her incredulous gaze, he continued. "There's a fine art to collecting information. You don't want to call someone too low on the chain of command, but you don't want to bother the top dog, either. It's a pretty safe bet to contact a mid-level agent and speak to him authoritatively. You can discover just about anything you need to know that way. Or, well, it worked out this time. I was able to brief General

XVIII

Stone before we even set foot on the premises. He was most impressed."

"Do you always brag about yourself so openly?" she asked.

Ben winked. "Only to the pretty girls. And here's General Stone bringing our precious little resources back outside. General, sir," he said, and he raised one finger to catch that man's attention.

General Stone looked like he was going to crush the next person who spoke to him. Emily surmised that all had not gone as anticipated inside the store. Secretly she hoped he would take his wrath out on Ben.

"What is it, Birchard?" he asked tersely.

That hostile tone of voice didn't faze Ben in the least. "I took the liberty of acquiring the suspicious properties list from Agent Knox this morning. One of the addresses is within half a mile of here. It might be worth sending someone over to investigate."

Stone grunted. "There's certainly nothing else for us to do here. Pull together the agents from the downtown office and give them that address. We'll leave the cleanup here for someone else."

By this Emily figured she was meant to escort Oliver back to the van. "What did you do in that store?" she asked as she rejoined him.

He grunted. "Nothing. It was filled with a flock of civilians in various stages of hysteria. They weren't under any projection, so there was nothing Quincy or I could do. Apparently," he added before Emily could ask any follow-up questions, "Honey West told them all that the government was coming to arrest them, and that they needed to hide or they'd never see their families again."

"But . . . that would have been a projection," said Emily in confusion. "So why . . . ?"

A Rumor of Real Irish Tea

"The projection wore off," Oliver said irritably. "It wore off a while ago. Honey just tapped into some primal fear these people have. It's brain-stem activity, fight or flight. She told them to hide, though, so they didn't get the chance to run away before the government actually *did* arrive. What were you talking to Birchard about?"

"His impressive information-gathering techniques," said Emily with a sour frown. "Honestly, that man is so full of himself it's a wonder he can talk without drooling his own guts out."

Oliver paused in the act of climbing up into the van to favor her with an incredulous look.

"What?" said Emily defensively.

"I'm trying to figure out if that even makes sense."

"Get in the van," she said, and she swatted the back of his head for emphasis. They were the first ones there, Quincy and Alyson having lingered behind by the electronics storefront. Emily and Oliver were already strapped into their seats before the other agents returned.

To her dismay, Ben appeared at the end of the line. "Are we all here?" he asked as he climbed in, briefcase in one hand. "Let's get on our way, then."

"What about Quincy and Alyson?" Emily asked.

He tipped his head behind, to the parking lot. "They're going with General Stone."

"Why?"

A mischievous grin flashed across his face. "You really want to know?" Before she could fashion a suitable reply, he climbed into the seat next to her. From his briefcase he extracted a hand-held device—the same one she had seen him using back at Prom-F—and flipped on the screen.

An unpleasantly familiar face appeared. "I'm on location

XVIII

in Phoenix, Arizona with breaking news in the kidnapping of Maddie and Alex North," Veronica Porcher was saying. Behind her, the strip mall and its parking lot acted as her backdrop.

Emily hissed. "When did *she* get here?"

Ben switched the screen off again. "About two minutes ago. General Stone's not about to take his chances around a projector like Veronica. The minute he realized she was here, he ordered Quincy to his side, leaving me to ride with the rest of you here in the van."

"If he doesn't trust her, why's he using her?"

"Because she's a tool," said Ben, as though this should have been perfectly clear to anyone. "To someone like General Stone, that's all projectors and null-projectors are, and he treats them accordingly. No offense, Oliver," he added apologetically.

Oliver rolled his eyes and turned his attention elsewhere.

"Is she following us to this second address?" Emily asked.

"Who, Veronica? No. Even if it is one of the Wests' lairs, they won't be there. They stole a car from a woman in the electronics store back there. They've probably hot-footed halfway across town by now. She'll need to come along when we do close in on them, though. Her adoring public is on tenterhooks waiting to hear how this case resolves. Now, I know it's terribly rude of me, but I do have a phone call or two to make. I hope you don't mind."

Emily didn't mind in the least. She didn't even really eavesdrop when he made the two calls. Not that there was much to eavesdrop on—Ben kept his phone volume low enough that she couldn't discern the speaker on the other end, and his side of the conversation consisted almost entirely of "Mm-hmm" and "Yes, I see." She suspected he was checking in with Genevieve Jones or another superior. He conveniently finished the second call as the van rolled to a stop in a residential neighborhood.

"Off we go," said Ben, and he led everyone out the back doors.

The house they had stopped in front of looked no more remarkable than any other house on the block. The front yard was xeriscaped as required by environmental statute, but it was also well-tended rather than overgrown. Curtains covered the windows to shield any glimpse of the interior, but a glance at the neighbors showed the same style of window treatments and thus nothing to be suspicious about.

General Stone's car parked in the driveway. He emerged with a domineering scowl. "What're you waiting for?" he demanded of the elite retrieval squad from the van. "Go break the door down."

Emily snagged Ben's sleeve in alarm. "Don't we need a warrant?"

He laughed unpleasantly, as though she were a child who had asked a very silly question. "No, the GCA doesn't need warrants. We're not technically a law-enforcement agency."

"But we can't just—" Her words cut off at the loud crack of the front door getting kicked in. Her breath hitched, her voice at a strangled whisper. "What if that's someone's house? What if it's not the Wests' hideout at all?"

"Then they'll get a new door. Housing is mostly government-subsidized anyway. The landlord doesn't need permission to enter if he thinks his property is being used illegally."

"But—" Her protest died as Ben swept past her toward the house, following in the wake of the other GCA agents.

"You're wasting your breath," said Oliver. He shoved his hands into his pockets and started forward. Emily fell into step behind him, hoping that Ben had been right, that this was one of the Wests' lairs and not the home of some unsuspecting family.

It took a moment for her eyes to adjust from the glaring sunshine to the shadowy interior gloom, but that moment was

XVIII

enough to fulfill her hopes. It was obvious at a single glance that no one lived here. There was no furniture. The air conditioning wasn't running. The place looked like it was in stasis, waiting for its next occupant to arrive.

"It's definitely theirs," said Oliver beside her.

She turned curious eyes upon him. "How can you be so sure?"

"Do you really think someone else would rent a house only to leave it vacant? Besides, there're bird droppings up on that fan."

Her gaze followed his pointing finger upward to discern a black-and-whitish lump stuck to the edge of one fan blade.

"Gross," she said.

"That's what happens when you keep wild animals as pets," Oliver replied. "Come on. Let's have a closer look around."

The elite retrieval squad had already made a quick sweep of the premises, and now they were undertaking a closer scrutiny. As far as Emily could tell, this meant digging through a meager pile of trash from the bin in the kitchen. The Wests had left behind nothing but a handful of food wrappers—candy and granola bars, mostly.

"How on earth are they surviving?" she asked.

"They're carrying everything they need, I guess," said Oliver.

"No—I mean, this is all junk food. They're not eating any fruits or vegetables!"

"You don't know that," said Quincy from the other side of the kitchen counter. "Revere used to eat Hawk's scraps all the time back at Prom-F. I don't think Hawk would feed him junk food, so it only stands to reason that they'd be eating some normal foods as well. You just might not get the remnants you'd expect."

It was the most Quincy had ever spoken to her. Alyson, scandalized that her young charge had broken the rules so extensively, hesitated over what to do in such an anomalous situation. Most Prometheus students didn't want to talk to their own handlers, let alone someone else's.

The awkward moment was destroyed by the entrance of General Stone from one of the back rooms. "Nothing but a few useless bread crumbs here," he said gruffly. "Where is Birchard with that list?"

"I'm here, sir," said Ben next to Emily. She jumped and wondered where he had materialized from. He held his cell phone in one hand. "Agent Knox says there are only five commercial and industrial properties on our list. We can set up surveillance without a problem."

General Stone grunted. "Good. Order it." Then, he swept past them, back to the front door. "I want field agents to bag and tag every dust particle in this house before the day's end and send it to the nearest lab for analysis. And Birchard, make sure the nulls get safely back to the downtown office." The door shut loudly behind him.

"What kind of analysis are they going to get off a candy wrapper?" one GCA agent muttered to another.

"Who cares? Just bag it."

Ben motioned Quincy and Alyson from the kitchen with a pleasant smile. "How do you know they're going to a commercial property next?" Emily asked as she followed Oliver past him.

"Because the residential ones have been poisoned," he said. "Veronica's been telling average civilians to be on the lookout in their neighborhoods. The Wests happened to see one of her reports back at that electronics store, so they'll know now that residential neighborhoods are dangerous for them."

She didn't bother to ask how he knew all of these details. The cell phone in his hand was answer enough. "But how do you know they're even still in Phoenix? Wouldn't it make more

XVIII

sense for them to hotfoot it out of town if the area's become so poisoned, as you put it?"

"Nope," said Birchard with utmost certainty. "We have our eyes on all the planes, buses, and trains going in and out of town. The car they stole was an electric model that has to re-charge after forty-seven miles—and they surely know we're looking for it—and all long-haul vehicles are currently under obligation to be searched when they exit the city. It's much easier for four kids to hunker down and blend into a town of millions than it is for them to break free onto the open road again."

"You hope it is," Emily muttered under her breath.

That only amused him all the more. "Quincy, Oliver, you heard the general—it's time to go back to the office." He herded them toward the front door.

Emily cast one final glance around the place as she left. It was abandoned now, but only a few hours ago their quarry had been holed up here, safely hidden from their pursuers. How had they passed their time? Were they getting tired of their life on the run? In her bones she felt it couldn't go on much longer. The GCA was tightening its net and closing in.

Soon it would all be over, of that she was oddly certain.

XIX
The Ever-Tightening Noose

AUGUST 2, 5:15PM MST, GCA REGIONAL OFFICE, CENTRAL PHOENIX

A HUM OF EXCITEMENT reverberated among the agents all afternoon. Stakeouts were ordered and people dispatched to the five suspicious locations. Those left behind kept busy orchestrating everything they would need for an ambush. Everyone looked grim, but their unspoken anticipation of success was almost palpable.

Emily wished she could waste away her time in the fifth-floor kitchenette. Instead, Oliver and Quincy had to stay in the second-floor conference room, near enough to General Stone that they could hurry with him to the parking garage the instant he gave the order. The general was on the phone for most of the afternoon requisitioning resources. He wanted a blitz, quick and dramatic, something that the public could gawk at in awe and admiration when NPNN reported it.

She worried that people were getting their hopes up too high. Every last detail of a retrieval plan might be in place, but it would all be meaningless if they didn't know where to go, and none of the surveillance crews had discovered anything yet.

When Ben strode into the room at a quarter after five, though,

XIX

she knew from the look on his face that something important had happened. He had been in and out all afternoon, always on his cell phone. General Stone had peppered him with orders, and he hopped to obey. This time was different, though. This time a solemnity in his eyes caught her attention and set her nerves on edge.

General Stone was on the phone and waved for him to wait. Mutely Ben shook his head and pointed to a specific piece of paper on the table in front of the austere man. Stone froze. Then, he covered the phone's mic with one hand.

"You're sure?" he asked, steel in his voice.

"Our men have made visual confirmation," said Ben. "I've ordered the other surveillance crews to the surrounding area, but everyone is keeping far enough away from the building itself."

A satisfied glint entered Stone's eyes. "I'll have to call you back," he said into the phone, and he ended the call. "Order the elite retrieval squad up here and contact the other offices."

Ben nodded. "I've already done both."

"Good job, Birchard." General Stone rocked back on his heels, the picture of self-satisfied importance. "We've solved in three days what it took the rest of the GCA a whole month to muddle through. I think you'll fit in quite nicely at Prom-E."

Next to Emily, Oliver gasped.

"Told you so," she hissed under her breath.

He spared her a dirty look before turning his attention back to Birchard and Stone.

"Agent Knox should be here any minute with aerial views," Ben said. "I thought you might like to use them in plotting the retrieval strategy."

"Sycophant," Oliver muttered, and Emily was inclined to agree.

The next hour passed at a whirlwind pace. Knox appeared

along with the black-clad members of the elite retrieval squad. They assembled around the table with several maps spread across its surface while a couple more GCA offices tapped into the meeting via webcam.

General Stone laid out their ambush strategy in quick, concise terms. Emily watched with ill-concealed awe as the plan was presented and orders given. The whole building seemed suddenly regimented, and the man running it had such an air of authority that she dared not even think a word out of line.

It might actually happen this time. Her heart hammered in her chest, pulsing anticipation through her.

After having their instructions so forcefully drummed into their brains, they proceeded to the basement parking garage. Here, the black-clad GCA agents received tranquilizer guns issued according to squad. They climbed into their assigned vehicle. Emily counted more than thirty heads.

Oliver had a place with one of the squads. He and Emily took their seats in the waiting van. Quincy, on the other hand, was to remain with General Stone. She and Alyson joined him in the much nicer government sedan. Ben would ride in yet another van, though Emily did not see which one. The arrangement of the two nulls made sense to her, though. Oliver's broader range would cancel out Honey and Happy. Quincy was the backup if anything went wrong.

It was past seven when they finally approached their destination, a row of industrial warehouses near a train yard. The setting sun stained the western sky with crimson and orange. Shadows stretched long across the ground, and the whole area seemed deserted despite its urban location. A short train rattled by on the nearby tracks, and birds chirped from the scraggly branches of a few sun-scorched trees.

XIX

The whole scene was surreal. If their information was right, the four Wests were holed up in a warehouse three units down the row. More than a hundred GCA agents from multiple branches were converging on the location, covering all exits. The lawless escapade was finally at an end.

As dusk turned to twilight, the squads crept into position. Emily kept a nervous eye on those few scraggly trees and on the warehouse rooftops, all too wary of the birds that roosted there. None had cried out an alarm yet. The whole world seemed to hold its breath, waiting for someone to pull the trigger.

It came. A coordinated blast of sonic waves blared. The birds scattered with caws of raucous terror, taking to the air as they sought refuge from the sounds.

Shouts echoed from the other side of the building and footsteps pounded in the alley that ran between. Oliver's squad advanced, just as the door ahead of them burst open and four children streamed out into the open yard. Troops scrambled from their hiding place across the train yard and from the sides of the building, weapons at the ready.

Hawk, Hummer, Honey, and Happy West stopped dead in their tracks, surrounded on all sides. Each wore a backpack and held a weapon of some sort—the stolen stun gun for Hummer, and discarded lengths of scrap metal or wood for the other three—which they raised defensively. Emily almost felt sorry for them when she saw the desperation mirrored on each of their faces.

Oliver's squad of ten fanned out around the foursome. "Hands in the air!" his squad leader commanded.

"You put your hands in the air!" Honey retorted, even as Hawk and Hummer moved to shield her and Happy from view.

Oliver spoke up at last. "Save your breath." He stepped forward triumphantly. "You're done. It's over."

A Rumor of Real Irish Tea

Silence blanketed the area as the four truants looked around themselves in growing hopelessness. Emily's gaze swept the area as well. A hundred black-clad GCA agents stood with tranquilizer guns at the ready. At the back, overseeing his tactical victory, General Stone wore a satisfied smirk on his face. Behind him, an NPNN van was parked, with Veronica Porcher already in position to announce the children's "rescue" to the country. All that remained was for Hawk and his siblings to officially surrender.

"There's no way out," Oliver said. "These men have orders to tranquilize you if you so much as make a false move. You don't want that. Just drop your weapons and put your hands in the air."

Overhead, a shrill cry sounded, and a black shape swooped down.

"Revere, no!" cried Hawk. "Get away!"

The great black raven screeched in fury, but the noise was clipped short as a tranquilizer dart slammed into him. His small, dark body plummeted to the ground, landing heavily, and his caws turned from piercing rage to wild pain.

"No!" Hawk screamed, his cry of dismay echoed by his siblings. When he surged toward the fallen bird, though, the agents pinned their tranquilizer guns directly on him. He checked his movement, stepping back again to act as a shield for Happy. His eyes kept darting to the place where Revere lay, downed so close to the black-clad GCA agents.

The raven flapped and fluttered its wings to no avail. Emily could see the white-tufted dart buried in his shoulder and didn't hold out much hope for his survival. The sedatives had been dosed for children, not for a bird like that.

"You need to surrender, Hawk," Oliver insisted. "Or do you want to risk getting tranquilized? It's your choice, but if you're smart you'll . . . you'll . . ."

XIX

He suddenly faltered. Emily watched in horror as one of his hands vaguely reached up to his neck. Then, his body wavered and crumpled to the ground. Instinct propelled her to his side, but the wave of emotion that smashed into her brought her to her knees: despair, panic, pure and utter terror.

Revere, Revere, poor Revere!

A little girl's voice shouted orders. "Get down on the ground! Put your weapons down and your hands behind your head! *Stay down!*"

Emily obeyed without even considering the source.

Not Revere. Please not Revere!

It was like a tidal wave, massive and untamed. She thought she heard shouting from somewhere behind her and a tumult around her, thought there should be something she should be more concerned about than the plight of a single raven, but she couldn't help it. Her heart was broken, her emotions raw and so finely tuned upon the bird's tragic fate. It was a child's despair, potent in its sheer innocence. Emily could focus on nothing else.

After what seemed like an eternity of absolute misery, the feelings began to ebb.

"Oliver," she whispered, trying to focus her mind. He lay a few feet from her, unconscious. Why was she so worried about a bird when Oliver was just lying there? Her blurred gaze caught a flash of red—the tranquilizer dart in his neck—and she trained her eyes upon it. "Oliver," she said again, and she inched forward. How long had he been like that? She didn't know. Everything around her seemed wrong.

A pair of hands hefted her up by her armpits. "Pull yourself together, Emily," said a voice beside her. The person moved to crouch over the motionless ten-year-old.

A Rumor of Real Irish Tea

"Come on, Oliver," muttered Ben as he turned the boy over. He felt for a pulse, checked beneath his eyelids, and then scooped him up from where he lay on the ground. "Come *on*, Emily," he said impatiently. "Tranquilizers are nothing to be meddled with, especially in children."

His calm, serious demeanor snapped some sense back into her. She picked herself up and looked around in a daze. A hundred GCA agents had begun to stir from their prone positions upon the ground. Ben had already broken into a run back to one of the waiting vans, Oliver unconscious in his arms. She started after him with a growing sense of purpose.

The Wests were nowhere in sight, but she didn't care. Something had gone horribly awry, and Oliver had been injured.

Really, nothing else mattered.

XX
Reversal of Fortunes

AUGUST 2, 7:56PM MST, PHOENIX

ONLY AN UNFORESEEN intervention allowed their escape. In the moment, it seemed like poor aim or accident was at fault for Oliver's unconsciousness. In the moment, the cause didn't matter. The four Wests could not afford to waste the opportunity it presented.

As Happy's unchecked emotions swept across the crowd, Hawk surged forward to claim his fallen pet. Revere shrieked in pain, and with that shriek came a stunning realization: the bird wasn't drugged. He was only hurt. Hawk clutched him protectively to his chest, careful of the white-tufted dart that stuck out of his shoulder joint. He was wary of removing it in all this chaos but silently assured the bird that all would be well.

Honey took quick measures to order everyone to the ground, but even if she hadn't, Happy's innocent despair had already rendered most of them harmless. A small bubble of GCA agents still stood, and one of them shouted orders in rage. In answer, Hummer snatched up two single-round tranquilizer guns and fired at the man. He cast these away and dove for two more.

Hawk scooped up another with his free hand. "Grab a gun

and go!" he yelled. Honey was more than willing to comply. Happy, tear-stricken, panicking Happy, couldn't collect his wits. Hawk was on the verge of falling apart. "Come on, Happy," he said to his little brother. "We have to go."

The sight of the raven nestled in the crook of Hawk's arm did more to calm Happy than any words could. He swallowed a shuddering breath and moved. Together the four ran, past the prostrate agents, across the train yard, and through a gap in the fence on the other side. They kept running until Happy started straggling behind.

"Hummer, wait!" Hawk called, his breath ragged.

Hummer had outstripped them all, despite the three tranquilizer guns and an extra set of darts he had hanging from one shoulder. At Hawk's command, he changed directions and jogged back.

"We're not far enough away," he said. "We have to keep moving."

"They're not going to follow us with Oliver out of commission," Hawk said. "Besides, I only wanted you to carry Happy piggyback for a bit. How'd you manage to get all of that stuff?"

Hummer glanced down at his newly acquired armory. "It was there to take. You'd have grabbed more if you didn't have to carry Revere."

"And the extra darts?" Hawk pressed.

"The squad leaders had 'em. The useless guns only fire one round, so it stands to reason that someone would have refills."

"They only fire one round so that there's less chance of an overdose," Hawk said. "At least we know they'd prefer not to kill us."

"As interesting as this conversation is," Honey interjected irritably, "could we please continue with our escape? Hummer, give me your stuff. You carry Happy."

XX

Hummer was halfway through complying when he realized it. "Hey!" he cried.

Honey snatched the shoulder straps of his backpack from his outstretched hand, the tranquilizer guns already slung around her neck. "Piggy-back ride for Happy, now! Don't argue!"

"Sorry, Hummer," Happy murmured as his brother crouched to pick him up.

"It's fine," Hummer said. "You're a lightweight anyway. We just need to get to some place we can hide."

Happy was small for his age, and Hummer was athletic enough to carry him for another block and a half before running out of steam. They stopped to rest in an alleyway behind a convenience store, careful to stay in the shadow of the huge dumpster there.

Revere let out a soft caw.

"How is he?" Honey asked in concern.

"He's hurt," said Hawk. Gingerly he settled on the ground and rested the bird in his lap. "I'm going to need some light."

"I'm on it," said Hummer, already digging around in his backpack.

Happy crouched next to Hawk and leaned in to get a closer view of the injured bird. "Is he going to die?" he asked, anxiety thick on his voice.

"I don't think so," Hawk said, "but he's got a tiny piece of metal jammed into his wing joint. It'd be like someone giving you a shot but forgetting to take out the needle."

Honey tilted her head. "What about the tranquilizer? Did it not work?"

Light blossomed in their shadowy corner. Hummer moved the flashlight closer, and Revere cringed away with an indignant shriek. Hawk's fingers closed around the dart and yanked it from the bird in one swift movement. Revere screeched and flapped his wings to get away.

"It wasn't that bad," Hawk told him.

The bird cawed and ruffled his feathers, then immediately preened the area around his injury. Hawk looked down at the dart in his hand.

The needle was colored with dried blood, but something along the metal shaft caught his eyes. "Hummer, shine the light here. What does that say?"

Four curious heads crowded together to study the tiny inscription.

Hummer suddenly hissed. "It says 'Real Irish Tea.'"

"What? No," said Hawk, and he squinted for a closer look.

"Yes," said Hummer, and he held the light closer. "I'd need a magnifying glass to make out the rest of it, though. It just looks like a bunch of numbers."

Honey abruptly stood and started rummaging around in her pockets.

"Don't tell me you have a magnifying glass," said Hawk.

She favored him with a flat look. "I have cash, and we're sitting behind a convenience store. My guess is they have a magnifying glass."

He bristled. "Maddie North is not walking into any convenience stores tonight."

"I'll go," said Hummer. "That sketch they showed on NPNN barely looked like me anyway."

"Get us something for dinner, too," Honey said as she handed over a wad of bills.

"Is anyone else at all concerned that a horde of GCA agents are within half a mile of us here?" Hawk asked.

"You said yourself they won't come after us with Oliver out of

XX

commission," Hummer retorted. "I'll bet that's the last time they try to use him. I'll be right back."

Much as Hawk disliked sending Hummer off on his own, he let him go. It was easy to think of the short linear distance between them and their recent traumatic encounter, but the fact was that in a city this densely populated, there was too much ground for the GCA to cover to find them, even in such a relatively small area.

"I'm pretty sure none of our safe houses are safe anymore," Hawk said as he studied the metal dart. "What do you think we should do, Honey?"

She sighed. "We each have a blanket, and it's a warm night. I think we're going to have to camp out. And tomorrow, we get out of town, regardless of the spotty train schedule."

He didn't respond, even though she was probably right. The GCA would be monitoring the trains, though. They'd be monitoring all transportation out of the city. He felt like he'd been painted into a corner and couldn't get out again. Absently his thumb ran over the engraving on the metal dart. "Real Irish Tea," he murmured.

"Looks like we owe them one," said Honey.

Hummer returned shortly thereafter. "There wasn't much of a selection," he said as he handed a sack over to Honey. "I got a hotdog for Revere—it's mostly soy and vegetable protein, but I thought he'd like it anyway."

"Did you get the magnifying glass?" asked Hawk.

He pulled that object from his pocket. "It's pretty cheap, but it should be good enough. Lemme see the dart." He received the white-tufted tranquilizer with one hand and raised the magnifying glass in the other. "Can you hold the flashlight, Hawk?"

Again four curious heads crowded together to have a look.

A Rumor of Real Irish Tea

The engraving read,

> REAL IRISH TEA 1400
> 19504 69990 +08520 59590
> 18365 63364 +38470 12910
> 20412 59000 +45164 90000
> 33475 30700 −11208 92760

"What the heck is that supposed to mean?" asked Honey. "It's just a string of numbers. Are we supposed to add them together?"

"Hang on," said Hummer, a frown furrowing his eyebrows. "I know that first line."

"We all know the first line," she said sarcastically. "'Real Irish Tea' means 'Altair is here.' It's a message from Altair. We got that."

"I'm talking about the first line of numbers, you pest," he retorted. "One, nine, five, zero, four, six, nine, nine, nine, zero . . . What was it?"

"It must be pretty obscure if you can't remember it," said Hawk.

"Nineteen, fifty, 46.9990," Hummer said abruptly. "It's the right ascension for Altair, the star. It was in those astronomy textbooks I was reading at the library back in Flagstaff. And the second half is the declination. The first line stands for Altair!"

"Great," said Hawk. "What are the other three?"

Hummer's face went blank. "I have no idea. They're probably stars as well, don't you think?"

"*Which* stars?" Honey asked.

He bristled. "I didn't memorize the entire catalogue. We were only looking for stuff on Altair."

"I don't think the last line's a star," Hawk said absently. "It has a negative instead of a positive. I don't think it's a star."

Hummer peered closer at the magnified script. "Thirty-three and negative eleven—no," he suddenly corrected himself,

XX

"negative one-twelve. You're right. It's latitude-longitude." When three stares bored into him, he scrunched up his face. "Thirty-third parallel, negative hundred-and-twelfth meridian? C'mon, guys. You've seen all the same maps I have."

"Where is it, Hummer?" Honey asked.

"It's here. Phoenix. It's a latitude and longitude in Phoenix, Arizona."

"*Where* in Phoenix?"

"I don't *know*, Honey! I've never gone and memorized every single exact point of latitude and longitude in the world. Sorry I can't be of more *help*." He grimaced at her on this final word.

"Calm down, everyone," said Hawk. "We don't have to figure it out tonight. In fact, there are a lot of other things we should be figuring out first, like where we can go to stay safe."

"Someone's back yard," said Honey promptly. "Preferably someone with a lot of vegetation and no pets roaming around at night. We can sleep under the bushes and be gone by morning."

"Wow," said Hummer. "I thought for sure you'd be demanding that we rent a room somewhere."

She made a face. "I'm not that stupid. Obviously the GCA's got its eyes on any cash rentals, if they were able to trace us to that warehouse. It's a warm night, so we should just camp out and consider it an adventure. We might even have enough time before curfew to buy ourselves a tent."

"That would risk drawing way too much attention to ourselves," Hawk said before she could latch onto the idea. "I think you're right about the camping, but we're going to have to rough it. Are there any libraries open tomorrow that we can look up the rest of these numbers, or will we have to wait until Monday?"

"Are we staying in Phoenix that long?" Honey asked, an edge to her voice.

A Rumor of Real Irish Tea

Hawk took the dart from Hummer and held it up for all of them to see. "Altair made the effort to reach out to us," he said solemnly. "This is what we've been waiting for. Are we going to stay and try to meet them, or run away and start again from square one?"

The answer was obvious. They all knew it.

"We stay," said Happy.

"We stay," said Hummer and Honey.

"And we tranquilize anyone that comes near us," said Hawk grimly, "especially if that someone is Oliver Dunn."

XXI
Rude Awakening

AUGUST 3, 2:23AM MST, GCA REGIONAL OFFICE, CENTRAL PHOENIX

OLIVER FELT LIKE he'd been clobbered with a ton of wet cement. It pulled on his limbs, weighing him down even as he struggled against it. After some exertion, he managed to open his eyelids, a monumental accomplishment.

"Erm-I?" he asked groggily. It was supposed to be "Where am I?" but his mouth refused to form the words properly.

He heard movement and slid his eyes toward the left side of the bed where he lay. He recognized his cell-like room at the GCA office now, but he couldn't remember how he had come here.

Emily's worried face swam into his vision. "Oliver? Are you awake? Can you hear me?"

"Not deaf," he sneered, and he struggled to sit up.

"Don't try to move," she said, pushing him back down. "That was a powerful sedative that hit you. You might need to sleep it off a little longer."

That explained why his arms and legs felt so heavy. He took her advice and relaxed back into the bed. His eyes shifted upward to stare at the ceiling above him. The longer he was awake, the more alert he felt. If he exercised patience, his strength would come back to him.

"They're still trying to figure out what went wrong," Emily said. "After you passed out, it was total chaos. The Wests got away."

He remembered now. "Someone shot me with a tranquilizer." His tongue felt like a dry, bloated potato in his mouth. "That's what went wrong. And what do you mean, they got away? No one followed them?"

Emily heaved an exasperated sigh. "It wasn't an option. The minute you were unconscious, Honey and Happy West unleashed their projections on us all. I finally understand why everyone keeps saying that Happy's the one to watch out for."

His attention flitted toward her. "It was that strong?" he asked with ill-suppressed interest.

"Yeah." Emily's lack of elaboration spoke more about the experience than any description she could have given. Closer assessment showed that her face was puffy around the eyes, as though she had been crying. Was that on his behalf, or was it a remnant of her ordeal back at the warehouse?

Probably the latter. No self-respecting handler would cry over her Prometheus student getting hurt.

A knock on the door interrupted this melancholy reflection. Oliver's gaze slid that direction to discover Ben Birchard in the doorway.

"Oh," he said when he saw Oliver looking back at him. "I thought I'd come spell your handler for a bit. How long has he been awake?" he asked Emily.

"Only a couple minutes," she said.

Birchard entered the room. Oliver would have ordered him away again, except that the man was a fount of information. Birchard would know everything that had happened back at the

XXI

warehouse and everything that had happened since. Much as it annoyed Oliver, he needed not to waste such a resource.

"Make yourself useful and tell me everything," he ordered, not bothering to conceal his objective.

Ben paused, startled to be dealt with so bluntly. He recovered his wits, though, and even had the cheek to pull up a chair next to Oliver's bedside. "You were struck by a rogue tranquilizer dart. The ensuing projections from Honey and Happy West rendered most of our forces ineffectual for, oh, two or three minutes at least."

"I know that already. What about Quincy?"

"What about her?" Birchard asked, much to Oliver's increasing ire.

"Was she hit with a tranquilizer as well?"

"No, but General Stone got one in the arm, courtesy of Hummer West. It didn't knock him out, but it left him extremely dizzy. And made him furious, of course."

"Did they figure out which agent shot Oliver?" Emily asked.

He sat back in his chair, a flat expression on his face. "It wasn't a matter of figuring out anything. Every tranquilizer dart has a serial number on it. We know exactly which gun it was loaded into, and exactly which agent that gun was issued to. All we had to do was look up the serial number of the dart in your neck."

"And?" Oliver prompted.

A wry expression pulled at Birchard's mouth. "As you might imagine, the agent responsible has been in questioning ever since the incident. General Stone conducted the first round of interrogations himself. He's letting Veronica have a go at the second."

"Then you don't believe it was a stray tranquilizer?" Emily asked, a hitch in her voice.

Oliver knew it wasn't. The timing and aim had been too perfect.

"That's where the trouble comes in," Birchard said slowly. "There's no way it was an accident, but the agent—Greene, his name is—claims he didn't pull the trigger."

"Even Veronica couldn't get him to confess?" asked Emily. Oliver suppressed a snort at her thinly veiled contempt.

Birchard ignored it. "Oh, she got a confession right away. She told him to admit he did it, and he did. If we needed a scapegoat, we'd have him, but with so many resources at stake here, we can't afford anything but the truth. Agent Greene has already undergone several interrogations, and the only thing we're really certain of at this point is that he genuinely believes he didn't do it."

"*Believes* he didn't do it?" Oliver repeated. "So what, maybe he did but just can't remember?"

Birchard shrugged. "General Stone is taking into account the possibility of hypnosis or brainwashing. I think it's far more likely that Greene is telling the truth, that he wasn't involved at all, but that would indicate sabotage from another agent, someone who had the opportunity to switch weapons with him. Our lives would be a whole lot easier if Greene actually was the perpetrator."

Oliver frowned.

"Because he's already in custody," Birchard said in response to that look. "If there was sabotage from another agent . . . Well, it doesn't really matter either way. There has to be a full-blown internal investigation into the matter as it stands. We've already started credit checks on every man that was there, and they've pulled them all in for questioning at the various branches. And to think, if everything had gone well tonight, we'd be done here."

XXI

Oliver could perfectly relate to the note of bitterness in Birchard's voice. Everything had been planned. The Wests should have been recovered, but some twist of fate had snatched victory from the GCA. "Who tranquilized the bird?" he asked. "Do you know? Or did they not recover the dart? I can't imagine that Hawk just ran off without his beloved pet, even if it was dying."

"It wasn't dying," said Birchard quietly. "There was no tranquilizer in that dart."

Oliver hissed. "What?"

"There was no tranquilizer," he said again. "I've reviewed our video footage multiple times—that was an injured bird, not a sedated one. And to answer your original question, we don't know. That dart wasn't one of ours, and we don't know where it came from—probably a nearby rooftop."

The weight of that pronouncement settled on Oliver. "And Greene knows nothing about it? Even when a projector asks him?"

"He's one piece in a much larger puzzle," said Birchard, who seemed suddenly very tired. "It wouldn't be out of the realm of possibility for one rogue agent not to know that another was stationed nearby—it might even be essential to the success of the plan. But, as I said earlier, I'm inclined to believe that Greene was framed. Most likely an insurgent organization paid one of the other agents to sabotage the mission. It'll all come out in the internal investigation."

"By insurgent organization, you mean Altair," said Oliver. Beside him, Emily stiffened in her chair. Mentioning the name in present company wouldn't get him in any trouble, he thought derisively. She worried too much.

A shrill ring sounded from Birchard's pocket. "They're at the top of the list," he confirmed as he withdrew his cell phone. "If you'll excuse me, this is probably an update on the situation."

A Rumor of Real Irish Tea

Oliver glanced Emily's way to meet her gaze. Together they shifted their attention to Birchard as he answered the call. He stood with his profile to them. His initial salutation was friendly enough, but then his whole body stilled.

"No trace at all?" he said in a strangled voice. "Have you checked his house? Is there a secondary address?"

His face went ashen, and his breath quickened as though he sought to control an oncoming panic attack. "If even the—" He checked his words with a self-conscious glance toward his two eavesdroppers. "Trigger an alert," he said abruptly. "There's no time to waste. I'll report this to General Stone immediately. If he has further orders you will be notified."

Then, he hung up.

"What's gone wrong now?" Emily asked before he could bolt out the door.

A muscle tightened along Birchard's jaw. "One of the agents from the South Phoenix office has vanished. He left their confinement area to use the bathroom, and then he just vanished."

"Then he's the traitor," said Oliver. "All you have to do is track him down."

"He has *vanished*," Birchard repeated, baring his teeth. "Not just the man—his personnel record has been cleared from the central database. He's gone, like he never existed in the first place. Oh, General Stone is going to have someone's head for this. I just hope it's not *mine*." On this last remark, he strode from the room.

A moment of silence followed his departure. When Oliver turned his attention toward Emily, her gaze was still fixed on the empty door.

"What's your problem?" he asked her. "You miss your boyfriend that much?"

XXI

"He—" she began, but her voice faltered. "That really upset him. Have you ever seen the blood drain from someone's face that quickly?"

Oliver shifted against his pillow. "Not from Birchard," he grudgingly said.

He didn't see what the big deal was. A GCA agent had disappeared right after a mission went horribly awry. Obviously the man was guilty of sabotage and had made his escape. Deleting his personnel file was just another means of covering his tracks.

Worse than Birchard's overreaction, though, was Emily's. "What're you so worried about him for?" Oliver asked jealously.

"I'm not—!" A blush rose to her cheeks. "You should be *more* worried. You should be *grateful* to him."

Oliver recoiled in utter disgust. "What? Why?"

"He carried you off that warehouse lot," she said, pointing toward the door where Birchard had disappeared. "Everyone else was coming out of the fog from Happy's projection, and his main priority was to get you to safety. If that sedative had been too strong or if you'd had any sort of reaction to it, you could have *died*. Ben made sure you were stable and got you help."

"So he wasn't affected by Happy's projection?" Oliver asked. "Why am I not surprised? He was probably standing right next to Quincy, wrapped in safety. Of course he should react quickly, if that was the case. And why should I be grateful to him for doing his job?"

Emily scowled. "You just don't like him."

"Neither do you," he reminded her nastily. Then, to emphasize his righteous indignation, he flopped over onto his side and covered his head with his blanket. "Go away. It's way past hours, and you're not supposed to be in here."

He heard her stand, but he didn't uncover his head. "You're welcome," she said sarcastically, and then she left the room.

She had sat with him all that time because she was concerned about him. Most handlers would have gone to bed. Some would have even rejoiced that their charge had gotten such a comeuppance.

Emily was different. She may have been an idiot, but her heart was sincere.

He was being childish, but he didn't care. No one had asked the infernal woman to get so worried about the welfare of *Ben Birchard*. And it wasn't like one missing agent was such an incredible setback anyway. They'd already known there was sabotage involved.

"The GCA is brimming with fools," he muttered as he burrowed deeper into his sheets. "Why is anyone surprised that tonight went so badly?"

XXII
The Morning After

AUGUST 3, 9:45AM MST, GCA REGIONAL OFFICE, CENTRAL PHOENIX

EMILY PASSED A perfectly awful night. She'd gone to bed after three o'clock. What should have been a deep, dreamless rest was instead fitful and filled with passing visions of fluttering wings and clandestine figures shooting one another with tranquilizer darts. She was chasing after a childlike version of herself, who ended up having the head of a raven when she finally caught up. She awoke with a start to morning sunlight through the slats of her window blinds.

It was Sunday. Under normal circumstances, the GCA office would have only a skeleton staff on hand, strictly for security purposes. Instead, the building almost burst at the seams with personnel. Even on the fifth floor there was extra activity from agents and analysts who had slept in the extra rooms before returning to work.

Emily checked on Oliver. To her surprise, he had already dressed and combed back his hair. A small red scab on his neck, right beneath his earlobe, served as the only evidence of his misfortune from the night before.

"I thought for sure you'd still be passed out," she said wryly.

"You're almost two hours later than usual," he retorted. "Even I have limits on how long I can sleep. And you look terrible."

It was true. One glance in the mirror had revealed puffy eyes and dull skin. Even after a long, hot shower she still felt sluggish.

"I know," she said. "I watched this crazy little kid get shot last night, and it kind of stressed me out."

He eyed her, a furrow between his brows. "You sure you weren't worked up about the woes of a middle-aged administrative assistant?"

"What middle-aged administrative assistant would that be? Maggie Lloyd's the only one I know, and I certainly wasn't worried about her." She beckoned him to the door. "If you're ready, come on. I'm starving."

Wordlessly he followed her down the hall to the kitchenette. It had been busy earlier, but Emily thought it might be deserted now. Much to her dismay, she was wrong.

Seated at the only table like a duchess at tea, Veronica Porcher sipped a cup of coffee as she idly flipped the pages of a news magazine. She glanced up when they entered, and Emily was annoyed to discover that her face was as flawless as ever. Veronica had been up into the wee hours as well, but she looked as fresh as a daisy.

She hummed a good morning—not the words themselves, but a vague noise of recognition that someone else had entered the room—before she returned her gaze to the magazine. Emily skirted past her to the countertop, where an array of bagels sat next to a scattered pile of jam and cream cheese packets. The breakfast supplies had been picked over already. Some had little gouges in them, as though someone had pinched a sample of the bagel and then decided against eating it. A few had been torn in half. One actually had teeth marks.

XXII

Emily sifted through the assortment, thankful to discover a couple of pristine bagels in the mix. "Do you want plain or onion?" she asked Oliver over her shoulder.

"Onion," he said promptly, "with orange marmalade, if they have it."

"Gross," said Emily.

"How do you know?"

He had her there. She'd certainly never tried the combination before. Dutifully she pulled a marmalade packet from the condiments, along with some cream cheese for her plain bagel. She slapped both orders on disposable plates and set them on the table, right across from Veronica. Then, she turned back to the fridge.

"What do you want to drink? Looks like your options are orange juice and soymilk."

"Orange juice," said Oliver. She could have guessed as much, but she knew he liked to state his preferences over having them anticipated. Just like her. She snatched up a box of each beverage and returned to the table.

They each prepared their breakfast in silence, her plain bagel with cream cheese and his onion one with marmalade. When he took his first bite, she asked, "How is it?"

He shrugged, mouth full.

The magazine across the table folded shut. "I thought for sure he was going to try to make you eat that," said Veronica. "We had a running prank at Prom-C where we'd see who could make their handler eat the grossest thing. I always won." She smiled proudly.

"I'll bet you did," Emily said before she could stop herself.

Veronica looked annoyed. "It wasn't a matter of simple projection. We had a null-projector at Prom-C back then, and he took delight in leveling the playing field. I couldn't just tell my handler to eat the scum off the bottom of the door-sweep. I had to use some genuine persuasive methods."

"You had to distract him so you could plop it in the middle of his food, you mean," Oliver said flatly. "We play that game at Prom-A, too."

Emily looked at him in horror. "What awful things have you made me eat?"

He screwed up his face. "There's no point to the game if you don't have other kids to witness it."

She'd never been with him at Prom-A, and he hadn't been chummy with any of the kids at Prom-F. Emily breathed a sigh of relief, glad that she hadn't unwittingly eaten any odd or disgusting items. Not yet, anyway. "I'm starting to wonder how any handler actually makes it through the full two years."

"Necessity," said Veronica and Oliver in unison. They exchanged a guarded look, irritated with one another. Veronica broke eye contact first.

"Is quitting an option for you?" she asked Emily.

Emily considered the mountains of school debt that this internship would erase and took another bite of her bagel, sufficiently humbled. If she had to pay back that debt herself, it would weigh her down for the rest of her life. She hated to admit that much to either Veronica or Oliver, though. Prometheus students were among the elite group that snatched up the few available scholarships and tuition waivers, so school debt was nonexistent for them.

And as a projector, Veronica had probably never experienced money problems in her life.

Emily changed the subject. "If there was a null-projector at Prom-C back when you were there, why aren't they using him now, for this mission?"

XXII

Veronica's brows arched. "How should I know?"

"Oh," said Emily, "I didn't mean . . . Um, what's he up to now?"

"Do you keep in touch with people who went to the same primary school you did?" Veronica asked. "I don't. But then, it's partly because of my job—when you're in the limelight like I am, you don't really have a lot of spare time for keeping track of old acquaintances."

Her glib tone chafed against Emily's sensibilities. "That's true. You're such an important person now, so busy that you probably never have any time to yourself."

Veronica smirked at the childish provocation and retreated behind her magazine again. Emily itched to snatch it from her hands and smack her across the head with it.

"Ooh, she gets under my skin," she confided to Oliver when they entered the elevator some ten minutes later. Veronica had sat in silence for the remainder of their breakfast, languidly reading her magazine and sipping her cup of coffee as though she had the entire day to herself. For all Emily knew, she did.

"You're jealous," said Oliver. "You wish you were a projector with the whole world groveling at your feet."

She stared at him. After a moment's consideration, she asked, "Can't I just wish that she *wasn't* a projector?"

"Jealous," he said again.

The doors opened on the second floor to a flurry of activity. No one had issued any instructions for Oliver yet today, so it seemed like a good idea to ask whether they needed him. Emily would have turned back when she saw how harrowed everyone looked, and when she heard General Stone's voice bellowing from his usual conference room, she actually grabbed Oliver's shoulder to waylay him. He shrugged away from her with a glare.

"I want eyes and ears glued to every single Altair network

we have record of! I don't care how old they are! Do you understand? Good!"

Emily presumed that General Stone made this declaration into a phone, because no vigorous "Yes, sir!" answered him. She and Oliver paused in the doorway as the general searched his contacts list for a new verbal punching bag. Next to him, Ben caught her eye and hastily motioned her to retreat.

She yanked Oliver out of sight just as General Stone looked up.

"What was that for?" the boy demanded, wrenching away from her again.

"We'll wait out here, I think," Emily said. From inside the room, General Stone barked orders at his new victim. "Or on second thought, maybe we should go back upstairs."

Suddenly, Ben poked his head out of the conference room. "It's better if you steer clear of the general for now. He's been on a rampage ever since they discovered the ghost."

"Ghost?" Oliver echoed sharply.

"The—" Ben started, but he caught himself with a self-conscious glance back into the room. He tipped his head down the hall. "There's another conference room two doors down. Wait for me there. I'll be right with you."

He disappeared back inside the room in time for General Stone to snap an order at him. "Birchard! Get me Secretary Allen on the phone, pronto! And where are those files I asked for?"

Emily felt a mixture of pity and relief as she guided Oliver away from the door—pity for Ben, who had to put up with that sort of behavior, and relief for herself, who didn't.

The second conference room was smaller, and it was oddly dark and empty. Most of the agents assigned to this branch probably had their own work space, so they had no need to retreat here. She flipped on the light and took a seat at the oblong table.

XXII

Oliver remained standing, his hands clasped behind his back. His critical gaze traveled the walls. There hung a picture of the President of the United States, right next to one of the Service Czar, Secretary Mary Rose Allen.

"She's probably having a conniption too," he said.

"I think this situation has blown up beyond what anyone expected," said Emily. "I mean, it's got to be pretty unsettling to discover a traitor rooted in your midst."

"Whatever." Dismissively, he turned to study a prestigious-looking plaque behind him.

His apathy was rather forced—he had been tranquilized last night because of that traitor, after all—but Emily didn't say anything. Instead she leaned back in her chair and closed her eyes as she waited for Ben to appear.

The conference room door opened. "What could have possibly possessed you to come downstairs this morning?" Ben asked as he slipped inside.

Oliver looked at Emily accusingly.

She folded her arms tight, shrinking away from both of them. "No one told us what we were supposed to do today. I didn't see Quincy or Alyson in the break room, so I assumed they were down here."

"I saw them at breakfast and told them to keep to their rooms today," said Ben. "Sorry. I should've put a note on your door. I just figured that Oliver would want to rest for a while after what happened last night."

"You thought I wanted to sulk for a while," Oliver intuitively said.

Ben tipped his head in honest acknowledgement. "Either way, you don't want to get in General Stone's crosshairs right now."

"What's this about a ghost?" asked Oliver.

A Rumor of Real Irish Tea

A pained look crossed Ben's face. "The agent that went missing last night, Thomas Fry, is what we call a ghost. He doesn't actually exist. Or rather," he quickly amended, "he does exist, but that's not his real name. The problem with having a national database of our citizenry is that it's relatively easy to forge records. All it takes is a name and date of birth. If a person—or a subversive group of persons—knows how to submit the information through the right channels, they could potentially create any number of false records."

"To use as aliases?" asked Emily. She wasn't comfortable talking about Altair, but at least he was trying to be discrete this time around.

Ben laughed cynically. "It's so much more than an alias. The false record is like a new life. The really well done forgeries come with medical histories, school transcripts, immunization records, you name it. They have national ID numbers, and some even have a sub-dermal tracking chip attached to the file. It's next to impossible to tell the difference between a real record and a forged one. It's the reason we need a mandatory national DNA database, but every time the issue is broached in Washington, you get protests about invasion of privacy. The international community in particular lobbies heavily against it."

"So how do you know the agent from last night was a ghost?" Emily asked. "I mean, if the forgeries are so good, how do you know?"

He shook his head ruefully. "There are two national databases: one for the living population, and one for the dead. Last night, someone—presumably the impostor himself—entered a death date for Thomas Fry of Phoenix, Arizona into the GCA system. That immediately transferred his personnel record into that secondary database. Once there, it was scrubbed clean of all vital

XXII

statistics, including fingerprint and DNA records. That used to be the common procedure that Altair used whenever one of their ghosts was no longer useful. It hasn't happened in quite a few years, because our system was supposed to be foolproof against that sort of tampering. Apparently someone got their hands on some necessary passwords. They cleaned up their tracks nicely, too. Basically, all we have left of him is his co-workers' memories and a fake death record."

"What about his family, his home?"

"No family," Ben said, "and his apartment conveniently caught fire last night at roughly the same time we were besieging that warehouse. Oh, this was a systematic operation on their part—they played us like a violin, and we never saw it coming."

"So they had this ghost waiting to help the Wests escape?" Oliver asked. "Exactly how long was that guy with the GCA? Two weeks?"

"Thirteen years," said Ben flatly. "He was a spy embedded deep in his enemy's camp. You've got to give them credit for patience, at least. We should've known they would try to use our efforts to reach out to the Wests, though. It's not like they could approach them any easier than we can."

Bitterness was thick on his voice. Not only did he have to deal with the chaotic aftermath, but he was also an information junkie. It probably killed him that something like this had slipped in under his radar.

"So you won't be needing Oliver today?" Emily guessed.

That at least got him to laugh, short though the sound was. "Not unless the Wests go walking in broad daylight, waving a white flag to draw attention to themselves. Right now we're trying to tap into Altair's channels of communication. If they haven't already talked to the Wests, they will soon, but they don't like dealing with hot property, so to speak. They'll want to smuggle them out of the country as soon as possible."

"How do you know?" asked Oliver.

"Because that's what they did with their parents," said Ben. "At least, that's what our sources say they did. Oh, did you not know that Mama and Papa West turned to Altair for their disappearing act? That's all the more reason to keep the four kids from escaping. Now, if I've spent sufficient time explaining the situation, you'd probably better make an escape of your own, back upstairs. I'm off to get yelled at again."

Emily and Oliver watched him leave before exchanging a wary look. "I guess we should probably go back upstairs," said Emily.

"How hard do you think it would be to hack the lock on the computer lab up there?" Oliver asked. "Hypothetically speaking, I mean."

"Hypothetically speaking, I'm pretty sure your handler would wring your scrawny neck if you tried. What do you want with a computer lab, anyway?"

"I want to see what's going on. You can't sit there and pretend you're not curious."

Emily leaned close, her voice cutting to a desperate whisper. "Do you not remember spending three weeks in confinement just because we heard the name Altair mentioned? It's only been a week since we got out, and we've been sucked even deeper into the same quagmire. I don't want to go back to a confinement cell."

He considered her words and seemed to concede her point. She wanted verbal confirmation, though.

"No hacking computer lab locks," she said sternly as they crossed the hall to the elevators.

"Yeah, yeah," said Oliver. "I got it."

XXII

Even though his reassurance was half-hearted at best, Emily had every intention of bolting straight for her room and leaving him to his own devices. It was Sunday, she was tired, and she didn't feel like watching a ten-year-old just to make sure he didn't do anything rash. She would retreat to her room, shut the door, and pretend that everything was fine. Crystal would be so proud, she thought wryly.

When the elevator opened to the fifth floor, though, she was met with a new road block—two road blocks, actually. Quincy and Alyson stood in front of the doors. Quincy's face was set hard with determination while Alyson fidgeted nervously.

"Is something wrong?" Emily asked, against her better judgment.

"Oh, um . . ." Alyson hemmed.

"I'm going to ask Birchard when they're sending us home," said Quincy. "I'm sick of being here. I don't want to do this. I'm going back to Prom-F."

"What brought this on?" Emily asked Alyson. Quincy answered, just as Emily intended.

"Seeing my friend and his brother cornered like animals brought this on," she said with an angry flash. "Watching Oliver get knocked out with a tranquilizer dart brought this on. Sitting here *twiddling my thumbs* while a bunch of morons in suits decide my fate brought this on. Prom-F is no picnic, but at least it's a slow poison, not a volatile one like this!"

She started to shove past them onto the elevator, but Oliver blocked her path. "You don't want to go down there right now. General Stone's on the warpath. He'll chew you up and spit you out again."

"The worst he can do is transfer me to Prom-E five years early," Quincy retorted. "I'm going to end up there anyway, so who cares? We *both* are."

"Prom-E is apocryphal at best," Oliver said. "And who says we're both going to end up there?"

She shoved his shoulders. "Open your eyes, Oliver! That's where all null-projectors end up! Come *on*, Alyson." She pushed her way past into the elevator.

Alyson managed a simpering smile toward Emily as she slipped by. Within the elevator, Quincy pushed the second-floor button impatiently. The doors slid shut.

"She's cracked," said Oliver.

Emily was inclined to agree, but she said curiously, "I wonder if that's where Veronica's null-projector ended up."

Oliver's attention snapped to her face. "Don't speculate like that. There's no point."

Then, he swept past her to his room. At least he wasn't completely discounting the existence of Prom-E anymore. He hadn't even bothered to call her an idiot for her speculation, either.

"What a strange day," said Emily to the ceiling, and she made a beeline for her own door.

XXIII
Altair Is Here

AUGUST 4, 10:35AM MST, PHOENIX

Sunday had proven to be a terrible day not to have a safe hiding place. Sleeping out in the open at night wasn't so bad, but the day had turned sweltering. The Wests spent it skulking from one back yard to the next, trying not to be seen by homeowners as they went. It was the one day of the week that people didn't have work or school to attend. Many braved the blistering heat to mow lawns or trim trees, which made the Wests' task of hiding that much more difficult.

Thus, when the Monday morning sun broke along the horizon, they were supremely grateful for a world returning to its weekly routine. A world in routine allowed them to move more freely about their own business.

They needed a library, and the easiest place for a group of kids to access one without drawing too much attention was at a school. Luckily, the area they were in had a couple of elementary schools. They chose the closer one to infiltrate.

"Are you going to blend in well enough?" Hawk asked dubiously. The students here wore uniforms of white collared shirts and dark slacks.

A Rumor of Real Irish Tea

"Our Prometheus duds should work," Hummer said as he dug through his backpack. "I hoped I'd never have to wear it again, but it's a close enough match, once you get rid of the tie and the coat and the sweater vest."

"You got rid of those back in California," Honey reminded him. "You'd have burned the whole thing if you didn't need an extra set of clothes."

"Guilty as charged." He favored her with a cheeky grin and whipped a wrinkled white shirt from the bottom of his bag.

She rolled her eyes and disappeared into the bushes to change. "Happy, you're going to be good for Hawk, aren't you?" she called. "We shouldn't be gone more than ten or fifteen minutes. We know exactly what we're looking for."

Happy didn't answer her. Instead, he turned his gaze on Hawk. "Where's Revere?" he asked quietly.

Hawk pointed up. "Playing lookout." The raven had recovered admirably from his adventure with the tranquilizer-free dart. He occasionally chattered to Hawk about soreness at the joint where the needle had struck him, but it had not debilitated him much, if at all, and he stubbornly refused to leave the four children.

They were currently positioned in the shrubbery of a side-yard across from the school. Children infested the playground, shrieking and running as they spent their pent-up energy on their morning recess.

"You two better hurry," said Hawk. "They're going to ring the bell soon."

Hummer stripped his old shirt to replace it with the new one. He'd already been wearing the dusty, dirt-stained pants. His final ensemble made him look like a disheveled mess. "How is it?" he asked.

XXIII

"You'll fit right in," Hawk said. Across the street, several children tackled each other in the sandbox while apathetic playground aides watched from a distance.

Honey emerged in her skirt and white shirt, far more pristine.

"Everyone over there is wearing pants," Hawk said, "even the girls."

She shrugged. "No one'll care. You ready, Hummer?"

Together they trotted across the street to the school entrance. Hawk and Happy watched apprehensively as the pair bypassed the fence and disappeared among the buildings beyond.

"Are you all right?" Hawk asked his youngest brother.

Happy studied him, intent. "Are you getting nervous because of me?"

A smile cracked across Hawk's face. "I'm fine. You do a good job of controlling your projections, you know."

Dissatisfaction crossed the little boy's face, but the expression smoothed almost immediately. He had an uncanny knack for neutralizing his feelings, especially for a six-year-old. In a way, that control made his projections that much more potent when he unleashed them full-force.

"The Prom-B people made me practice," Happy said. "They told me I was bothering the whole school and that if I didn't learn to control my projections I wouldn't get to see Honey anymore."

"Those jerks," said Hawk, looping a protective arm around him. "You're allowed to feel whatever you want, okay?"

Happy smiled wanly but said nothing in return. Taciturn as he was now, he was still far more open than he had been a month ago when they first escaped. The longer they were away from the influence of the Prometheus Institute, the more he would open up. He would never again be the bright, joy-filled baby of Hawk's memories, though. Prometheus had left its mark on them all.

The bell across the street rang, and the children scrambled to line up and return to class. The shouts and games gave way to stillness, and the minutes afterward passed at a snail's pace. At long last, two figures emerged from the main entrance. Hummer and Honey broke into a full run as soon as they were beyond the fence.

"Come on," said Hawk, and he snatched up his bag and Hummer's. "Grab Honey's stuff, and let's go."

Happy followed the orders, and together they met the pair at the sidewalk.

"We've got to hurry if we want to get there in time to scout things out," said Hummer as he retrieved his backpack from Hawk's extended hand. "The latitude and longitude are for a park in Central Phoenix. I'm pretty sure that the 1400 next to 'Real Irish Tea' is a time, two o'clock in the afternoon. That gives us a little over three hours to get there and get a feel for the area."

"What about the other numbers?" Hawk asked.

"Vega and Deneb," said Hummer vaguely.

"Come again?"

"Vega and Deneb—they're the other two stars that make up the Summer Triangle with Altair. Look." He stopped and pulled a sheet from his pocket, a printout from the school's library. "This is a satellite image of the coordinates. They're here, where these two paths converge into one. But if you look, you can see three ramada roofs positioned out from around this point—they're at roughly the same angles from one another as Vega, Deneb, and Altair in the Summer Triangle."

"Meaning we want to go to Altair," said Hawk, "and not to this point on the map where the paths meet."

"As best I can figure," said Hummer.

XXIII

"But if that's the case, then there's no date in the code. How do we know they'll be there today? How do we know we didn't miss them yesterday?"

"I think they'll be there precisely *because* there's no date. They gave us a code to figure out, so they probably gave us a grace period too. Plus, there's no way they could be certain we even got the code to begin with. If you had thrown it away and someone else picked it up—like someone from the GCA trying to track us—then having a specific date along with the time would put them in danger. As it is, anyone sitting at that ramada at two o'clock in the afternoon can claim ignorance of a meeting."

"This is crazy," Hawk said.

"What's even crazier is that we're going to miss our bus if you two don't pick up the pace," said Honey. "We have two transfers to make to get where we want to go, so there's not a whole lot of time."

"We figured out a bus route in the library too," Hummer said in explanation. "Happy, try to keep your thoughts from focusing too much—we don't want anyone to notice us, if we can help it."

"Happy knows what to do," said Honey. "He gets plenty enough practice. Come on, now."

Her hurry proved unnecessary. They arrived at the bus stop a few minutes before the lumbering transport rolled up the road in front of them. Honey paid the four fares and advised the bus driver not to remember them before she skipped back to her seat. Midday public transportation was not over-crowded, and stops were less frequent than during the rush hours of morning and afternoon, but it was still slow-going. The buses ran less often, and the children were forced to wait between transfers, but roughly an hour and a half later they descended to the street next to a large public park.

A Rumor of Real Irish Tea

They had their plan of attack already decided, but Hawk repeated it nonetheless. "Happy, you're with Hummer. Honey, you're with me. Keep an eye out for anyone suspicious, especially any government types. Revere is going to circle above, and I'll try to enlist as many of the local birds here to keep watch for us. Stay out of open areas, if you can."

The park was not overpopulated, since afternoon in August was hardly the time local residents wanted to be out and about, but there were still several groups of people scattered across its expanse. Many were older, retirees who were masters of their own time. Some of the younger people walked with baby strollers, and a cluster of small children played in an expanse of grass while their caregivers watched from the shaded benches nearby.

In all, the place was quiet, peaceful.

Hawk and Honey went one direction while Hummer and Happy went another. Gradually, both groups wove their way toward the latitude and longitude cross-point. They were only going to observe the spot from afar, and for a relatively short time. If Hummer was right, it wasn't the actual rendezvous but merely a point of reference, but it couldn't hurt to know what sort of people were walking those paths.

This area of the park was fashioned around a man-made lagoon, a relic of eras past when such water features were allowed and even encouraged on community lands in the arid climate. This worked to Hawk's advantage: the waterways were inhabited with ducks and swans. He chattered with them and made quick friends by feeding them bits of crackers—more so with the social little ducks, who were eager to interact with a potential food source. At first Honey stood idly by and allowed him to do his job, but soon enough she fished a granola bar from

XXIII

her backpack and started throwing pieces, much to the delight of the growing flock of birds.

"Oh, they're so on our side now," said Hawk.

Honey tutted. "Tell them to get back in the water. We're starting to make a spectacle of ourselves." She crumbled the remainder of her granola bar and tossed it into the nearby lagoon. Most of the ducks gladly followed, with no need of interference from Hawk.

"Come on," he said wryly. "Hummer and Happy have gotten way ahead of us."

The point given to them on the dart was near a bridge, where two paths merged into one. Hawk and Honey took refuge beneath a bay of trees on the other side of the bridge while Hummer and Happy circled around to watch from a different angle.

After fifteen minutes, only three people had ventured past the point, and none of them looked particularly suspicious. Hawk decided it was time to move on and gave the signal, which Revere cheerfully cawed from above.

Across the water, Hummer and Happy slinked away from their hiding place.

"We still have almost an hour before the meeting," said Honey nervously. "If we get too close to the meeting place too early, we'll be that much easier to spot."

"The birds in the area haven't noticed anything out of the ordinary," Hawk said. "We're the only ones here who are loitering."

"Are you sure?"

"Honey, it's a hundred degrees out. No one's staying in the park for more than a half-hour. They come in their air-conditioned cars, get out and walk around until they start to sweat, and then get back into their cars and leave. The only exceptions are the handful of crazy golfers across the lagoon, and they're all focused on their games."

"The birds told you that?" she said skeptically.

"They're pretty used to the daily routine here."

His reassurance placated her worries. She fell in step behind him with no other protest but a wary glance at their surroundings. They had to cross another bridge to get in the area of the ramada that Hummer had pegged as Altair. Instead of following the path toward that spot, though, they veered and circled around the water's edge, feigning interest in the algae-filled lagoon and the waterfowl that played there.

The ramada was empty. Hawk and Honey settled in the shade of a tree to watch and wait. Hawk plucked at the dry, scruffy grass beneath him.

Next to him, Honey tensed. "There are people coming."

He looked up to see two golfers—both the age of retirees—walking up the path toward the ramada. Each of them pulled a golf bag behind him.

"It's still forty minutes to two," he said. "They're probably just taking a rest from their game, or else having a late lunch."

Sure enough, the two men stopped at the ramada, and each produced a brown lunch bag from his things. They chatted together as they ate their sandwiches and drank from water bottles.

"I'm starving," said Honey.

"You have a whole stash of food in your bag," Hawk reminded her. "If you're starving, it's your own fault."

"I'm sick of granola bars and fruit. I want some real food."

"Like they served back at the Prometheus cafeteria?"

She favored him with a narrow-eyed glare before returning her attention to the two dining golfers. "Like something Mom used to cook, back before the world collapsed."

XXIII

Hawk didn't immediately answer. He knew that Honey's memories before Prometheus were scattered and few, so for her to bring up this kind of desire was out of the ordinary. "If everything goes well today, you might get that wish sooner than you expected," he finally said, and he couldn't hide the quiet hope he felt.

The two golfers took their time eating. They talked and chuckled at one another and seemed to be in absolutely no hurry whatsoever.

"They're going to ruin our meeting if they stay there much longer," said Honey after a half-hour had elapsed.

"No," Hawk said. "Look—they're cleaning up. They'll be gone before two."

He was half-right. While both golfers gathered together their things and packed them away in their bags, only one of them stood. He shook his fellow's hand with a smile and then waved goodbye before he turned and retreated up the path. The other one pulled out a deck of cards and began a game of solitaire.

"You don't think—" Honey began, but her attention diverted to one side. Hummer and Happy were quickly moving along the water's edge to join them.

Hawk and Honey both hunched closer to the ground.

"What are you doing?" Hawk hissed.

"That's the guy!" Hummer said as he joined them.

"You don't know that for sure."

"Look—the golf course might be right across the water, but there's no direct path from there to here. He just lugged his golf bag halfway around the park to have lunch with his friend at that particular ramada on a scorching afternoon like this? I don't think so. It's two o'clock, and he's there. Go talk to him."

Hawk and Honey exchanged wary glances.

A Rumor of Real Irish Tea

"We've got nothing to lose," said Honey.

"Not unless this is a really elaborate scheme the GCA put in place to make us come to them," Hawk retorted, but even he knew this was a moot point. The GCA may have set up such an involved sting, but the Wests were in no position to back out. Everything they had worked for thus far had led them down this path, and they couldn't risk abandoning it now.

"Come on," he said to Honey. "Hummer, you and Happy get away from here like we planned. I'm sending Revere with you. If anyone comes after you, he'll let me know. I'll have one of the local birds find you if anything goes wrong on our end."

Hummer and Happy obediently continued down the water's edge. Hawk and Honey cut across the grass toward the golfer under the ramada. Hawk wished that his nerves were as steady as his footsteps. Everyone within a square mile could probably hear the pounding of his heart.

The golfer was angled away from them, so rather than approach him from behind, they cut an oblique path as though taking a wide berth around him. It seemed only fair that he should see them coming. Contrary to their expectations, though, he kept his eyes fixed on the table and his cards as they neared.

"Excuse me," said Hawk, and his nerves were more flustered than ever. "Do you happen to have any Real Irish Tea?"

He didn't know if the code word was needed; he didn't know what to say in this situation at all, but if this man had no affiliation with Altair, he wouldn't find the phrase too notable.

A laugh broke through the man's lips. "Subtle," he remarked as he raised his eyes at last. They were a twinkling brown, shrewd and cautious and bordered by pleasant wrinkles. "They told me you kids were smart. I'm glad. I don't think I could've

XXIII

handled a midday golf game every day this week. Here." He fished a baseball cap out of the golf bag beside him.

Hawk took it in confusion. When the man only smiled, he hesitantly put it on his head.

"Sit down. We'll pretend we're a grandfather treating his grandkids to a school-day outing. You can call me Smith, by the way."

"Is that your real name?" Honey asked.

He shook his head. "No. And please don't ask me what my real name is. I'm taking my life into my hands by meeting with you."

"You're the ones who set up this meeting," Hawk said. "You shot my bird."

"It was either that or shoot one of you kids. We figured there was a better chance of you seeing the message if the dart went to the bird, though. And we only set up the meeting because you were looking for us. Shadow organizations don't much like having lights shined their direction. That was a clever little run on the downtown GCA office, by the way."

Hawk felt the blood rush to his face. Next to him, Honey smiled impertinently. "Thank you," she said.

"What is it you want from us?" Smith asked bluntly.

The two children glanced at one another. Hawk took a deep breath before he spoke. "We're looking for our parents, and someone told us that you might be able to help."

To their dismay, Smith shook his head. "We're not in the business of finding. We're in the business of hiding."

"But if you hid someone in the past—" Hawk started.

"There are avenues to track that someone down," Smith interrupted, "but it's not such a simple matter. We're not like the national government, with a giant database of records to consult. You could say we're exactly the opposite: every cell keeps its own secrets, and they guard them jealously."

A Rumor of Real Irish Tea

Hawk's hopes fast dwindled. "So . . . you're *not* one big organization?"

"You might say we're a conglomerate of little organizations—individual franchises with the same brand name, perhaps. It's the only way we've been able to survive, by being local and tight-knit. The cells—that's what we call each local unit, a cell—they do communicate with each other, but the information they pass is limited."

"Such as?" Honey prompted.

"Such as whether there're any good hiding places in their region," he told her. "But you didn't come to us to hide, and even if you had, there's nothing we can do for you as long as your faces are on the news every hour. Right now, you're untouchable."

"So that's why you wanted this meeting?" Hawk asked, suddenly bitter. "So you could tell us to quit trying to find you?"

Smith smiled, but there was more apology and regret in his expression than pleasure. "Not quite. We do have a couple of options for you, but you're probably not going to like either of them. I don't really like either of them, to be honest."

Hawk wished that the man would quit equivocating. "What are they?"

"The first is to smuggle you out of the country. We have the channels to get you across the border and from there to any number of places around the world. You'd be fugitives for the rest of your lives, and you might never be able to return to the States, but you wouldn't have to look over your shoulder for the GCA anymore. You'd have relative safety, but very little stability."

"And what about our parents?" asked Hawk.

"You'd have to give up your search for them, at least until you're adults who can blend into a crowd. But then, you're probably going to have to give up your search anyway. There

XXIII

isn't very much that a group of children can do without drawing attention to themselves."

Hawk and Honey glanced at one another, mutinous expressions mirrored on their faces.

"What's the second option?" Honey asked.

"You're not going to like it," said Smith, "but it's the one I'd strongly advise you to take. That option runs you back into the custody of the GCA."

Hawk wrenched away from the table. "No! What are you saying? That we should turn ourselves in?"

"You could, but it would be a lot better if you were caught," Smith replied, unfazed by his violent reaction. "Understand that we've already had to sacrifice one of our men to set up this meeting. The GCA will never stop searching for you, and with the entire country waiting with bated breath for little Maddie and Alex North to be delivered from their captors, that search is only going to pick up steam. Under ordinary circumstances, time would reduce people's interest, but in this case they're kept glued to their screens by the likes of Veronica Porcher at NPNN, and every time they leave their houses, they're on the lookout for the poor children in those news clips. The case has even garnered international interest. Our hands are tied. If you were to get caught, though—"

"We're *never* going back," Honey interrupted with quiet determination.

"I think we're done here," said Hawk. "Come on, Honey." He stood and stubbornly pulled the ball cap from his head to return it.

Smith looked down at the hat, then back up. "Keep it. There's a key and an address to a safe house in the brim. All of the information we have about your situation is in a file there, along with our two proposals. You don't need to decide today, but we can't give you more than forty-eight hours. After that, you'll be on your own again, and this time for good."

Hawk wanted to fling the cap in the man's face, but necessity made him stop. "Is the house really safe?" he asked resentfully.

"Yes," said Smith.

"Tell the truth," Honey commanded.

"It's safe," Smith said again. "I give you my word."

Hawk was still riddled with hesitation. Honey interceded. "Beggars can't be choosers." She took the cap from his hand and fit it on her own head. "Thanks, Smith," she said sarcastically to the old golfer. Then she tugged her brother behind her, away from the scene.

One final glance toward the ramada showed Smith gathering up his cards, preparing to leave.

"What a waste," said Hawk.

"He's given us information to look over and a roof to sleep under for the night," Honey said woodenly. "That might've been all he could do."

This was probably true, but that didn't quell Hawk's disappointment. "All this time looking for Altair, only to have them tell us to go back to the GCA," he muttered. "Hummer's going to throw a fit."

It was a fairly accurate assessment. Hummer and Happy saw them coming from a distance and met them beneath a row of trees near the park's exit. Hawk summarized the situation.

"So they're completely useless," Hummer declared.

"Maybe they know something we don't," Honey interjected. "We can't really blame them for not wanting to take the GCA head-on when we don't want to do that ourselves."

"Since when have you been the voice of reason?" he asked.

XXIII

"Since you both started throwing fits whenever everything didn't go as planned. This is *progress*. They're giving us information and hiding us for a couple of days. They don't owe us anything, and certainly not if it involves risking their necks for us."

"They're grown-ups," Hummer said. "They should be braver than we are. So where's this safe house?" he added grudgingly.

Hawk pulled the ball cap from Honey's head and fumbled around with the inner lining. His brothers and sister watched with eager interest. The key was easy to find, secured at the front of the hat just above the bill. He had to fold down the lining to discover the address; it was scrawled in black marker halfway around the inside brim.

"That's only a couple of streets away from here," Hummer said.

"Did you memorize the entire city grid?" Honey asked impertinently.

He bristled. "What of it?"

"What should we do?" asked Hawk before a fight could break out between the two. "We're treading dangerous waters here, so we should all agree on our plan of action."

"Are you kidding?" asked Honey. "We go to the house."

Indecision danced across Hummer's face. "We should at least have a look, don't you think? Maybe there'll be something useful in the file he left us. At the very least we can walk by the place on our way to the train depot."

Next to him, Happy nodded.

"And what do we do if Altair is leading us into the hands of the GCA to get them off their own backs?" Hawk asked.

"They're not," said Honey. "Smith said it was a safe house, even when I asked him."

A Rumor of Real Irish Tea

"And no one's ever been able to withstand one of your projections," said Hummer sarcastically. "There's no way he could've been a null."

She pursed her lips in a sulk. "I thought you wanted to go to the house."

"I do. I just don't like you acting like the high and mighty infallible projector. Come on, Hawk," he said. "We need to follow this through to the end. If we skip town without having a look at that file, we'll be starting from square one again. Besides, I'm roasting here. We're each losing a quart of water every ten minutes we're out in this inferno."

Hawk glanced to Revere perched in a tree branch overhead. The bird looked back at him as though to ask what he was waiting for. A sigh escaped his lips. "Lead the way," he said to Hummer.

The house was in a quiet neighborhood with little traffic. It was small but well kept. Hummer volunteered to go first and, key in hand, he trotted across the street alone. His siblings nervously watched as he disappeared inside. After a few tense moments passed, he opened the door again and beckoned them to come. They tried to be as inconspicuous as three children and their pet raven could be, but there was a collective sigh of relief when they finally shut the front door behind them.

The air-conditioning was on, and the house was blissfully cool. The inside was furnished, much nicer than any place the Wests had stayed for the past couple of weeks. Hummer pointed them toward the tidy coffee table in the front room, where lay an overflowing fruit basket next to a thick manila file with the words "Burn after reading" printed in broad red letters across its cover.

"Points for hospitality," said Honey, and she cheerfully plucked up an apple.

XXIII

"Did you look through the file?" Hawk asked Hummer.

"Just a glance. They've got a roster of all the people looking for us, for starters, including the two Prometheus null-projectors."

"Two?" Hawk said sharply.

Hummer gestured to the file. "According to that, Quincy's there with Oliver. The other night at the warehouse, there was a pocket of people who were unaffected by Happy or Honey—I guess she must've been standing with them."

Honey glanced between her two older brothers as she chewed on her apple. "Quincy—she's your friend, isn't she, Hawk? So she's helping them catch us?"

A muscle along his jaw clenched. "She probably doesn't have a choice. Or maybe she's really mad at Hummer and me for taking off in the middle of the night. Either way, it's one more reason to steer clear of the GCA. Let's have a full look at that file."

Soon enough, they had its contents strewn out across the floor. It was more than just a roster of people. It was their life histories, including those of Hawk, Hummer, Honey, and Happy.

"I thought that Smith guy told you they couldn't help us find our parents," said Hummer, confusion thick on his voice.

"He did," Hawk said.

Hummer held up the page he was reviewing. "They know where Oliver's parents live. So why not ours?"

Honey scrambled from her place on the floor to have a look. Hawk remained where he was. "Oliver's parents didn't ask to be hidden, I'm guessing."

"Wow," said Honey as she took the page. "They know all of this about Oliver and next to nothing about us? What about Quincy? What do they know about her?"

"Name, birth date, and basic history with Prometheus," said Hawk from his corner. "Just about the same information they have on us. But they've got a truckload on this General Bradford Stone."

"That's the guy I shot at," said Hummer proudly. "According to that report, I hit him once, too. And he's the principal of Prom-E, the *shadow campus*. If he ever gets us there he'll make our lives absolutely miserable."

"You know how many kids back at Prom-F would kill for this information?" Hawk asked.

"All of 'em," answered Hummer. He rifled through a couple more pages. "I hate to say this, but it looks like the GCA isn't going to pull their punches anymore. Their plans are getting more aggressive. Your friend Smith may have been right about our options."

The file was divided into four distinct sections: first, a roster; second, the individual bios; third, a record of the Wests' known movements and the GCA's counter-movements thus far; and fourth, Altair's two options to resolve the situation. The first of these options was a clear-cut plan to smuggle the children from the country, just as Smith had said. The second was branded under the ominous label, "Return to GCA Custody."

Hummer flipped through the options section with a deepening frown. "Hawk, you really need to have a look at this." He proffered the pages to his older brother. "These people know what they're doing. They have everything planned, right down to the minute. There's definitely some risk, but I think we should at least consider the help they're offering us."

This speech was intriguing enough to get Hawk up off the floor. He took the pages from Hummer with a wary glance and settled down to read. Honey and Happy joined him on either side, curious.

"This is too dangerous," he said as he scanned the text. "If

XXIII

even one thing goes wrong—one vehicle transfer, one checkpoint inspection—we'd be back in the GCA's clutches forever."

"We'll be back in their clutches anyway if we keep running around blind like we are," Hummer said. "But if Altair can deliver the results they're promising—"

"That's a pretty big if."

He wasn't going to let the issue drop. "How much longer can we do this on our own? We're living out of backpacks from day to day and place to place, and we all know that sooner or later we're going to slip up and get caught unless we catch a break. This might *be* our only break."

"If we can trust them," said Honey grimly.

"We only have forty-eight hours to decide," Hummer reminded them both. "I think after that, the window of opportunity will close. There's a number here to call once we've made our decision, and it says they left a cell phone in the fruit basket. Our contact's name is Ruth."

Hawk shook his head and looked away. He didn't know how to answer, because he didn't know what kind of sense to make of Altair. They provided options to help, but those options were nothing that the Wests had anticipated or wanted. If they accepted, the four children would have to give up searching for their parents, and they would spend the rest of their adolescent years wherever Altair deposited them.

The past month on the run had taught him one thing, though. "We have to get away from the GCA. We'll never be able to do anything as long as they're tracking us."

The four siblings exchanged a solemn glance. On that one point they were in total agreement.

XXIV
The Big Break

AUGUST 4, 7:14PM MST, GCA REGIONAL OFFICE, CENTRAL PHOENIX

"How much longer are we going to be here?"

Emily glanced toward Quincy, who had asked the question, and Alyson, who studied the wall as though she hadn't heard. The pair, along with Emily and Oliver, had spent their entire afternoon and evening in one corner of General Stone's conference room doing absolutely nothing.

Everything was still a mess. Even though General Stone had calmed from his furor of the day before, he was still short-tempered and expected his orders to be obeyed almost before he gave them. He had kept the two null-projectors in his sight for most of the day, but with no work for them to do.

A few new faces had cycled through to speak with him, though, which made Emily wonder if there were projectors among them.

"How much longer?" Quincy asked again, an edge to her voice.

Alyson ventured a timid glance toward the austere general at the far end of the conference table. She whispered, "I'm sure it won't be long. Maybe we can ask Mr. Birchard when he comes back again."

XXIV

Quincy made a contemptuous face and fixed her eyes on the ceiling. Ben had waylaid her attempt to speak with General Stone the day before in much the same manner that he had kept Emily and Oliver away. Quincy had been in a sulk ever since, with very little charity to spare toward anyone, especially the ubiquitous "Mr. Birchard."

Ben had been in and out of the room all day, always on his phone as he came and went. He had paid the group in the corner little heed, except to check that they had food and drinks available to them. Emily had her doubts on whether he would be able to give them an estimate on their time of departure. He was just as much General Stone's pawn as they were.

It surprised her that her opinion of someone could change in such a short period of time. Her gratitude toward Ben for his quick actions on Saturday night had been the catalyst. He had interceded to help Oliver—and in so doing, her as well—when everyone else had been focused on the chaos around them. Her previous dislike of him was mostly petty, born from irritation at his smug, sure knowledge of the world around him. She had seen a different side of him since that night, though. He was rattled just like everyone else, scrambling to get the information he needed to make things right.

It wasn't a sudden crush on the hero who had swooped in to save her. She just understood him a little better, that was all.

Alyson, now, she did have a crush. She got flustered and nervous every time he entered the room. Since she was generally a flustered person anyway, her heightened mannerisms became that much more obvious.

He appeared again, finishing yet another phone call. Alyson straightened in a pathetic attempt to catch his eye. Next to Emily, Oliver emitted a scornful grunt. She glanced to him in disapproval.

A Rumor of Real Irish Tea

Ben remained oblivious to any of these movements, his attention fixed only on his boss. "Agent Knox is on his way with the intel reports from this afternoon."

"About time," Stone said grumpily. "Have you learned anything from your little network of contacts?"

"Not yet, but they all know to keep their ears to the ground."

The general raised suspicious eyes. For a moment he said nothing. Then, "You will inform me the moment anything comes through."

"Of course," said Ben with a curt nod. He shifted his attention to the corner as Agent Knox appeared at the doorway. The man's advent gave him excuse to move away from his belligerent superior.

"How are things over here?" he asked the group of four in a low voice.

"When can we go?" Quincy demanded outright.

Ben laughed, a brief indulgence of levity in the midst of what had obviously been a stressful day. "I have no idea. You must be bored silly by now."

"Quit sucking up, Birchard," she snapped, much to Alyson's horror.

He didn't take offense. Instead, he replied in modest protest, "But that's what I do best. You know that, Quincy."

"Has there been any word about the Wests?" Oliver asked.

"The hotline's had its usual share of reports," he said. "Until we have something concrete, we're back to the old plan of attack, which is not to attack at all. None of the reports panned out for the GCA agents sent to investigate, though."

"They're long gone," said Quincy. "There's nothing to keep them here."

He shrugged. "Nothing but Altair. Whether that's enough of

XXIV

an incentive for them to stay in the area, we don't know, but we should shortly."

"What's that supposed to mean?" Emily asked sharply.

"The GCA has a long list of alleged insurrectionists, and an even longer list of phone taps. Altair has stayed below the radar for the last few years, but they're traceable. If they make contact with the Wests and agree to help them, we'll know and we'll intercede. We'll be the ones to ambush them this time."

"Only if they don't outsmart you again first," said Oliver darkly.

Ben grimaced, but he was saved the trouble of replying when his phone rang. "Hello?" he said, more than willing to turn away from the present conversation. "Yes, that's right. How can I help you? You have? Are you sure?" He made a sudden, swift motion to catch General Stone's attention. "Understood," he said into the phone. He grabbed a pen and scribbled something on the nearest piece of paper. "You know what procedure to follow? We'll do our part on this end, then. Thank you."

He hung up, well aware that all eyes in the room were fixed upon him. "That was my contact at Central," he said grimly. "They've picked up chatter on one of the phone taps. Altair made contact with the kids, and they're planning to smuggle them out of the country within the next twenty-four hours. And this," he added, holding up his scribble for the man to see, "is the safe house where they're staying until then."

General Stone was out of his chair in an instant. Ben met him halfway to pass the address into his eager hands. "You're sure this is the right place?" the general asked suspiciously.

"No," said Ben. "What do you want to do?"

"I want to kick in the front door and wrap this up before the nine o'clock news. Knox! Cross-reference this address in our database to see if it raises any red flags. And get the elite retrieval squad ready. I want that house surrounded with agents in ten minutes flat. Birchard, call Veronica at NPNN. Where are the satellite images of this area?"

He was in full assault mode, storming about the room and shouting orders at everyone.

Ben turned on his phone only to have it chirp at him. "Are you kidding?" he muttered in disbelief, to no one in particular. Then, he turned to Emily with a desperate expression. "Can I borrow your phone? My battery's dying, and if I don't get this call made, Stone's going to tear my head off."

Out of the corner of her eye she saw Alyson scrambling to locate her cell phone instead. Emily slipped her own from her pocket and handed it over.

"You're a lifesaver," said Ben gratefully. He turned away as he punched in the numbers for his phone call to Veronica.

Emily patently ignored Alyson's venomous glare. Oliver's was more difficult to avoid. "What?" she asked him defensively.

"Nothing," he grumbled, and he fixed his gaze on the wall.

"Veronica's on her way to the site," Ben said to General Stone two minutes later. He handed back Emily her phone.

Stone looked up from the maps he was poring over. "Good. Call the South Phoenix branch and make sure their men have mobilized. Then get everyone down to the vans."

Alyson leapt forward with her cell before Ben could ask for Emily's again. "Thank you," he said as he took it, a charming smile on his face.

She blushed and tittered.

"We're just moving out?" Emily asked Oliver in a low voice. "What about all of the planning, like on Saturday night?"

"I'm guessing the elite retrieval squad has infiltrated their fair

XXIV

share of homes," he replied dryly. "It doesn't take as much preparation as the warehouse district."

"They could do this sort of thing in their sleep," said Ben, who had finished his quick phone call. He proffered the phone to Alyson.

"You . . . you can keep it longer. Y'know, in case you need to make any more calls," she nervously said.

"Creepy," Oliver muttered under his breath.

Ben thanked her with a charming smile and tucked the phone into his pocket. "Let's go," he said. "Same procedure as last time: Quincy, you're in General Stone's car. Oliver, you're in the second retrieval van."

Emily experienced a keen sense of déjà vu as they filed to the basement garage, where black-clad agents were receiving their tranquilizer guns. "How can they be sure there's not another rat?" she asked Ben.

"There's not," he said with complete certainty. "Not among this group—they've all been questioned by Veronica and a couple other projectors that Secretary Allen sent. This time there'll be no mistakes."

"There'd better not be," said Oliver.

They split up to climb into their appropriate vehicles. In no time at all, they were barreling down the road to a central Phoenix neighborhood. Emily could see the same grim determination on Oliver's face reflected in the face of every agent around her. She only hoped that Ben's informant was correct, that this was the right house.

They parked halfway down the block to let all the agents out. To Emily's great surprise, she and Oliver were ordered to remain behind. "This is going to be the command van," said the driver in answer to her confused expression. The next moment,

General Stone himself climbed up into the front seat, and Quincy appeared at the back with Alyson and Ben in tow.

Stone had a handheld radio. "Is everyone in position?" he asked into it.

A man's voice on the other end answered. "Front and back doors are both covered. Waiting for your command."

"Where's Veronica?" General Stone asked Ben.

"She's with the news van, parked at the other end of the street."

"Remind them not to record us entering the house."

"Yes, sir," said Ben, and he immediately phoned the news reporter to relay that information.

"All units at the ready," Stone commanded. Each squad leader reported back a confirmation. Then, "Go ahead," said Stone to the driver.

Emily had wondered how Oliver was supposed to block a projection from halfway down the street, but now the van drove boldly forward and parked in the driveway of the presumed safe house.

"We're in position," said General Stone. "Take the house."

She leaned forward, and through the driver's window she saw several dark figures emerge from the shadows to rush the front door. They kicked it in with a loud clatter and shouted commands for the occupants to put their hands on their heads.

"Front door breached," said a voice on the radio.

"Back door breached," said another.

"We have visual contact."

"Put your weapons down! Weapons down, and hands on your heads!"

There was shouting and the sound of some scuffling. Emily thought she might die from the pressure of that tense moment.

XXIV

Then, "Four targets have been captured, General," said the first voice. "The rest of the house is clear."

"Let's go," said General Stone smugly, and he exited the vehicle.

Ben motioned Quincy and Oliver to go in front of him. "Now comes the fun part," he said to Emily. "The cover-up."

She followed at the rear of the column that entered the house: General Stone first, then Oliver, Quincy, Alyson, and Ben. The inside was a sea of black-clad agents. "Get that van out of the driveway, Birchard," General Stone barked, "and tell Veronica to get ready to record."

"I'm on it," said Ben, and he slipped back out the door.

The sea of agents parted for Stone and his minions. Emily half-expected some innocent family under arrest in front of her. Her stomach twisted when she saw Hawk, Hummer, Honey, and Happy West sitting in a row on the couch. Their hands had been cuffed, and their faces wore mirror-image rebellious expressions.

General Stone paced in front of them. "Your little run is finally at an end. I'm here to offer you back your home at Prometheus—at the E campus this time, of course."

They sullenly ignored him.

Agent Knox in his black uniform stepped forward to report. "They were carrying the tranquilizer guns they stole. We've confiscated them, along with their supplies. How do you want to proceed?"

"Was there anything else in the house?"

"Just a basket of fruit. There are some ashes in the fireplace, though, so we suspect they burned something."

"What was it?" he asked Hawk, who raised his nose haughtily. General Stone caught his chin. "What was it, *boy*?" he repeated in a menacing tone.

A Rumor of Real Irish Tea

Hawk jerked away with a voiceless sneer. At the other end of the couch, Happy burrowed his face into his sister's shoulder. "We didn't burn anything," she said belligerently.

"Honey, shush," Hummer said.

"I'll have the truth from all of you soon enough," said General Stone. "Where's Birchard?"

"Here, sir." Ben pushed his way in from the door, a box in his hands. "Veronica's in the right spot, and I've brought the blankets. Did you want to add these two to the list of victims?" He tipped his head toward Quincy and Oliver. "Six instead of four would heighten the drama and vilify the insurrectionists that much more."

Emily looked between the two men in alarm. Ben seemed almost to be enjoying himself, and General Stone had a steely look in his eyes that did not bode well.

"If there are enough blankets, I don't see why we shouldn't put the nulls with them," said Stone. "They'll have to be transported with them anyway. Is Veronica ready to record? I need all but five of you men out of here. Those who stay behind need to keep their weapons out of sight when they escort our rescued little lambs out to safety."

"The public doesn't like to see armed men leading children around," Ben told Emily in a low voice. "At least, that's what all our focus groups say."

Then, he handed a blanket to Oliver. "Put that around your shoulders and act like you've just been rescued from the most harrowing experience of your life." He moved on to Quincy, to whom he issued the same instructions.

Emily noticed the girl looking in Hawk's direction, trying to catch his eye with a wordless apology. Hawk kept his gaze fixed on the ceiling, though.

XXIV

"Stand up, you four," Ben said. "We're going to put blankets around you, and you're going to keep them around you until you're loaded safely into the van." He made a great show of slinging the first blanket around Hummer's shoulders and tucking the ends into his handcuffed hands. Hummer glared at him.

"There's a good lad," said Ben wryly, and he patted him on the head before moving to the other three children.

"The public doesn't like to see children led out in handcuffs either, I suppose," Emily whispered grimly to Oliver. This whole situation felt wrong. A cover-up had to happen—enough lies had already been told about kidnapping rings and the precious North children not to continue along that path—but this seemed too calculated.

Oliver had a perturbed expression on his face. "Something's not right."

"What do you mean?" she asked.

His frown deepened, his eyes fixed on the four Wests. "Something's not right. This was too easy."

Emily bit back a scoff. "You're joking, right?"

"Where's Revere?" he suddenly asked Hawk. "Your bird, where is he?"

Hawk's gaze jerked away from the ceiling. "He got shot, remember?"

"But he was only injured. So where is he now?"

"Everyone in a line," Birchard interrupted, and he prodded Hawk toward the door. "Escorts, keep a protective arm around your poor little victims as you lead them to the van. That means you two as well," he added to Alyson and Emily.

"I think I'm going to be sick," Emily murmured as she complied. It was all so contrived.

A Rumor of Real Irish Tea

"*You're* going to be sick?" Oliver retorted.

She squeezed his shoulders in a mock-comforting gesture.

"All ready out there?" Ben said into his phone. A voice responded to the affirmative. "Let's go, everyone. Single-file, straight out to the van, but take your time so that we have some nice footage for the news reels."

He really was enjoying himself, but it only made sense that an information junkie would delight in twisting that information around. She led Oliver from the house, conscious to keep her head down. The last thing she wanted was for her mother to recognize her face on the evening news. Veronica was broadcasting from the front porch, with General Stone standing next to her to comment on the case. Emily heard snippets of her report as she dutifully helped Oliver up into the van.

The back could only fit two agents more in addition to the children and the two legitimate handlers. A third moved toward the front seat, only to be cut off by Ben. "Sorry," he said with a smile. "General's orders. You're with the sedan."

The man nodded and immediately crossed to the black sedan ahead, where he joined the other extra escorts.

"Switch places with me," Ben told one of the agents in the back. "I think these kids might like to watch the broadcast of their rescue." He produced his handheld screen from one pocket and waved it enticingly.

The agent laughed and gladly complied.

Ben plopped down between Emily and Hawk. "It should be just about ready to air," he said. "I can't imagine that General Stone had a very long statement to give." The screen in his hand flared to life.

"It's not a live broadcast?" Emily asked.

"No way. We had to be sure none of these little miscreants

XXIV

made a scene on live television. It can start any time now, though, since you all behaved so well. Here we go."

He flipped a switch on the side, and the sound blared through the van. "For breaking news in the Maddie and Alex North kidnapping case, we go live to Veronica Porcher in Phoenix. Veronica?"

Veronica's beautiful face flashed into view, with the safe house as her backdrop. She smiled into the camera. "Thanks, Ted. I'm standing here in a quiet neighborhood where, just moments ago and acting on a tip from a concerned citizen, the Government-Civilian Alliance entered a suspected kidnapper's den. Inside, a bone-chilling scene: not two, not four, but *six* children, ranging in age from six to thirteen years old. You can see behind me those children being escorted to safety, even at this very moment rescued from what had to be the most horrific ordeal of their young lives.

"I have with me General Bradford Stone, who led this rescue effort. General Stone, can you confirm that two of those children are Maddie and Alex North of Seattle, Washington?"

General Stone looked as grim as ever. "I can confirm that."

"And the other four? Who are they?"

"At this time we're not releasing their names. We need to get into contact with their parents or guardians, but I can say with complete certainty that they have been saved from a most unsettling situation."

"And what of the kidnappers?" Veronica asked.

"Unfortunately," said General Stone with a self-conscious glance toward the camera, "the kidnappers escaped out the back door moments before we entered the house. We have men tracking them, and we urge citizens to be vigilant about their surroundings and any strangers they might encounter. We will do everything in our power to bring these vile criminals to justice."

The van had begun to move away down the street, following the black sedan in front of it. Emily barely noticed, her attention fixed on the tiny screen. Every so often, she glanced up at the other riders to discover that they were just as mesmerized.

"Do you have any words of thanks you'd like to say to those whose time has been so focused on this rescue effort?" Veronica asked the general.

"Of course. We owe an enormous debt to the Government-Civilian Alliance and its continued endeavors to bring justice to those who need it most. I'd also like to thank the many civilians who called in tips that led to this rescue tonight, as would the parents of these children, I'm sure. And, of course, a big thank you to NPNN for keeping this kidnapping fresh in our minds, for reminding us never to give up the fight. Maddie and Alex North thank you very much, I'm sure."

"Like fun we do," said Honey sourly. Hummer immediately shushed her.

"And there you have it, Ted," said Veronica to the NPNN anchor. "A month-long nightmare brought to a happy end. From Phoenix, I'm Veronica Porcher."

Ted's face flashed back on screen. "Thanks, Veronica. We're waiting for a statement from the North parents, but first—"

Ben flipped the screen off. "And that's that," he said cheerfully as he tucked it away in his pocket. "The manhunt is over."

Then he took out a gun and shot the agent sitting across from him.

XXV
Turnabout Is Fair Play

ALYSON SHRIEKED, AND the van erupted into chaos. Hummer and Hawk West both lunged for the fallen agent's tranquilizer gun. The agent in the front passenger's seat started from his chair, only to slump down the next moment, a tranquilizer dart in his neck. The shot hadn't come from either of the West boys, but from the driver.

"What are you doing?" Emily screamed at Ben.

"What does it look like I'm doing?" he asked as he turned his gun on her.

"That's a tranquilizer gun," said Oliver from behind her, his voice trembling. "It only fires one round."

"True," said Ben, and he carelessly cast it away. "This one's a bit different, though." He pulled a heavy weapon from beneath his jacket, a bona fide pistol, the kind that had been outlawed decades ago. "Good thing I didn't grab it first by mistake. I'd prefer not to use it, but I will if I have to."

On the other side of the van, Alyson whimpered.

"I don't know what you two are waiting for," Ben said to Hawk and Hummer.

A Rumor of Real Irish Tea

Hawk hesitated, but Hummer snatched up the second tranquilizer gun and pointed it straight at Alyson. "Sorry, lady. It's nothing personal." He pulled the trigger. Alyson's eyes rolled back in her head, and she slumped in her seat.

"How did you two get free of your handcuffs?" asked Oliver sullenly.

"He gave us each a master key with our blankets," Hummer said, and he moved to undo Honey's cuffs. Hawk did the same for Happy.

"You four have followed the plan magnificently," said Ben. "I'll have to admit, I was a little worried going into it. Smith, you know where the first drop-off point is, don't you? Because I don't."

The driver grunted his affirmative.

"So there were two traitors," said Emily bitterly.

"No, just me," said Ben. "Smith left the real driver knocked out somewhere back by the safe house."

"Across the street, in the bushes," said Smith from the front seat. "He'll have quite the headache when he wakes up."

"And really, I'm not a traitor," Ben continued lightly. "My loyalties have been fixed from the very beginning. It's not my fault the GCA didn't figure that out sooner. Quincy Ivers, whose side are you on?"

Quincy, tucked away in the corner across from her unconscious handler, jumped when he said her name. "Do I get to choose?" she asked.

"According to Altair you do. This is your chance to get out. Will you take it or leave it?"

"I'll take it," she said without an ounce of hesitation. "I'm sorry, Hawk. I never wanted to help them."

"I figured as much," he replied with a wan smile.

XXV

"You'll be sent in a different direction than the Wests," Ben said. "You'll probably never see each other again. Is that all right?"

Quincy nodded.

Hawk and Hummer made short work of Honey's and Happy's handcuffs, which they readily transferred to Alyson and the unconscious agent in the back. Hummer held up the other two sets. "One of these goes to Emily, right?"

"Right," said Ben, and he kept his gun steadily aimed.

"What about Oliver?" asked Hummer as he gingerly moved to comply.

"What about him?"

"Does he get to choose?"

Oliver jerked in his seat. A sneer leapt to his face. "You think I'd willingly side with any of you? You're crazy. The GCA's going to track you all down just like before."

"Not like before," Ben said before Hummer could answer. "They've just broadcasted on the national news that they successfully recovered precious little Maddie and Alex North, along with four other children, two of whom look remarkably like Hawk and Hummer. What are they supposed to do now, admit that they botched the rescue, that one of their own men sabotaged them and carried the kids away? Or do they say that someone went and kidnapped Maddie and Alex a second time? That hardly builds public confidence in an organization like the GCA. They'll still hunt the Wests, sure, but it'll have to be done in secret, without relying on the general population to be their eyes and ears. That sort of hunting can be dealt with quite easily."

"You should come with us," Honey suddenly said to Oliver. "You should get away from Prometheus while you can."

His face twisted in contempt. "Your words have no effect on me."

"My projections have no effect," she retorted. "My words have merit of their own."

"There is nothing you could possibly say to make me switch over to your side," Oliver told her disdainfully.

Honey sat back in her chair, and the flat look in her eyes sent a chill up Emily's spine. "Henry and Iris Dunn," she recited, "married June 15, 2040. One son, Oliver Henry Dunn, born September 18, 2042, currently under guardianship of the Government-Civilian Alliance at the Prometheus Institute, F Campus."

"Shut up," said Oliver.

"One daughter," Honey continued, "Ruby Cecilia Dunn, born January 7, 2046."

"Shut up!" he shouted.

"The Dunn family, except Oliver, currently resides in Silver Meadows, Nevada, and has lived there for nine years."

He was almost beside himself with rage. "I'm not listening to you! *Shut up!*"

Honey's mouth turned up in an impertinent smirk. "I thought you said my words had no effect on you."

"That's a cruel trick," said Emily. "Who knows if what you said was even true?"

"You'd better hope, for the Dunn family's sake, that it isn't," Ben remarked mildly. "Silver Meadows is a government-planned community. A century ago we would've called it an internment camp. That's the sort of place the GCA sends civilians who don't want to do their bidding, especially parents who don't want to give their little ones over into government care. I should know," he added. "I lived in one for the first ten years of my life."

"So what, this was a personal vendetta?" Emily asked.

Ben smiled wryly. "Something like that."

"The sedan's been detoured," Smith said from the front seat.

XXV

"We're almost to the first drop-off, and it needs to go as quickly as possible."

"Come with us, Oliver," said Quincy. "There's nothing waiting for you at Prometheus."

"There's nothing waiting for me away from Prometheus," he replied bitterly.

Her voice turned urgent. "They're not going to send you back to Prom-A. In another couple years, they won't even use you to solve problems with projectors on other campuses, especially now that they have Cedric at Prom-C. You're going to end up at Prom-F until you're eighteen, and from there you'll be transferred to Prom-E and never see the light of day again."

"I don't believe you," he said stubbornly.

"You think I was transferred to Prom-F by a fluke?" she asked. "I turned twelve and that was it. No explanation, no excuses. Genevieve just smiled and put me on a plane. Haven't you ever wanted to choose your own path in life instead of having it handed to you by a bunch of adults?"

His face was unyielding. He didn't even bother to answer her.

"Unfortunately, Quincy's right," Ben said quietly. "Null-projectors always go to Prom-E. This government doesn't trust people they can't control, especially the smart ones."

"That's ridiculous," said Emily.

"It's policy," Ben replied. "You've seen how they use projectors like Veronica. Imagine if Oliver were standing in a crowd she was supposed to indoctrinate. The powers-that-be wouldn't be able to control how their message was received. Obviously their best plan of prevention is to keep null-projectors isolated from everyone else, and that means Prom-E. That's the future you have to look forward to, Oliver."

"Out of the mouth of a snake," Oliver sneered.

A Rumor of Real Irish Tea

The van abruptly stopped, and the back doors swung open. "I've got an angry caged bird and a waiting car," said a man in a black ski mask. "Four Wests come with me."

"And one Ivers," Ben said. He tipped his head to motion for Quincy to go as well.

"Oliver," said Quincy haltingly.

"We don't have time for negotiations," Ben interrupted. "Just go without him."

The four Wests paused outside the van.

"Thanks, Ruth," said Hawk.

"Thanks, Ruth," said Hummer.

"Thanks, Ruth," said Honey and Happy together.

"Thanks, Birchard," Quincy said, and the doors shut.

"Ruth is short for Rutherford," Ben said in explanation to Emily as the van started to move again. "You know, Rutherford B. Hayes? Rutherford *Birchard* Hayes?"

"Very clever," she said insincerely.

"Well, now, you're not very fun at all." He put the gun back into his coat and moved to sit across from them.

Just because the weapon was out of sight didn't mean it was out of Emily's mind. He could draw it out again at any time. She thought it best to keep him distracted. "Is that even your real name? Birchard, I mean."

"No. Neither is Ben, for what it's worth."

"I thought that was short for Benedict Arnold."

He smiled wanly. "I suppose there's no point in trying to persuade you to my way of seeing things. It's sad, really, because I think if we'd met under different circumstances, we could've gotten along together quite well."

"You mean different circumstances like where you weren't a conniving traitor?"

XXV

"No, just where you weren't a blind idealist," he said. "But then, that's part of your charm, so I wouldn't wish that to be otherwise. You and I have differing views, that's all. You are content to live in a world where the government can steal a couple's children at gun-point on a whim. I'm not."

"That's never happened," said Emily hotly.

"You're naïve," Ben replied, his voice like steel. "How do you think the Wests ended up at Prometheus in the first place? A judge declared the parents incompetent and issued a warrant in the middle of the night for the children to be taken away."

"Maybe they *were* incompetent."

"They had gifted children that the government wanted to control. They could've been the most competent people on the planet, and the government still would've taken those children away. I lost a sister to Prometheus," he added with growing anger. "I was lucky not to bear the same genetic curse that she did, but I saw firsthand the destruction that her disappearance caused in my own family. And she and the Wests aren't the only ones. At least half the kids at Prometheus have that same story, including Oliver."

Emily had nothing to say to this.

Oliver spoke up instead. "You don't know that."

"The GCA doesn't relocate willing donor-parents," Ben said in a flat voice. "It's only the unwilling ones that need to be watched. It doesn't matter, though. I know perfectly well that nothing I say will convince you that I'm telling the truth."

"So what's your real name?" Emily asked. One hand rested on her pocket, where her cell phone lay hidden. The microphone would be recording everything. If she could get him to divulge some useful information . . .

Ben seemed to read her thoughts. "I reprogrammed your

phone," he said bluntly. "Earlier, when you let me borrow it. Alyson's too." He withdrew that object from his pocket and tossed it to the floor. "They're both stuck on a two-hour loop of audio from this afternoon. Members of the elite retrieval squad aren't allowed to carry phones into a mission like this—no one wants home invasions recorded, you know—so we're all basically free to say whatever we want right now."

"You twisted son-of-a—"

"Language, Emily," he admonished before she could finish her insult. "There's a child present."

"You really are a piece of work, Birchard," said Oliver.

"Thank you," Ben said mildly. "I've worked for quite some time to become what I am. Do you have any idea how much practice is required to gain resistance toward projectors? And then, after you get that, you have to practice acting like they're affecting you so that people who are looking to see whether you're resistant can't tell that you really are. Years of my life I lost to gaining that trait alone. It paid off in the end, though."

"You want an award or something?" Emily asked.

He laughed agreeably, not in the least fazed by her sarcasm. "I wouldn't mind one. I never thought I'd make it this high up the administrative ladder. Becoming Genevieve Jones's personal assistant was like being handed the entire organization on a silver platter. I had access to everything that happened, and I could pass the pertinent information along as needed. I was such a good little ghost, but then General Stone had to come along and ruin everything. I was a moth who got too close to the flame. The minute he chose me, my days were numbered.

"But then to have another ghost show up at that warehouse siege—that hit me hard. I don't have a clue how many of us there are, but it stands to reason that when one is discovered,

XXV

any others in the organization are under greater risk. Luckily, Stone kept his attention on the Phoenix GCA staff. I half-worried that Altair might leave me to fend for myself, since they'd already used their resources to get rid of the ghost of Thomas Fry. I knew my exit would have to be of a different sort than his."

His countenance suddenly changed, solemn and pensive. "It's all right, though," he said absently. "I've lived past my usefulness, but I can take heart knowing that I was very useful indeed."

The van came to a sudden halt. Emily glanced through the front window to the interior of an empty parking garage.

"You ready?" Smith said from the front seat, and he turned to hand Ben another tranquilizer gun.

"Does it matter?" Ben asked as he took the weapon. He shifted his attention to his two captives. "Last chance, Oliver," he said.

The driver's door opened; Smith disappeared outside the vehicle.

"Never," said Oliver hatefully.

"I thought as much," said Ben with a shrug, and he fired the tranquilizer gun.

Emily shrieked as Oliver toppled from his seat, unconscious. "You monster! What have you done?"

"Believe me, it's far more merciful to tranquilize him," said Ben grimly. He set the empty gun down on the seat beside him. "It'll save him some trauma."

"When you carry him off against his will?" she accused.

His expression turned caustic. "Unlike the GCA, Altair doesn't force anyone to do something against his will, even if they believe it's better for him. Oliver stays with you here in the van. Don't worry—they'll be along shortly to rescue you."

"Why didn't you shoot me?" Emily asked. "Why does everyone else get a tranquilizer?"

A Rumor of Real Irish Tea

"Someone has to be the messenger," he said. Then, to her utmost astonishment, he leaned in and gently kissed her forehead. "Sorry," he whispered, and he retreated to the back door. He didn't look her way again; her last view of him was the back of his gray suit before the door slammed shut.

"You've outlived your usefulness, Ben Birchard," said a voice outside. Smith had left his window halfway rolled down, Emily realized with growing confusion.

"Yes," Ben calmly said.

"Are you ready?"

"Yes," he said again. "Goodbye."

Gunshots—real gunshots, three of them—cracked the air and echoed off the concrete of the parking garage. The metal panel next to Emily's head dented with the impact of a bullet. She cringed into her seat as her blood ran cold.

In the aftermath came a horrible, deafening silence.

"Get the body moved, quickly," said the unknown man. It took a moment for Emily's brain to register the sounds that followed: something heavy being dragged, people grunting as they hefted it from the ground, a car trunk slamming shut, an engine starting and a car driving away.

Logically she knew what had just happened. Emotionally, she refused to acknowledge it. Her breath came in short, ragged gasps, and she dimly realized that tears were spilling down her cheeks. She sat as though in a trance, unseeing, uncaring. It was only a few minutes before wheels screeched against the concrete outside, but it felt like an eternity.

There were sirens and shouts, and footsteps running toward her. The back of the van was thrown open, and Emily flinched away from the sudden brightness. A pair of headlights shone directly on her.

XXV

"Get those people out of the vehicle!" General Stone bellowed.

Her eyes strayed to Oliver, unconscious at her feet, to Alyson in the back corner, and the two GCA agents sprawled in their seats. Her whole body was in shock, unable to move.

The agents began to drag the unconscious people out of the way. Someone jumped inside and grabbed onto her arm, pulling her toward the exit. Emily forced herself to go with the man. They helped her get down. Someone removed the handcuffs from her hands. They were a blur of nameless faces. The only image that truly stuck in her mind was the large, smeared bloodstain next to the van.

General Stone was beside her, she realized in her odd lack of focus. She looked up at him helplessly. "They killed him," she said in a hollow voice. "He wasn't useful anymore, so they killed him."

"Get this woman back to the office for questioning," General Stone callously ordered one of his men. "And put out an alert for a fugitive matching Ben Birchard's description!"

"He's dead," Emily protested with growing hysteria. "They killed him!"

"Get her out of here!" cried Stone again.

XXVI
The Long Ride Home, Part 1

AUGUST 11, 2:42PM CDT, SOMEWHERE IN THE MIDWEST

It was blatantly illegal for four children to ride in the back of a double-cab truck, because there were only three seatbelts there. The man who was driving didn't seem to care, and neither did the young woman in the passenger's seat. If they didn't have a problem with it, the four Wests certainly wouldn't complain.

"We'll be there in another ten minutes," said the driver. "Pumpkin, can you hand them those file folders now?"

"Sure, Dad," said his teenaged passenger. She pulled four blue files from beneath the cage that sat between them. The raven within cawed at the slight jostle, which caused her to jump. "Here ya go," she said as she handed the files to Hawk just behind her.

He flipped open the first only to shut it again and hand it to Honey. The next went to Happy. He paused at the third one. "This profile is for a fifteen-year-old," he said.

"We fudged on your age," said the driver. "We've found we can get away with up to two years' discrepancy. You and your brother are now both a bit older, so try to act like it."

XXVI

"I can drive next year," Hawk said to Hummer as he handed over the last file.

"I can drive right now," Hummer retorted. "Just not legally."

"You keep the laws in this new life," the driver said abruptly. "You're not allowed to do anything that'll draw attention to yourselves."

"And we really get to stay together, all four of us?" Hawk asked.

The man grunted. "In a manner of speaking, yes. Noah and Jacob—that would be you two older boys—are live-in hired hands. You'll notice your Career Aptitude Assessment scores indicate that you'll make perfect farmers or ranchers. That CAA allows you to be entered into an apprenticeship instead of finishing out formal high school. You'll walk away with a specialized degree in farming—and who knows? You might even like it.

"The McGill farm, where you'll be living, has been family-owned for nine generations. The current head-of-family, Jay McGill, has a wife, Helen, and a two-year-old daughter, Grace. We've doctored their records to give them an older daughter and son, Mia and Aaron. The Rural Population Retention Act allows farming families in communities of fewer than five thousand people to have three children, so this won't raise any red flags."

"Mia McGill," said Honey with satisfaction at how the name rolled off her tongue.

"From now onwards, Jefferson, Franklin, Madison, and Washington West no longer exist," the driver said. "In order to ensure your safety and that you remain hidden, you're never to use those names again. Understood?"

"We never used them anyway," said Hummer. "But what about Hawk, Hummer, Honey, and Happy?"

The man glanced up into the rearview mirror. "What you call yourselves in private is none of our concern."

A Rumor of Real Irish Tea

"And what about our parents?" asked Hawk.

"The McGills will call you by your new names."

"I meant our real parents. When can we start looking for them?"

"When you're eighteen and legal to be off on your own," he said. "There's a word out on the Altair network, and if anything turns up, we'll let you know." He brought the truck to a sudden halt and turned stern eyes upon them. "I cannot emphasize enough that Jay and Helen McGill are putting their lives and the life of their daughter at risk to take you four in right now. Do not do anything rash."

"We'd never," said Hummer innocently.

The man started the car forward again. "We've heard of some of your antics, even out here in the sticks. You're in our hands now, though, and you're going to have to trust us."

"That's fair enough," Hawk said for the rest of his siblings. They had no room to complain. Altair had successfully extracted them from the clutches of the GCA. They had parted ways with Quincy back in Phoenix, and over the ensuing week, they had been adeptly smuggled through half a dozen places, passed from one Altair cell to another without incident. They had been clothed, fed, and now they were going to have a place to call home, for a few years at least. It might involve some extra work, but Hawk liked animals and Hummer liked machines, and both could be found on a farm. Honey and Happy would have the freedom to run and play, and they'd be able to grow without the threat of the GCA constantly looming over their heads.

There wasn't a whole lot more that they could ask for.

The surrounding land was painfully flat and populated entirely with fields of corn and wheat. They were so far removed from civilization that it had been several miles since they'd seen a farmhouse, let alone a person. The little dirt lane that the

XXVI

truck finally turned down looked like something out of an era long past. A cheery arch overhead welcomed them to McGill's Family Farm, established 1873. The blue farmhouse and bright red barn were nowhere near that old, and were kept in very good condition.

The driver pulled to a stop in front of a wide white porch and honked a staccato rhythm on his horn. "Down you go to meet the folks," he said to the kids as he climbed out and opened the door for them. "You need to memorize the information in those files and then keep them somewhere safe. Mr. McGill might know a good spot."

His daughter descended from her side with Revere's cage in hand. This she set aside to pull four duffle bags from the truck bed—clothes supplied by their cell for the newcomers. She handed each to its appropriate recipient as they came around. Up on the porch, a woman opened the screen door and emerged. Her expression was a strange mixture of eagerness and hesitation. Behind her came a curious two-year-old girl in the arms of her smiling father.

Hawk's duffle bag hit the ground. "Mom," he whispered in shock. "Mom! Dad!"

Four children scrambled forward, met halfway by their tearful parents, who embraced them in a reunion long overdue. Emotions choked any words they tried to speak, and for several moments the family simply clung to one another in joy.

"I can't believe you're really here," said Sara West when she finally regained her voice. "Oh, my sweet Happy! You've grown so big, and I missed it!"

"Everyone, grab your things and come inside," said James West, unsuccessfully fighting his tears. "We have your rooms all ready for you. We've had them ready for ages."

A Rumor of Real Irish Tea

Next to the truck, Revere cawed his indignation at having been forgotten. Hawk trotted back to flip the latch on his cage door, and the great black bird immediately flapped out of its confines and up to the rooftop.

The nameless man and his daughter watched as the family waved their gratitude and disappeared into the farmhouse. "Did you know those were their real parents, Dad?" asked the girl as she wiped her eyes.

"Are you kidding?" he replied with a soft smile. "It was all I could do to make those people stay put when that kidnapping story broke a month ago. The whole reason we placed them here was so that they could have a place for their other children, if the opportunity ever came. And, against all odds, it did."

"But you said that this farm has belonged to the same family for nine generations," she argued.

He grinned. "The eighth generation Mr. McGill and his wife were unable to have children, but they didn't want to lose the farm to the government. So, we created a couple of sons for them a few decades back. On paper, it is nine generations, and that's all that really matters these days. Come on now," he said, and he put an arm around her in a fatherly hug. "Let's go home."

They climbed into their truck and drove away, knowing that all was right with the world in this little corner, at least.

XXVII
The Long Ride Home, Part 2

AUGUST 12, 8:15AM MDT, IN TRANSIT TO PROM-F

THE MIDNIGHT PLANE ride and two-hour morning drive were so familiar to Emily's mind that she thought she had been transported back in time by two weeks. Maggie Lloyd met them at the airport with the same greeting and the same packaged pastries for their breakfast. Oliver shunned his in the same way, and Emily couldn't manage to swallow anything past the first bite.

At least they hadn't spent three weeks in confinement this time around. There was no question of Emily or Oliver being responsible for the events that had taken place on the night of the fourth, but both of them had been subjected to multiple interrogations to glean as many facts as possible. Emily had received counseling for trauma, too. She understood what Ben had meant when he said the tranquilizer dart was a mercy to Oliver. The sickening sounds of gunshots and a body being dragged still rang in her ears, and when she closed her eyes she could see that blood smear on the concrete.

It had matched the DNA profile they had for Ben Birchard, one of the GCA agents had confirmed. Emily didn't understand.

A Rumor of Real Irish Tea

Ben had served Altair superbly, if the chaos he caused was any indication, and in return they disposed of him like yesterday's trash. Furious as she had been with him moments before his death, he didn't deserve that. His sorrowful face as he left the van remained fresh in her memory. He had known what was coming and accepted it readily.

That made even less sense to Emily.

Alyson went back to Prom-F three days earlier, or so they said. Emily hoped the nervous young woman didn't receive any censure for coming back without her student. Alyson couldn't have stopped Quincy from jumping ship, even if she had been conscious at the time. No one could have stopped it. The plan had been too well orchestrated.

"You're to go straight to Principal Gates's office when we arrive," Maggie said as she turned off the highway onto the road that led to campus. "You've been excused from your first period, Oliver."

He grunted a wordless acknowledgment, his gaze fixed on the scenery beyond the window. Emily studied him with a frown.

Did he regret his decision not to leave with the other kids? Would he regret it someday?

Soon enough, Prom-F loomed before them. They left the car and climbed the stairs. The reception area was as unwelcoming as ever.

"Upstairs with you both," said Maggie. "No need to keep the principals waiting any longer than necessary."

"Principals?" Oliver repeated, his keen ears catching the plural of that word.

Maggie nodded. "Principal Jones arrived last night especially to speak with you."

XXVII

Oliver bolted forward, renewed energy in his steps as he mounted the staircase. Emily kept pace behind him, silently praying for the little boy not to get his hopes too high. There was no telling what Principal Jones might say to him, but the chances of him being transferred back to Prom-A seemed almost nonexistent.

They stopped outside Principal Gates's office long enough for Oliver to straighten his clothing and smooth down his hair. When he was sufficiently composed, Emily knocked on the door. A voice within bid them enter.

Principal Gates sat at his desk, and Principal Jones stood behind him. Both of them looked more somber than usual. "Shut the door, please, Ms. Brent," said Principal Jones, and Emily meekly complied.

"Well, Oliver," said Principal Gates, "we've heard you had quite the adventure."

Oliver stood at perfect attention, but Emily could see the fidgets in his fingers. "Things didn't go as planned," he said in what was possibly the understatement of the century.

Principal Gates and Principal Jones exchanged a glance. "We've decided that it would be better for you to remain here at Prometheus-F," Principal Jones said emotionlessly.

He started. "But—!"

"Our agreement was that you would return to Prom-A when the Wests returned to Prom-F," she reminded him. "The Wests didn't return to Prom-F, though, did they?"

Emily took a jarring step forward, unable to stop herself. "But they were never going to return. General Stone was going to take them straight to Prom-E." The pair of principals exchanged another glance, and reality struck her full in the face. "You . . . knew that all along, didn't you."

A Rumor of Real Irish Tea

"You're out of line, Ms. Brent," said Principal Gates.

"I know," said Emily, her resolve strengthening, "but it wasn't my personal assistant who was moonlighting for Altair." Principal Jones stiffened, which only encouraged Emily to continue. "Oliver did everything he was asked to do. He even chose to remain behind when they offered him a chance to escape. And now he's being punished for it?"

"This isn't a punishment, Ms. Brent," Principal Jones said, but there was no substance to her words. "This is just the way things are."

"So Quincy was telling the truth," Oliver abruptly said. "I was going to end up here regardless, and I'm going to end up at Prom-E after this."

The two principals exchanged another telling glance.

"Fine," said Oliver firmly. "I understand."

Principal Gates folded his hands atop his desk, the picture of administrative decorum. "In order to restore normalcy here, our student body was told that the Wests were caught and expelled, and that Quincy was transferred. Any discussion of Prometheus-E or the events that you witnessed beyond this campus are strictly forbidden. That goes for both of you. You would be wise to watch your words, Ms. Brent."

"Under normal circumstances, any affiliation with Altair would be enough to get you expelled from our internship program," Principal Jones added. "It's been obvious that you were merely collateral damage in these incidents, though, and we are taking that into account. You've had a very rough start here, but we have good faith that the remainder of your service will pass without further incident."

"Three strikes and you're out, Ms. Brent," Principal Gates told her flatly. "Do you understand?"

XXVII

"Yes," said Emily. "I'm not allowed to talk about Altair or the treachery of Principal Jones's administrative assistant."

"We'll deal with Birchard when we find him," Principal Jones said in iron tones, an attempt to drive home her own innocence in the man's treachery.

"He's dead," said Emily. "Why does everyone keep acting like he's still alive?" The GCA agents back in Phoenix had been the same way, as though the gun casings and bloodstains had not been proof enough for them.

"No body, no crime," said Principal Jones. "You think he's dead because that's what you were meant to think. Why would they leave a witness to report that detail back to us?"

"Why would they pretend to kill a colleague?" Emily asked. True enough she had not seen the shooting, but she had heard it, and she had seen its aftermath.

"Altair always kills their ghosts," Principal Gates said. "They don't kill the person who's playing the ghost, though. The man formerly known as Ben Birchard is still out there, and we're going to find him. In the meantime, you're to forget everything you know about him. Do you understand?"

"Yes," she said bitterly.

"Good. That is all. The two of you may go."

Oliver wordlessly led the way from the room. Emily resisted the urge to glare at the pair of principals as she followed him. She shut the door and was halfway down the hall before Oliver suddenly paused in front of her.

"We're a danger to them," he said in a low voice, so quiet that Emily almost missed his words entirely.

She leaned forward. "What? What do you mean?"

"We're a danger to them," he repeated. "Principal Jones is the most powerful person at the Prometheus Institute, except

A Rumor of Real Irish Tea

General Stone, maybe. If word gets out that her personal assistant was an embedded spy who used his position to pass sensitive information to a group of domestic terrorists, and that she was completely unaware of this, she'll be a laughingstock. It could potentially ruin her career. Watch your back, Emily."

She self-consciously glanced over one shoulder before returning her attention to him. Her voice lowered to the barest whisper. "Do you regret not escaping when you had the chance?"

A strange array of emotions flitted across his face. "I'm not stupid enough to admit that out loud," he muttered, which was answer enough. "Come on. I might be able to catch the last bit of first period if we hurry."

"Why so eager?" Emily asked.

"People to meet and friends to make," Oliver said nonchalantly. "If this is going to be my home, I might as well make the best of it, right?"

She didn't buy that explanation for a second, but she let it slide. Oliver boldly joined his class for the last ten minutes, but Emily entered the observation room with far less bravado.

"New girl!" Crystal cried from the couch, and she beckoned her over. "I was half-scared they wouldn't send you back. You'll never guess what's been happening here since you left."

Emily settled into the seat next to her, grateful that Crystal was willing to gossip rather than ask any questions.

The morning passed in a blur. Lunch found her and Oliver in the cafeteria, amid an unusually somber sea of students. To her great surprise, he approached a table of three boys.

"Tyler, Arthur, Pierce," he said in greeting.

"If it isn't the principals' lapdog," Tyler sneered, while Arthur and Pierce both glared. "What treats did they give you for betraying your own this time?"

XXVII

"Nothing," said Oliver. "The Wests got away, and Quincy went with them. The admins lied to all of you so you'd stop thinking it was possible. You guys still plotting your escape?"

"That project is confidential," Tyler said with an upturned nose. "Null-projectors need not apply."

Oliver leaned forward and said in a low voice, "Any exceptions for null-projectors who can confirm the existence of a shadow campus and know about a subversive group that can hide potential escapees?"

The three boys exchanged a wary glance with one another. Tyler grudgingly scooted over to make room on the bench.

"I think I'll go check my mailbox," said Emily perceptively. "You boys have fun."

She felt not the slightest bit of remorse as she left them to their plotting. At worst, it would land Oliver at Prom-E a few years early. If he made some good friends before then, though, it would be time well spent.

The tiny mail room was crowded, as many handlers took refuge there for that free hour. Crystal waved a hello and beckoned her to the row of bins on the far wall.

"I forgot to tell you that you have a package," she said when Emily approached. "It's been in your box for a couple of days now."

Emily curiously pulled out the small rectangular parcel that awaited her. She recognized the return address typed on the label. "It's from my mom," she said in wonder. "I should probably call her. I haven't talked to her in weeks."

"Ooh, care package," said Crystal. She guided her to a small table in the corner. "What does she usually send you?"

"She doesn't," said Emily, but she eagerly tore off the brown tape to see what was inside. A package of her mother's favorite cookies nestled there, along with her father's favorite hard candy. "She knows I don't eat any of this," Emily said, but she couldn't suppress the nostalgic smile that pulled on the corners of her mouth. "What am I supposed to do with it?"

"Share and share alike." Crystal snatched up the bag of hard candy to pass among the other handlers.

Emily's blood froze when she saw what was beneath that bag: an orange box with a green design encompassing the label, "Real Irish Tea." It was her mother's favorite flavor, so it made sense for it to be there. The words on the box had just startled her.

She picked it up in a daze and opened the lid to view the individual tea packets. Taped to the inside of the lid was the purchase receipt, folded in thirds. Emily pulled it off in growing confusion. The store's address jumped out at her first: it was located in a California town forty minutes north of her parents' home. The box of tea had been purchased there, along with the cookies and hard candy, on the sixth of August.

A strange foreboding twisted through Emily as she turned the receipt over. The message scrawled there was not in her mother's handwriting or her father's. It read,

The question now is, do you tell anyone or not?
~C
(The man in the gray suit)

Emily's jaw dropped. "That evil jerk," she muttered. "Three strikes, and I'm out."

"What was that?" said Crystal, who had returned to her side in time to hear the last two words.

Emily quickly folded the receipt again. "Nothing," she said as she tucked it away. "I was reading my mother's note. I'll have to give her a call this evening, after class gets out."

XXVII

"Tell her thanks for the candy," Crystal said with a grin.

Emily assured her that she would do just that. And she really did intend to call her mother, too—right after she burned a sales receipt to ashes.

Further adventures continue in

ANNALS OF ALTAIR BOOK 3

Oliver INVICTUS

Available September 2019

About the Author

KATE STRADLING was born on a military base in Louisiana to a father who served in the dental corps and a mother who kept the hospital receipt (just in case). She grew up in the Arizona desert, the neglected fifth of six children and has lived a generally unremarkable life. In her spare time, she enjoys twisting information, diminishing her accomplishments, and staring blankly at the wall.

Made in United States
Troutdale, OR
09/16/2023